Nevermere

Devon De'Ath

Copyright © 2018 Devon De'Ath

All rights reserved.

ISBN-13: 978-1-73108-515-3

This is a work of fiction. Names, characters, businesses, places,
events, locales and incidents are either the products of the
author's imagination or used in a fictitious manner.
Any resemblance to actual persons, living or dead,
or actual events is purely coincidental.

DEDICATION

In loving memory of Gerald Stewart (1925 – 2013)

A true, modest, salt of the earth Cotswold gent.

Sleep well, kind Sir.

CONTENTS

1	Ordeal by Water	7
2	Big City Blues	25
3	Pennycress Cottage	45
4	Points West	64
5	Settling in the Valley	83
6	A Walk in the Woods	103
7	Some Relief	123
8	Echoes of the Past	145
9	Cheese and Wine	168
10	Fallacious Fermentations	188
11	Demon Drink	208
12	Robed and Disrobed	228
13	Sinister Spinster	248
14	The Contract	268
15	Rural Isolation	291
16	Something in the Water	316
17	Milk and Honey	340

1
Ordeal by Water

"Susan Blackwood. You have been found guilty via ordeal by water of the crime of witchcraft. That you did send out your spirit to attack Goodwife Parsons in an act of maleficium has now been irrefutably established." The sombre, monotone voice cut through crisp, cold, misty air that writhed atop the recently disturbed depths of a deep, dark pond. In a rowing boat on its rippling surface, a raven-haired young woman in her early twenties coughed up some murky water. She choked and spluttered as her entire torso dripped into the tiny craft. She spasmed and shook but remained held firm by two strong men. On the bank, an assembled throng of local villagers had watched as those men hauled her out of the pond by a rope. One of the villagers bore a striking resemblance to the accused. Her knuckles whitened from the strain of willing her twin sister to sink. An act that would show her innocence. Then the men could retrieve her and she'd come home a free woman. But Susan hadn't sunk, though she had taken in a sizable amount of fluid.

"I'm so sorry, Mary," the cracking voice of old Annie

Moore - a family friend - mumbled in the girl's ear.

Mary Blackwood glanced from the kindly old spinster across to Goody Parsons. She was a plain, thirty-year-old woman with beady eyes and a severe aspect to her thin face. She stood clutching the hand of her husband, Jacob. That Susan had been carrying on with Jacob for some months now wasn't news to her. But for his wife to accuse Susan of witchcraft was the greater evil. An accusation made following the discovery of her spouse's adultery. A discovery that caused her an attack of the vapours.

The local assizes judge cleared his throat to pronounce sentence. "As it says in the book of Exodus: *'Thou shalt not suffer a witch to live.'* In this year of Our Lord, 1644, I pronounce that you, Susan Blackwood, be weighted down and thrown into the water until you are drowned." He paused and rocked in elevated position on the bank, to regard the men holding Susan in the boat. "Carry out the sentence."

Without a word, the fellows strapped a series of weights onto Susan's trembling legs. She stared across the water to where her sister watched. Her face creased with heartsick agony. Susan was not the first accused soul charged and executed for witchcraft. Not the first slain in the village pond that sat atop a wooded hill near their tiny rural hamlet. For more than two years the Parliamentarians and Royalists had been at war, tearing England asunder. Small wonder amidst such death and everyday injustice, those with an axe to grind could gain. It was easy to monopolise the pervasive puritanical hysteria to destroy their enemies.

The men in the small, bobbing vessel hurled the weights over the side with a dull splashing sound.

"No!" Mary shrieked. She stepped into the freezing pond to stand in ankle-deep solidarity with her twin.

Susan called across the surface through her own sobs. "I love you, Mary."

The unravelling ropes went taut and dragged the young woman into the water. Her body sank with a shower of spray. It vanished to the imperceptible bottom of the foreboding watery pit of execution. In the stillness of that cold morning, only one sound remained. It came from the heaving, grief-stricken lungs of Mary Blackwood. Jacob Parsons bowed his head, along with Annie Moore and several of the other villagers. Goody Parsons held her chin aloft. She stared across the calming pond surface with self-righteous zeal.

Mary caught sight of the aloof glint in the accuser's eye. She turned where she still stood, ankle-deep at the miry edge. "I suppose you are happy with yourself?" she spat at the startled woman. "Do you think to have done the will of God? My sister was no witch as you well know, Margaret Parsons." Mary extended a finger in one fluid motion to point straight at her quarry. "May you be struck down in endless suffering and torment for this falsehood, and your belly remain forever barren."

A gasp rippled through the assembled crowd, as if the pointing finger were a magic wand. An occult device firing off a dramatic spell like a lightning bolt. Annie Moore ambled to the water's edge with creaking limbs. She reached out both hands to try to calm the distraught and furious girl. "Hush now, Mary. Give them no cause to condemn you as well." She twisted round to face the assizes judge and villagers. They appeared to be eyeing the pretty, black-haired maiden with a questionable look. One that suggested something more than 'guilt by association' with Susan. She coughed and moved a pleading gaze from one to the other. "Good neighbours. Pay no heed to the distressed cries of this unfortunate child. She has suffered cruelly from the outcome today. But the girl only speaks words borne out of grief and love for her sister. Which among us would do any less under such circumstances?"

The assizes judge tweaked a thin, grey waxed moustache. "Best to take her home." Then he shifted his gaze to Mary. "Pray none of your curses against Goodwife Parsons come to fruition, girl. It would be far better for you if they did not, lest you join your accursed sister in hell."

Mary regarded him with indignant defiance. Her pale cheeks flushed and her eyes brimmed with tears.

Annie Moore helped Mary from the pond. She ushered her out of sight back down to the village with care. Ever since fever took Henry and Constance Blackwood, the spinster had watched over the daughters of her deceased friends. The woman had no husband or children of her own. As such, Annie always regarded the Blackwood girls in a motherly manner. Like the offspring her now-ageing body never produced. This attitude made the tragic events of the past day even harder to bear. Not to mention the very real danger in which Mary's outburst had placed her. The two women clutched onto each other. They approached the tiny limestone cottage that had always been Susan and Mary's home. Its thick walls sagged with age. The structure appeared to squat alongside the village stream, which formed a tributary of the River Coln. Annie took Mary inside and closed the door behind them with a gentle click.

* * *

Mary Blackwood had stayed away from the village pond for several days. She remained secluded, shut up in the tiny cottage. When the girl could actually face it, she spent some lonely hours at her spinning wheel. The fruit of the Blackwood sisters' labours provided a meagre living. Now the output would be halved, but there was of course one less mouth to feed as well. In fact, there was now only one mouth in the entire household as it happened - hers. Ruminating on this reality brought back the sting of grief afresh to her breast. But grieving wasn't the only thing keeping the young woman indoors. Annie Moore had advised her to maintain a low profile in the community for a time. At least until talk of her angry charge against Margaret Parsons faded from local gossip. There would - no doubt - soon be a new and interesting matter to discuss in its place. Then the girl could resume life as normal. Or at least as normal as one could manage, after the false accusation of a beloved sibling for witchcraft. An accusation that led to their execution. In her heart of hearts Mary knew nothing would ever be the same again, either within or without. Her heartbreak and anguish festered and fomented into rage and a desire for vengeance.

I need to get outside before I go completely mad. The thought caused her to place a set of carding brushes down. She had been using them to prepare woollen staples for a rolag to spin. Mary slipped a home-made shawl about her shoulders. She opened the cottage door and peered out into the fading light. *No-one about. I'll take a turn up the hill.* The girl latched the door behind her. With deft steps, she nipped between the spread-out collection of tumbledown stone hovels. The less folk who saw her, the better. The air in that interwoven landscape fabric of sheep hills felt damp. This was often the case, but more so in the vicinity of the hilltop village pond. The place had always been a source of legends and fables. Ever since the witchcraft trials and executions, nobody dared venture there after nightfall. It was a safe bet that visiting this site - more than any other - at that hour, would enable her to go about unnoticed. Plus, she needed to 'talk' with Susan. It seemed to her that the place of her twin's execution (or murder as she considered it) would be the most appropriate spot. Dainty fingers reached up to rub tired, smoky coloured eyes. They looked puffed and reddened from days of almost unblinking concentration. She had remained indoors while spinning, struggling sometimes with unreliable light levels. It felt good to focus on trees, rivers, hills -

anything that enabled her distance vision to correct itself.

A cloud of birds erupted into flight from the treetops, amidst a cacophony of flapping wings. Mary watched them swoop away from the minor clearing in which the pond was situated. The surface of the water was still, like a mirror. Weeds, algae, leaves and other waterborne vegetation floated on top, swayed beneath, or poked through into the fading light. Not far from the bank, the bottom soon disappeared from view into silent depths. The pit where they had killed her sister. Mary squatted at the edge in movements evidencing a lack of energy. Her back hunched over, arms across her chest to clutch their opposite shoulders. She closed her eyes and let out a faint sigh. It was an exhalation of the hopelessness that continued to steal away any zest for life, or the desire to live it. In the silence, a sudden but subtle ice-cold breeze blew across the back of her neck, causing the girl to shudder.

"If you speak to her, she will hear you." A sultry, feminine voice followed the breeze from the trees behind the mourner.

Mary started, turned from her crouch and rose to peer through the undergrowth.

"Who's there?"

No reply.

"Show yourself. Please." She added the second word as rather a pathetic afterthought. Mary didn't have the strength to be angry at yet another person.

A faint, sickly aroma like too-sweet strawberries teased the Blackwood girl's nostrils. It was March.

Where could the smell be emanating from? "Who are you?"

The voice spoke again. "Allow me to show you."

"Mary?" A different vocal timbre sounded from further along the water's edge to the right. A call Mary thought she would never hear again.

"Susan. How can it be?" Tears streamed down Mary's face as she tore through the waving grass to embrace her sister. "You're so cold. Did you manage to slip away from the pond unseen?" Mary shivered at the dry yet glacial feel of her twin's freezing skin.

"No Mary," the condemned girl regarded her sister with empty eyes. Her face was pale, the expression distant. Yet it was definitely Susan.

"B-but, you're alive," Mary stammered.

"Not as you are," this last sentence seemed to echo. A stronger wind blew through the clearing, causing a cloud of dust to blow into Mary's face. When she rubbed her eyes clear, the figure of her sister was nowhere to be seen.

"Susan? Susan?" she roamed the banks, spinning around and calling in different directions.

"Such a touching reunion," the voice from the trees bore a hint of mockery beneath its silvery siren song.

Mary stood still, arms hanging limp at her sides. "I must be going mad." She uttered the words with a resigned groan.

"Nay. But madness killed your sister. Madness drove those simpering religious fools in your village to stand by and see her slain." This time there was a keen, sibilant hiss cutting through the words. "And for what,

Mary? So a frigid, barren woman could take revenge? Vengeance on the joy of her husband's union with another who partook in the pleasures of the flesh. Pleasures she rarely afforded him herself."

"W-who are you? How do you know my name and what my sister did?" Mary shivered. *Is this some illusion or sickness of the mind brought on by grief and anger?*

"I am Nemesis, Rhamnusia, Adrestia. I am the inescapable bringer of retribution. The giver of justice and zephyr that announces the storm." The tone of that voice throbbed with hidden power and dripped with nebulous intent. From out of the rustling bushes a tall, shapely naked woman strode into the clearing. A long mane of rich, thick red hair cascaded over her shoulders and swirled about her curvaceous torso. Her eyes shone like burning torches. Their glowing luminosity blinded and obscured any attempt to read what lurked beneath.

A chill swept through Mary Blackwood and froze her to the spot. "Are you a demon?" she struggled to get the words out.

The naked woman laughed and placed one leg in front of the other. Her hips slunk as she strode closer to the terrified maiden. "And what is that, Mary? One who is an enemy of your religion? Behold what that religion has done to your sister." The creature arced one upturned hand across the surface of the water. Its unseen power swept back the floating detritus and dragged Mary's gaze with it. The blackness of the dark water cleared, allowing the girl to see all the way to the bottom. There was Susan. She struggled and fought with ropes that secured weights to her lower limbs. The panicked victim writhed in terror. Bubbles escaped her mouth. Her eyes widened in horror at the realisation her final moments had come.

"Stop it, stop it!" Mary screamed. She choked back stinging tears.

The vision faded.

"Are you not angry at such injustice? Does not your heart burn to see the guilty receive due recompense for their actions?" the naked woman walked around behind the Blackwood girl as she spoke.

Mary wiped her nose with one finger. "But how? What can I do? Annie Moore says the village may well suspect me of witchcraft too, after my popping off at Goody Parsons."

"But you are not a witch."

"No. Neither was my sister. I don't know if anyone convicted hereabouts through ordeal by water was guilty of anything much. They never hurt Susan or I. Though, the village accused Goody Mason of causing the fever that killed our parents."

The naked woman raised one long, thin eyebrow and regarded the girl with a faint smirk. "Did they now? And how many have had their lives taken in the waters of Nevermere on account of such charges?"

"Seven to date."

"Seven," the redhead exhaled the word, closing her eyes as if lost in absolute ecstasy. "Then that shall be the price."

"W-what price?" Mary shook, still unsure if she was going completely mad.

"The price of your sister's return."

"Return. How? Can you really do that?"

"No. But The Master can."

"Master? You mean... Satan?"

The creature hissed and spat. "Satan! Adversary? And what are those who murdered Susan? My prince is not your enemy. He is..." She thrust her nose close to Mary's left cheek, hot breath blowing out between sharp, steely teeth. "The Light Bringer." Her tongue licked Mary's cheek in a long, seductive and wet motion.

The body of water blazed with an intense aura. Beneath its surface, Mary could see seven figures - including her twin. They reached out as if trying to make their escape back into the world of the living. She recognised each face: those condemned of witchcraft in the village. Condemned and drowned here in the pond.

"Only He can imbue someone with such powers on earth. This is His realm, and The Master rewards His faithful servants." The naked creature moved her head aside, and the waters returned to their natural state.

Mary remained staring into the blackness, long after Susan's face disappeared from view. Her fists clenched. Her mind swam with the self-righteous, satisfied countenance of Goody Parsons. After much thought - and feeling the numb emptiness of loss wash over her again - she finally spoke. "What must I do?"

"A contract shall be the bond and promise between us. A contract signed in blood. When you are ready, you will write it."

"But I cannot write. Mother and Father taught Susan and I to read, but-"

"When you are ready, the words will come. Seven souls must you take in vengeance from the village. The murdered victims of Nevermere will aid you in this endeavour. They will come to help at any hour, once summoned during the night watches."

"And then my sister will return?"

"And then you will receive power." The redhead's eyes glittered at Mary and she turned to wander off into the bushes whence she first appeared.

Among the reeds at the water's edge, a frog plopped into the murky mire.

Mary swallowed hard and picked her way past the trees to stand on the lip of the hill. In the little valley below, wood smoke rose in wispy curls from abundant chimneys. She drew in a sharp breath and regarded the 12th Century St. Mark's Church on a rise beyond the village. A frown creased her forehead, and the girl moved her gaze from house to house. Her eyes half-closed with resolute intention. She whispered in an almost animalistic growl. "Brethren, your judgement cometh."

* * *

"You heard her curse Goody Parsons. She extended her hand and called for endless suffering and torment," a red-faced man bellowed. He slammed down a pewter tankard on the bar of 'The Woolpack Inn.' The air hung heavy with smoke and the stench of stale beer.

"And don't forget her charge that Margaret should remain barren," added a meeker tone from one side.

"Aye, there's that too," roared the first. "How much longer are we to allow the Blackwood daughters license to persist? Daughters of darkness foisting their evil curses upon our God-fearing community. One has met her judgement, but the other still remains. What say you?"

The bar erupted with determined shouts and calls for justice upon Mary Blackwood.

In the dark lane outside, a cloud of moths flocked around a lantern. Beneath, Annie Moore listened with mounting concern. She shuffled away with tentative steps. Her mind searched for options to save her only remaining vicarious daughter.

Logs snapped and crackled in the cottage fireplace. Intermittent sparks flew up the chimney. A puff of smoke followed from wood not yet dry and seasoned for use.

Mary Blackwood rested on a stool, hunched over a rough wooden table. Before her, a blank piece of parchment and quill that once belonged to her father, sat alongside a pot of ink. The creature at the pond had informed her that she would find the words of their contract when she was ready. *Does that mean I must learn to write first?* The girl placed her head in her hands at the seeming impossibility of the situation. Images of Goody Parsons gloating about her victory and the murder of Susan chased through her brain. Mary closed her eyes and thought of the promise of power. A reward delivered after the demise of seven new souls from the village. She didn't notice her own hand reaching out to pick up the quill and dip it in the ink pot. Nor did she have any sensation of the writing implement in motion. It whipped back and forth, tip scratching across the surface of the parchment in vigorous strokes. Only when the top of the feather brushed against her cheek as her head fell forward, did the tickling sensation rouse the girl from her trance. She sat up and stared in disbelief at the document. A collection of words had appeared in the centre of the page. They were neat and well arranged. Mary snapped her head around, looking for anyone who may have entered the cottage. Was this some joke or trick to indict her with the self-righteous witch hunter crowd? Those hypocrites ever baying for blood and justice? Satisfied that she was still alone, the young woman picked up the parchment. She held it near a sputtering candle flame to read:

'The undersigned do hereby attest that they will - by all necessary means - deliver the mortal stroke upon seven souls from this village and its immediate environs. Said souls are offered in tribute to The Master, whereupon such sacrifice will witness him afford the undersigned power beyond all natural reckoning in this life. In the course of this undertaking, those souls already in thrall to The Master pursuant to their execution for witchcraft at Nevermere, will aid any signatory upon nocturnal request for the same. Once

expiry occurs in relation to this mortal realm for the beneficiaries, they do hereby surrender their own souls forever to the ruler of this world. This promise shall be considered binding upon signature in blood.'

Mary drew a sharp breath at the final condition. *Am I selling my soul to the devil for vengeance and to bring Susan back?* She thought about the cost and the alternative. *Do I want to go to a heaven populated by the likes of Margaret Parsons and her God, anyway?* She reached for a blade that she had used to sharpen the quill.

A sudden banging on the cottage door caused the young woman to jump.

"Mary. Mary, it's Annie. Please, you must let me in right away. Your life is in danger."

Mary unbolted the door and drew back at the strained expression on the old spinster's face.

Annie raced across the threshold and tugged at the girl's arms. "I heard men talking down at 'The Woolpack.' They're fixing to come for you on a charge of witchcraft, Mary. You must go, now."

Mary's face paled. She spun and picked up the parchment, before holding its edge over the candle. It wouldn't burn! She screwed the paper up in a ball and tossed it into the fireplace. Flames licked all around it, but the document was neither blackened nor consumed.

"What is it, Mary?" Annie watched the anxious expression on the girl's face without comprehension.

"My certain death if it's discovered. Whether or not I

sink or float in the pond." Mary collected a pair of iron tongs from the fireside and retrieved the hellish contract. From down the lane a murmur of angry voices became audible. Mary turned to her matronly neighbour. "Annie, can you stall them for me?"

Annie shrugged and looked confused.

"Please," Mary shook her.

"Okay child. I'll do my best." The spinster hurried outside.

Mary tossed a bucket of water from beside the front door onto the fire. The flames died in an instant, filling the tiny cottage with choking smoke and fumes. She was now in almost total darkness, the room only illuminated by that small candle resting on the table. The young woman crouched by the chimney breast and reached a hand up inside to feel for a loose chunk of limestone. Her father had always kept some spare money in a little metal box there. He hid it away in that secret space behind the concealed stop-gap. The box retrieved, she folded the paper contract with trembling fingers. Outside, the angry voices approached. In the near pitch-black room, illumination from their lanterns and torches announced its presence. The mob would be here at any moment.

"Out of the way, you old crone." Mary could distinguish the voice of Jethro Cullen. He was a bawdy, red-faced drunkard who liked the importance of leading a crowd in pretence of God's service. She hoped the murderous hypocrite hadn't hurt Annie while pushing her aside. The metal box slid back into its hole and Mary replaced the chunk of limestone by feel. At that moment, the first footsteps reached the cottage exterior.

A male voice coughed. "What trickery is this? No good hiding in the night, daughter of darkness." Jethro Cullen stuck his crimson visage through the doorway, raising a lantern aloft. "There you are." He belched and leered at the terrified, raven-haired figure cringing in the corner. The rest of the mob surrounded the building. Jethro drew himself up to his full height and puffed out his chest, better to bellow with authority. "Mary Blackwood, you stand accused by your peers of witchcraft against the people of this village. You will be taken from here to a place of confinement to await the next visit from the assizes judge. Whereupon you will stand trial for your accursed deeds." He looked round and called to some of the figures peering through the little cottage windows. His face shone with glee as they fogged the glass with their breath. "Take her away, lads."

Mary's skin flushed, her nostrils flared. All the pent-up emotions of recent days burst forth from her lungs in a scream of hatred. "I'll kill you!"

Jethro swung his lantern back round and jerked his head. The pendulum-like beam of light flashed across the length of the blade. It still rested on the table between them. With a growl, the Blackwood girl launched herself at the ringleader. One hand swept up the knife, and she put her entire body weight behind it in that final charge. The large man stumbled backwards, eyes bulging. He placed one wavering hand on the door, then fell with a crash, the metal buried deep in his stomach.

Mary didn't have time to comprehend what she had done. A cudgel blow struck the side of her head and she reeled across the table top, before plummeting to the floor. Her temple struck the hearth, ending her motion.

"No!" the wailing voice of Annie Moore broke through the male shouts. The old spinster pushed past the girl's assailants to crouch by her side. Blood poured from Mary's mouth and the room began to fade as Annie clutched onto her weakening hands. "Mary. Mary, don't leave me. Please."

Annie's face faded into a tunnel of light. Mary Blackwood's eyes rolled back in her head. The lids closed, never to re-open.

2
Big City Blues

"So, once we reach the next milestone of the project, our developers can bring geofencing into play. The resulting mobile app delivered to your customers, will lead to greater engagement. They'll receive Push Notifications whenever they near the boundaries of your commercial outlets." He might have sounded like a techno geek. But, six foot one, well-built and square-jawed Douglas Ashbourne didn't reinforce the stereotype. Hazel eyes peered out beneath thin eyebrows. He regarded the clients sat around the firm's shiny conference table. Doug scratched his broad nose. Fingers moved down to stroke a semi-grey, short stubble beard. The salt and pepper appearance blended with his neat, dark brown, side-parted hair. A crop that also showed the natural silver highlights of middle age. He caught the eye of Jack Morris - a colleague at 'Hyde & Clarke Project Management.' The pair were quite a team in the 'Geospatial Division.'

Jack shrugged; these clients were difficult to read.

Doug gazed out the tinted plate-glass window. Eight floors below, London traffic stopped and started between sets of lights. Someone dressed as Father

Christmas avoided getting splattered across the front of a BMW. The vehicle darted round a red double-decker bus. Its driver noticed the pedestrian at the last moment and swerved.

"It's good to know we have so many options." Harry Johnson - senior manager of the visiting client team, mouthed the nondescript response.

Doug winced. That didn't sound like the kind of enthusiasm he was after. The kind that came with appreciating what GIS technology could do for their business. *Didn't I explain things well enough during the presentation? Why aren't these people getting it?* He shook the thoughts aside, taken aback by the attendees rising to leave.

"Thanks for the presentation," Harry Johnson shook first his hand and then Jack's. It was a lacklustre example of gratitude. The man neither emoted nor made eye contact, beyond the polite bare minimum.

"What was all that about?" Jack stood open-mouthed when only the two of them remained in the conference room.

"Was I unclear? Did my presentation suck?" Douglas regarded his thirty-nine-year-old colleague with punctilious scrutiny.

"Baby, it rocked!" Jack slapped him on the shoulder.

"Doug, Jack, can I see you in my office for a minute please?" Eckhard Kaufmann, their wiry German senior manager poked his read around the door. He straightened his thin rectangular glasses.

"Well this doesn't sound good," Jack muttered. They

followed their boss back to his plush corner office.

"Close the door, would you Jack," Eckhard motioned with one hand and took his seat.

Jack Morris swallowed and clicked the door shut. He joined Doug on a pair of chairs facing the German's desk.

Eckhard cleared his throat. "There's no easy way to break this news, so I'll just come out and say it. The firm have decided to drop geospatial from its management portfolio."

"What?" Doug blinked and lifted a wrinkled brow.

Eckhard raised both his hands and sucked in his cheeks. "Now before you start, Douglas, we all know what a 'GIS Evangelist' you are. Nobody understands or implements the technology better than you."

"Better than *us*," Doug motioned to his colleague.

"Cheers mate," Jack added, his own brow furrowing.

"True," the German conceded, although without appearing convinced over the addition.

"So what's the problem then?" Doug leaned forward.

Eckhard drummed his fingers on the desk. "The thing is, senior management have noticed a real drop in client adoption of this technology. We're in difficult times. People are always asking us for tighter budgetary options with their projects. GIS is one very logical arena to cut back on. I don't need to tell you that it hasn't been a particularly good year for the company, with fewer client wins than ever. It's a competitive market and everyone is tightening their belts."

"All the more reason to implement tech that gives you a significant edge, wouldn't you say?" Doug countered.

Eckhard sighed.

"But the bean counters don't see it that way," Jack spoke for him, his tone thick with sarcasm. "So where does that leave us, Eckhard?"

Eckhard opened a draw and pulled out two envelopes. "I'm sorry, gentlemen. You have both been very dependable and hard-working employees."

"Very dependable and hard-working employees, my arse!" Jack spat. He slammed his mug of high-street chain coffee down on a bar. With a grunt, the fellow hoisted his overweight frame onto a stool alongside Doug. "Didn't count for shit when they wanted to save a couple of quid though, did it?"

Douglas took a bite out of a panini and peered through the window across the street. A light, pre-Christmas snow flurry blew in the air. It whipped about the huddled figures of a Salvation Army band playing *'Joy to the World.'* Their efforts seemed to delight passers-by. Behind the musicians, an old meeting hall bore a bright neon sign. This should have read: *'Glory to God in the Highest.'* Instead, the final letter 'e' had blown. Doug grinned to himself. It was an appropriate irony: Christmas shoppers rushing past a church band, beneath a sign declaring: *'Glory to God in the High st.'*

"What's so bloody funny?" Jack chided him. "How

are Lizzie and the kids going to react when you tell them you got shit-canned from work?"

"I don't know," Doug shook his head and sipped his own coffee.

"Redundant right on top of Christmas. My wife is going to go nuts. You would think 'Hyde & Clarke' could have at least waited a couple of months before lowering the boom on us." Jack placed his head in his hands.

"You'll find something else."

"If I'm lucky. I'm almost forty, mate."

"So?"

"So? Do you have any idea how hard it is to get a job at my age? And you're forty-six, going on forty-seven for Chrissake."

Douglas shrugged. "I'm sure there are jobs out there for guys with our skills and experience, willing to work."

"News flash, Dougie: Nobody wants blokes our age any more. You know all that experience and those qualifications we worked so hard to get? Well, it actually counts against us in the world of paying as little as possible for as much as possible."

"Are you serious?"

Jack nodded, eyes wide. "Let me tell you about my cousin, Ashley. He got laid off from a successful career as an IT Trainer in the public sector. Years of experience and awards, and all the tickets an employer could ask for. He was forty-two. Do you think he could get another job?"

"Why not; aren't law firms and the like always

looking for IT Trainers? Heck, we've even recruited a few on projects ourselves over the years."

"And how old were they, Doug?"

"Oh I don't know, thirty-two or so, I guess."

"Uh huh. Ashley rarely got a response to his applications and CV e-mails. If he did, it was usually something like: *'Sorry, you're too qualified.'* Code for *'Sorry, you're too old and expensive to hire. Plus you won't take a lot of shit and be a yes man,'* if you catch my drift. It's no good being a 'self-starter' these days, unless you also happen to be a 'just-starter' along with it."

"Did he need to raise his sights then?"

"Nope. He tried everything from top-flight training jobs to minimum wage local admin posts. The whole employment gamut. Age discrimination might be illegal, buddy, but it happens every single day. And don't even get me started on the number of fake jobs he applied for, time after time."

"Fake jobs?"

"Yeah. You don't have to be on the market too long, before you realise that a whole host of supposedly available jobs are permanently advertised. I mean, to the point where you can actually recite the same job description by heart. One post read: *'We need an experienced IT Trainer for a short-term contract, with the possibility of a permanent extension. The applicant must be able to start Monday, to fill an immediate staff vacancy.'* Fun huh?"

"What's wrong with that? Sounds ideal to me."

"Yeah, it did to Ashley too. But after watching the same advert appear every week for over a year -

demanding someone who could start on Monday - he realised it was all bullshit."

"What happened to him? Is he working now?"

"His troubles are over."

"Well that's something."

"His troubles are over because he's dead, mate. After his wife and kids left him and she got the house, he couldn't afford to keep a roof over his head. Last Christmas the cops pulled his frozen corpse out of a ditch. Ho Ho Ho and joy to the fucking world," Jack flipped his nose upwards in the direction of the worship band."

"That's terrible. I'm sorry, Jack. I had no idea."

"This throwaway culture of ours doesn't just dispose of things, Doug. It wastes people too. Good people."

Doug's previously confident posture slackened somewhat. He was anxious to inject some positivity. "Do you think you'll stay in project management, if you can?"

"Unless I can find another game to up-skill in, I guess. If Kaufmann was right about the cutbacks on geospatial adoption, a sideways move might be sensible. You won't like that though, hey? GIS has been your baby for so many years."

"So, I'm over the hill as a prospective employee at forty-six and geospatial roles are thinning out. Does that mean I have to create my own job then?"

"It's what a few folk are doing. Either that or you could drop out and become some kind of new age hippie. Can't quite imagine you milking goats and knitting tofu sweaters though, mate." Jack grinned and motioned his head towards Doug's chin. "But if you grew that beard a little longer…"

Doug snorted and finished his coffee. "I'm gonna miss you, Jack. We've had a good run of things one way and another, haven't we?"

Jack nodded. His eyes watered as his face softened. "The very best. Spotty dog."

The two men climbed down off their stools, shook hands and clapped each other on the back.

At the tube station they parted, each wondering if they would ever meet again.

Doug shuffled along a Circle Line platform to allow train passengers to disembark. A recorded loudspeaker announcement crackled overhead. "Mind the gap. Mind the gap."

The gap? That's where I am right now with my work. Question is: how do I bridge it, and what does the other side even look like? He adjusted his tie, squeezed the handle of his briefcase and climbed aboard the train.

* * *

"Hi Hun. Hey, you're home early. Don't tell me: you took a few hours off to get some Christmas shopping? Where have you hidden the presents this time?" Elizabeth Ashbourne beamed from ear to ear. She dropped her car keys into a bowl near the front door of the family's London Victorian mid-terrace home. The forty-one-year-old, five foot one female still looked as pretty to Douglas as the day he married her. If anything, twenty years of marriage had improved her, like the ageing of fine wine. That was something Doug knew a thing or two about. Lizzie had a round face with side-parted hair in a bottle blonde, shoulder-length bob. Dark roots *added to* rather than *detracted from* her appearance. Grey eyes beneath plucked brows, sparkled either side of a long, slender nose. This led down to a wide triangular mouth with pale pink lips.

"No. No shopping today," Doug kissed his wife. "Where are the kids?"

"Becky is taking Bethany to one of those shops where you can make your own teddy bear."

"Are you sure you trust our eleven-year-old with that rebel?" Doug frowned with mock concern.

Elizabeth revealed an array of perfect white teeth and squeezed her husband. "She's too much like I was at eighteen."

"I know. That's what scares me," Doug winced as his wife poked him mischievously in the ribs. "How about Josh?"

"He's round at Alan's, painting some of their fantasy miniatures. I asked him to be back for dinner at seven. Stir fry. Nothing special. So, how was your day?" she walked into the kitchen. "Oh, I see you've started early." Elizabeth motioned to a clear wine bottle, now only half full of a golden liquid. It stood alongside a fat beeswax candle that flickered on the dining table. "Is that from last year's batch of mead? You must be running out by now. Go easy, you won't be bottling the new lot until spring. Unless I can persuade my bees to produce some extra honey on overtime. And if I could perform miracles like that? Well, I'd make so many extra soaps and candles to sell that I could quit my job as an office manager." Laughter flashed in her eyes, but soon dimmed as she caught Doug's expression at her quip. "Honey, whatever is the matter?"

"I got made redundant today." The words came out with a flat, even tone.

Elizabeth's mouth fell open. She hugged her husband. Doug wasn't given to emotional outbursts. But, Jack's assertions about how difficult it might be to find new work actually knocked him for six. He struggled to get hold of himself and not blub while Elizabeth sat him down at the table. She reached over and retrieved an extra wine glass from a rack. The woman poured them both a measure of mead, emptying the bottle. "Tell me all about it. What happened?"

Doug relayed the events of the day and the content of his final coffee shop chat with his - now former - colleague.

"And right on top of Christmas, too. Bastards," Elizabeth clenched her teeth.

"That's pretty much what Jack said. So, what do you think? I took a look at the recruitment websites when I first got in. Nothing doing in my line at present."

"Those sites are enough to drive anyone over the edge." She put her glass down. "Or drive them to drink."

"It wasn't that. You know the mead and country

wine making has never been about getting wasted for me. I hate that feeling, anyway."

"I know, Darling. I'm guessing you went down into your meadery (once known as the Ashbourne family basement) because it's a hobby that takes your mind off things."

"Exactly."

The front door opened and closed with a bang.

"Mummy, Mummy, look at my new bear," an over-excitable eleven-year-old girl burst into the kitchen. She clutched a well-dressed, plush teddy. The youngster stood four foot ten, with a round face like her mother. Light brown hair in shoulder-length waves accompanied a fringe down to her eyebrows. The maternal thick-set frame, nose, mouth and pale grey eyes were also distinguishable.

"He's lovely, Bethany. What are you going to call him?"

"Reginald."

"Reginald?" Elizabeth and Doug spoke in unison.

"Well, he looks like a Reginald."

Doug shrugged, and a smile broke across his previously troubled face. "I guess he does at that. Is your sister with you?"

"Hi Dad. Hi Mum," a bored, female voice called from the hallway.

"Thank you for taking her to the shop, Becky." Elizabeth stood up and walked to the kitchen door.

"Sure."

Rebecca Ashbourne had blonde hair - also with dark roots - although in short, messy curls. Eyeliner decorated her familial grey eyes. It caused that feature to dominate her rounded facial aspect. Bushy yet feminine eyebrows, a thin nose and small mouth completed the countenance. Combined with her five and a half foot frame, this presented an attractive eighteen-year-old. One who could turn a head or two. Even a head or three, if she ever got over that teenage need to not actually smile at anything. Especially anything that wasn't considered rebellious or cool. "So, why is Dad home early?"

Elizabeth looked at her husband. He nodded.

"Well, I'm afraid your father was made redundant today."

"No way." Rebecca dashed down the hallway and poked her head around the kitchen door frame. "Are you okay, Dad? Are you going to sue them?"

"No. They haven't done anything wrong, though their timing could have been better." Doug patted Reginald as Bethany waved the bear under his nose.

"Bummer," Rebecca snorted. "Hey, you know suicides are high at this time of year over things like that."

"Becky!" Elizabeth snapped, eyes bulging and teeth gritted.

"What? I was only saying. Gosh, take a chill pill, Mum. I'll be in my room chatting on-line to Kate if you need me," the teenager tutted, spun and walked upstairs.

The front door went again.

"And there's the other Ashbourne," Elizabeth sighed.

"What? What did I do?" a six foot tall, gangly sixteen-year-old boy hung up his coat to reveal a t-shirt depicting a wizard and dragon. He had eyes like his father, but spaced far apart of his long, rounded nose. Spiky brown hair with minimal sideburns formed up high above a broad forehead.

"Nothing, Josh. We've all arrived home within a short space of one another." The boy's mother smiled at first, then her eyes widened. "What happened?" She pointed at a bandage on her son's lower arm.

"A gang jumped Alan and I right after school. My arm got sliced by a knife. Alan's Mum took me to the surgery, but it's only superficial. Nothing to worry about. Life in modern London, I guess."

"Nothing to worry about? Come here," Mrs Ashbourne demanded of her dismissive offspring.

"Oh, hi Dad," Joshua acknowledged the presence of his father upon entering the kitchen.

Elizabeth held up the bandaged arm in front of the lad's face. "This isn't nothing, Joshua. What if they had stabbed you?" her face went taut.

"Hey, we pushed them off as best we could and made a run for it like you always told me to," the boy protested. "Jeez, Mum. What more could I have done? We were only walking home from school. It's not like we went somewhere dodgy looking for trouble or anything."

Elizabeth's head sunk.

Josh motioned to the seated man. "So, why is Dad home early? Did they fire him or something?"

"Pretty much. Made me redundant, anyway."

Joshua slapped his forehead. "Oh man, I'm so clumsy. Dad, I'm sorry. Are you alright?"

"That's okay, son. Yeah, I'll live."

"Well make sure you do. Suicides are high at this time of year over things like that, you know."

"Thanks, we've already been informed," his father tweaked an eyebrow.

Joshua caught his mother shaking her head at him in disbelief. The boy's shoulders sank. "Oh no, I did it again, didn't I?"

Doug laughed and stood to pat his son across the shoulders. "Well done for getting away from the gang. Has Alan's mother reported this to the police?"

"For all the good it will do, yeah. We didn't know the guys. They weren't from our school."

"Is Alan okay?"

"He took a beating. Got a couple of bruises, but other than that he's fine."

"Alright then. Well, you'd better go sit down and rest. If you need the dressing changed, tell us right away. You should keep the wound clean."

"Thanks Dad." Joshua loped off down the hallway.

"Why did your company make you impotent, Dad?" Bethany piped up from where she had been sitting Reginald alongside the empty bottle of mead.

"Where did you hear a word like that?" Mrs Ashbourne wheeled, her expression a mixture of shock and amusement.

"It was in one of Becky's magazines," Bethany muttered, eyes scanning from side to side in bewilderment.

"I wasn't made impotent, I was made redundant. It means they don't need me to work there anymore," Doug looked from his youngest daughter to his wife. "Though it certainly makes a guy feel impotent."

Elizabeth blew him a kiss. "You'll find a new direction."

* * *

"What's going on in that sexy brain of yours?" Doug placed his arms around Elizabeth's waist, nuzzling her neck. It was after ten at night and the kids were all in their rooms. Elizabeth Ashbourne stared out the kitchen window. A fox tripped their back garden security light. The animal turned first to face the kitchen window, then to some bee hives sited at the opposite end of the lawn. Ascertaining there was nothing further of interest to study, it leapt over the neighbouring fence. Its bushy tail swung behind.

"Hey, hey, hey, what's all this now?" Doug noticed the silent tears. They rolled down across pretty, feminine cheeks. He felt his wife shudder.

"I'm so fed up with London. First your job situation, then Josh suffering a knife injury on the way home from school. On the way home from school, Doug! What is this city coming to? Next year Bethany starts at secondary, and I don't want her anywhere near this place."

"I know, I know," Doug squeezed her and rocked from side to side. "Hey, how about we open a bottle of my fruit wine? It's not a *school night* and we don't have to be up early."

"Sounds good," Elizabeth blew her nose, frown lines subsiding.

"Want to come down and help me choose one?"

"Why not? As long as you don't take advantage of me in your private space."

"Spoil sport," Doug teased and dragged her by the hand to the cellar door.

The basement light flicked on. It revealed shelves crowded with one-gallon glass demijohns. These were filled with all manner of various coloured liquids. Each had a rubber bung and bubbler airlock fitted. At the far end, some larger glass vessels contained higher volume batches. A large, stainless steel bucket with racking arm completed the array of home-brew equipment. It featured a soft blow-off tube for escaping gas during vigorous fermentation. This curled into a glass jar of sterilised water. From time to time it emitted a large bubble. On the other side against the wall, a ceiling-height wine rack stood crowded with bottles.

"What do you fancy: Strawberry, Blackberry, Blackcurrant?" Doug descended the stairs to admire his collection.

"Ooh, Blackcurrant." Elizabeth's demeanour had lightened.

"The king of the fruit wines. Good choice," her husband stepped back and took a deep breath. He fished around on the rack for a wine bottle containing a deep red liquid.

"It always reminds me of a decent Beaujolais. What do you think, Mr Winemaker?"

"If it's well made, it should," Doug nodded. "Here we are. Is a two-year-old vintage alright for Madame?"

"That will be fine." She paused. "Doug?"

"Yeah?" the man replied in a distracted tone. He studied the fermenter airlocks to check their fluid hadn't run dry and exposed the contents to the air.

"Why don't you do *this* for a living?"

Doug snorted. "Be serious. Come on, I've filled the basement with kit and taken it over. Sure, we have enough to enjoy a bottle whenever we want, and our friends and neighbours do very nicely thank you. But, making meads, melomels and country wines on a commercial basis requires space, equipment and money. Things we don't have spare at present."

"Yeah, we do. Or we could have."

"Huh?"

"Grandpa's cottage."

The words stopped Doug dead in his tracks. She had his full attention now. "Are you suggesting what I think you're suggesting?"

"Come on, Doug. Grandpa died in September and I've been pondering what to do with the cottage ever since."

"Why didn't he leave it to either of your aunts or your Dad, they're still alive?"

"The memories of all those summer holidays I spent staying there as a child, I imagine. Plus, none of his kids ever took to beekeeping like I did. He was a great mentor." She indicated the array of fermenters. "And you haven't done badly out of that knowledge yourself, with all that free honey."

Doug thought for a moment. "You want to sell up and move to Gloucestershire? You know it would take at least a year after we've moved down there before I've got any products ready for sale. If we combined your present hives and your grandfather's, how many would that make?"

"Around thirteen."

Doug whipped his mobile phone out of a back pocket. He launched a spreadsheet application he had toyed with many times. A document loaded entitled *'Mead and Wine Costings.'* Doug tapped in the number of hives. "Ten hectolitres of mead a year, based on a typical hive production rate. Direct selling after costs including duty, I'd clear 13K profit. Maybe eleven or so at market stalls and eight or less with retailers."

"What about if you combined fruit wines? There's plenty of space for bushes at the cottage."

Doug tapped in a few more figures. "We could do a fifty-fifty split, producing another ten hectolitres of fruit wine. I'd need around thirty plants. More if we plan on making melomels along with standard meads. That would add about seven grand with direct selling. A little under six at markets, and three and a half or so via retailers."

"And don't forget my soaps and candles. If we're moving to the Cotswolds, I'm hardly going to commute and be an office manager. With thirteen hives I could be looking at around six kilos of beeswax. At the price my products go for, we'd see a little under five thousand in profit."

"So, we sell this house, then combine the equity we have in it with my redundancy payment. The idea being to keep us afloat until we start making some money?"

"Plus, I'm only going to need to tend the hives between April and August. About three hours a week given that number, but more if we expand. There must be some extra local work I can pick up to help."

"It's a bold plan, Lizzie. Are you sure you want to do this? Having nice memories of summer holidays with your grandfather is one thing. Moving into the house where he died and trying to scrape a living out of nothing is quite another. What sort of state is the place in, anyway? Is it definitely big enough for the children?"

"I haven't been there in quite a while, but it will need some TLC. After my father and aunts all left home and Grandma died, he barely touched, changed or maintained anything. But it was home to a family of five when Dad, Auntie Amy and Auntie Sandra lived there."

"Great. What about planning permission for a meadery/winery on-site? No way can we afford an extra premises elsewhere."

"There are several outbuildings you could convert. Why don't we at least go up there and have a look? Come on. How many years have you been playing with that spreadsheet? You've always dreamt about turning your hobby into a proper business."

"I guess we have nothing to lose. I could use a pre-

Christmas break after everything that's happened. Imagine the kids might enjoy it too. I've never been to the Cotswolds. Is it nice?"

"Nice? Oh Doug, it's beautiful."

"Well, let's head back up to the kitchen. You can tell me all about it over a couple of glasses of this little baby," he waved the bottle at her. "Night boys," he turned and grinned at his fermenters.

"Are you going to tuck them in later and read them a bedtime story too?" Elizabeth teased.

"I might at that," Doug toddled away with a comic but defiant gait.

It was well after midnight when Douglas Ashbourne's head finally came to rest on his pillow. He lay holding Elizabeth close. Her warm breath blew against his chest. The blackcurrant wine had been as smooth as velvet. A stout competitor for any grape variety. New excitement at their wild plans combined with the loosening effect of alcohol. That and a desire to overcome the anxieties of the day, flowed into effortless lovemaking. Now in the darkness, his mind swam with possibilities. *I can hardly believe what she's willing to do. This old pipe dream of mine is about to become our next endeavour to earn a living for the family. Thank God for Lizzie. None of this could happen without her.*

3
Pennycress Cottage

"You're not really bringing that bear with you, Bethany?" Rebecca Ashbourne climbed into the family's silver Subaru estate, behind the driver's position.

"Why not? Reginald wants to see the Cotswolds."

"For goodness' sake, you're eleven years old."

Elizabeth twisted in the front passenger seat. "I seem to remember someone taking a stuffed dog everywhere with her until she was thirteen. Isn't Rufus still sat on your bed? Perhaps Bethany might like him, now you're so grown up you no longer enjoy the company of soft toys?"

"No." Rebecca frowned at Bethany. Her stern expression halted the rising sparkle of excitement on her younger sister's face.

"Leave her alone, Becky." Joshua clicked his seatbelt into place on the other side of the rear seat. He patted Reginald on the head. The bear sat in the lap of its owner, who occupied the middle spot.

"Who asked you, nerd face?" Becky said.

Joshua started to speak but sucked the words back

down at a hand raised in warning from their mother. "Don't start, you two. We're not having a row all the way to Gloucestershire."

"Everyone set?" Doug eased himself behind the steering wheel and shut the driver's door with a solid clunk.

"Ready as we'll ever be," Elizabeth replied with a perfunctory tone. She examined her offspring in hopes they'd finished their outbursts for now.

"Cotswolds, here we come." Doug keyed the ignition. He signalled to pull away. The SRS warning light hadn't even yet extinguished itself during the start-up procedure.

Elizabeth checked the mirror her side and clamped her lips together. "Eager much?" she said to her husband following a brief pause. He completed their departure from the kerb side.

Doug snorted and shot his wife a wink.

The car drove out of their relatively quiet residential London street. It soon merged with the throng of jostling vehicles in Saturday traffic.

The constant stop-start at red lights eased off. The All-Wheel drive estate joined with the Oxfordshire bound M40. At Beaconsfield Services, Bethany decided she needed the loo. A temporary halt to their steady progress felt welcome to the whole family.

Joshua stood in a newsagent that formed part of a ring of shops. They skirted an open food court at the motorway rest area. He buried his head in a computer gaming magazine.

"Anything good?" Doug sidled up to him. "Your Mum was wondering if there was something extra to put on your Christmas list."

"A new RPG. Didn't think it was going to be out before Christmas, but the developers seem to have turned it around in the nick of time."

"That's the joy of Internet connectivity. If they missed something, your console will pick up the patch when they release it - after the fact." Doug's eyes misted in a faint but perceptible manner for a moment. The old world of projects, slippage, deadlines, and hot fixes was almost part of his nature. He'd worked in IT delivery for so many years.

"This would be great. I loved the last game they did."

"Well, write it down for us. I'd hate to get the wrong one."

"Sure Dad. Will do."

"Have you seen Becky?"

"She's glued to her mobile phone out there somewhere." The boy waved in the general direction of the seating area.

Doug emerged from the shop to spy his eldest perched on the edge of a seat at a small, round table in the food court. She was attempting to focus on her phone. A task interrupted by two barely shaven, swarthy-looking fellows in their late twenties. They appeared to be hitting on her. The former project manager caught sight of someone sat to one side reading a newspaper. Details of the latest grooming gang scandal covered the front page.

"We're all done. Where's Becky?" Elizabeth reappeared from the ladies toilet, Bethany close in tow.

"I was about to call her." Doug stepped into his wife's field of vision. "Becky." His voice rang across the general hubbub and noise of crowds milling about.

The girl caught sight of her father with a relieved expression. She rose to her feet and walked straight towards him. The two pests received no further acknowledgement. They exchanged glances and scowled at the middle-aged man. A moment later, the pair wandered over to a pretty brunette teenager. She wiggled a shapely bum and queued up for a burger, oblivious of their interest. Seconds later, the interruption routine began again.

Doug frowned. *I hope there's someone looking out for that kid, or she has a sensible head on her shoulders.*

"Ready to go?" Becky joined her family.

The M40 climbed on a right-hand curve above the town of High Wycombe. Picturesque undulations of the Chilterns rose on every side.

"Hey, you *did* remember the keys, I assume?" Doug signalled to change lanes.

"Yes. I'd have been popular if I'd forgotten those, wouldn't I?" Elizabeth retrieved a bunch of jangling metal from her handbag to show all was well.

"What number is Great Grandpa's house?" Bethany tried to lean forwards too rapidly. Her seatbelt held the girl rigid.

"Number?" Elizabeth looked round.

"Yes. You know, like our house is number twenty-eight."

"Oh, I see. Well, a lot of places in the countryside don't have numbers as such. My grandfather's house sits on its own plot of land adjoining a quiet lane on the edge of a village. Houses out there tend to have names rather than numbers."

"Wow. So-"

"Pennycress Cottage." Elizabeth could discern the next question long before her daughter finished vocalising it.

"What's a Pennycress?"

"Cotswold Pennycress is a flower. Actually it's a very rare member of the cabbage family, though you wouldn't think so to look at it. The cottage has any number of the plants growing all around it."

"Will we be able to see the flowers?"

"We'll be able to see the plants. But it only flowers in spring, so not today. The flowers are white, and very tiny in small clusters that appear on top."

"Oh. Did Great Grandpa keep bees like you do?"

"Yes he did. That's where I learnt about beekeeping. I spent my summer holidays at Pennycress Cottage as a young girl."

"Was that when everything was still black and white, like in the old films?"

Elizabeth caught a minx-like expression on the face of her youngest.

"Don't be stupid, Bethany." Rebecca rolled her eyes.

"She's joking, dimbo." Joshua's brow creased.

"Get stuffed, dickwad."

"Hey hey hey." Doug raised his eyes to glare at them in the rear-view mirror. "Shit!" He stomped on the brakes as a lorry cut him up in front. The action caused the occupants of the estate to lunge forwards. Their restraints locked in place. The man gave a loud blast on his horn.

"Feeling better?" Elizabeth pursed her lips, eyes narrowing.

"Yeah Dad, language. There's a couple of kids back here." Rebecca indicated her siblings with a shake of that rough-curled head.

"That's quite enough from you, young lady," her mother said.

Doug took the Oxford and Cheltenham turn off onto the A40. Shortly after a large roundabout at Headington, the dual carriageway reduced to a friendlier scale. Things became more residential at Cutteslowe. A much smaller roundabout appeared on Elsfield Way. The Subaru went straight across in the direction of Witney.

"If we'd have taken a right back there, you could have seen Wolvercote Cemetery." The man glanced up to see if his son was paying attention.

"What's at Wolvercote Cemetery, Dad?"

"That's where Tolkien is buried."

"Are you serious? Oh man, I would love to visit his grave. Can we stop there on the way back?"

"We'll see how we're fixed for time."

Rebecca scowled at her brother. "Who's Tolkien?

Not another one of your geeky authors."

"Shut up, Becky. Tolkien was a genius. He wrote *'The Hobbit'* and *'The Lord of the Rings,'* among others."

"Oh great. So now I've got to spend my weekend watching a live nerd mourn at the grave of a dead one."

"A little more respect might be appropriate." Doug cleared his throat. "Professor John Tolkien was an Oxford don. Along with writing some of the most successful books of all time, that is. Even if they're not your cup of tea."

"You shouldn't encourage him, Dad. My loser of a brother is never going to get a girlfriend if he doesn't drop this stupid fascination with elves and wizards. It's bad enough that you let him listen to those crusty big old vinyl discs of yours."

"Those crusty big old vinyl discs are called LPs. And some of those prog rock bands produced world class music in their day." Doug fought hard to restrain the annoyance in his voice.

"Rebecca. Why don't you enjoy the view in silence, if you haven't got anything nice to say." Elizabeth's tone was sharp.

"I would if there was anything worth looking at." Rebecca crossed her arms.

"Give it a few minutes. Once we're past Witney, you'll catch sight of the River Windrush out your window on that side. When we hit Burford, I'm sure you'll change your tune."

"What's in Burford then? Not more dead nerds?"

"Burford is 'The gateway to the Cotswolds.' That's

where you'll see the characteristic limestone buildings appear. People come from all over the world to admire them."

"It's also been voted one of the top ten idyllic places to live in Europe," Doug said.

"But we're not going to *live* there, are we?" Rebecca raised an eyebrow.

Her mother sighed. "No, but Coln Abbots isn't that far away. It's quiet and not overcrowded with tourists like Burford gets during the day. But the place is still beautiful. Give it a chance, will you?"

Rebecca remained silent.

"That's a thought," Elizabeth said to her husband. "Why don't we stop in Burford for a bite to eat and a wander? We only need drive down the hill to park and it's not far off the road to Bibury and the Coln Valley."

"Sure. I'm keen to see it after everything I've read."

"Go right here," Elizabeth pointed across a roundabout. She turned to rouse her children. "See that stone with a picture of a sheep down here on the left? We are now entering the Cotswolds Area of Outstanding Natural Beauty."

"Why has it got a sheep on it, Mum?" Bethany rose in her seat to get a better look.

"Because 'Cotswolds' means 'Sheep Hills,' or pretty much close to it in modern translation. Once upon a time the wool industry in this country was famous around the world for the quality of its fleeces. Many merchants in this area became very wealthy off the back of their lions."

"Lions? But I thought you said they were sheep?"

"Yes Darling. Cotswold Lions are a breed of stocky, broad-backed sheep indigenous to the region."

"Oh. Hey look at that street."

The occupants of the vehicle sat transfixed at the view ahead. The road ran down a steep hill. Tumbledown, honey-coloured limestone cottages lined either side. Further on, the buildings became shops and inns. At the foot of the hill, the road paused at a set of traffic lights. These controlled the right of way over a single lane, medieval stone river bridge.

"Okay, I have to admit this is pretty cool. Hey, look at those boutiques." It was the first time Rebecca's mood had improved throughout the whole trip.

Lines of amusement formed around the edges of Elizabeth's eyes.

Doug breathed out, mouth wide and upturned, teeth showing. "The pictures don't do it justice. This was a great idea, Lizzie."

"Take another right here. There's a free car park near an offshoot of the Windrush, close to the church." An overwhelming sense of joy and pride swelled in her breast. It was good to show off this first example of wonder from her childhood, to her own family.

The Ashbournes spent a pleasant couple of hours wandering around Burford. They enjoyed a light lunch before a crackling log fire in a quaint, traditional English tea room. As afternoon wore on with a wintry red sky, the Subaru re-ascended the hill. It turned right and continued on to a hotel near the outskirts of Bibury.

"We should still have time for a quick turn around the village before it gets dark," Elizabeth said to her husband. They dropped a couple of bags in their double room. Rebecca and Bethany had a twin. Joshua got tucked up in a tiny single, jammed underneath the eaves down the hallway.

"This is 'Arlington Row.' A famous collection of cottages. They were once occupied by weavers who lived here on the rack isle; a water meadow of the River Coln." Elizabeth led them over a low stone footbridge across a wide but shallow river.

"You're enjoying the whole *tour guide* thing, aren't you Mum?" Rebecca squinted and rocked on her heels. "Perhaps you should do that for a living if we move here."

Doug dropped a few coins into a wall mounted collection box. A sign indicated it as being for the preservation of the historic site.

"Does anyone live in them now?" Bethany peered through a tiny, leaded light window on the ground floor of the first house. The whole collection seemed concertinaed together, with nary a straight line nor parallel surface in sight. The triangular roofed organic-looking structures had a natural feel. It was a common characteristic of cottages in the region. They appeared to have been grown, rather than built. Almost as if the landscape itself spawned them.

"Come away from the window, Darling." Elizabeth retrieved her daughter with gentle hands. "This is somebody's home."

Joshua thrust his chest out and surveyed the scene.

"Don't tell me. You're having one of your fantasy dreams about living here like a bobbit." Rebecca frowned at her brother.

"That's Hobbit, not bobbit." Joshua didn't even look at her.

"Why are there bags in front of the doors, Mum?" Bethany walked along pointing at several of the entryways.

"They're sandbags. As you can see, the meadow is very low. It's prone to flooding at this time of year."

The family continued their stroll. At last they reconnected with the principal thoroughfare. It ran through the village near a trout farm.

"Where's Pennycress Cottage then?" Bethany looked from side to side, as if they might have walked past it without telling her.

"That's up the road at a much smaller village called Coln Abbots," Doug said. "We'll go there first thing tomorrow."

"A much smaller village," Rebecca repeated the words in hesitant, staccato fashion. "You've got to be kidding. I mean Burford was quite trendy and all. This is alright to look at for tourists, but there's nothing much here. And we're going to view a house in a place even more remote and empty? Does it even have running water?"

Elizabeth raised her nose with a stern countenance. "Yes. Actually the cottage has its own water source from one of the many natural springs that rise here in the valley."

"Oh joy." Rebecca's mood sunk back into sullenness.

"You didn't tell me Pennycress had a spring-fed water source." Doug's face lit up at his wife.

"Didn't think about it. Oh, I guess that'll help with the mead. I know you tend to buy spring water rather than use the tap variety, but it's not that expensive is it?"

"No. It's not so much the cost saving as the added provenance that will help out with marketing. Mead fermented from local honey with natural, Coln Valley water. It's a winner."

The family made their way back to the hotel.

* * *

The Subaru pulled into a long gravel drive, through an opening between a wall of thick hedges.

"Are you alright?" Doug caught sight of the dreamy - if sad - expression on his wife's face.

Elizabeth raised a hand with curled fingers and brushed her lips. A thousand memories of endless happy summer days came flooding back. She remained silent and opened the passenger door. They climbed out into a typical, mist-heavy Cotswold valley December morning.

Pennycress Cottage was a detached, four bedroom oolitic limestone building laid out in an L-shape. Its twisted and sweeping tile roof sagged in the middle. Two chimneys poked through it and dormer windows adorned half the upper storey. Windows to the main structure bore thick, stone mullions. The place sat against a wooded bank which rose high above. Sweeping hills climbed upwards on either side. Lawns adorned with wildflower beds stretched in front and all around. Many of them contained a green mass of stalks that would bloom in spring. The eponymous Pennycress that gave birth to the cottage's name.

"Where are your grandpa's bees?" Doug asked. He stood and admired the attractive but somewhat rundown home. It wasn't exactly a hovel, but the place needed a lot of work. More than a lick of paint, but less than a total rebuild.

Elizabeth waved to the right. "Behind those bushes, along from the outbuildings."

Doug's ears pricked up at the word 'outbuildings.' He was keen to take a peek at what he had to work with on this new project.

"Can we at least get a look inside this dump, before Dad starts enthusing about his possible new mead shed. I'm freezing." Rebecca accentuated her statement by flapping arms across her chest. She rubbed her shoulders with a vigorous impatience.

"It's like fairyland." Bethany wandered around between the flowerbeds, eyes shining, mouth wide.

"Don't *you* start. One fantasy crazed lunatic in the family is quite enough." Rebecca looked from her kid sister to her brother.

Joshua surveyed the exterior of the building and its

setting. An appreciative smile arose that he couldn't contain.

Elizabeth fished the front door keys out of her handbag and inserted one into the lock. She gave it a twist, but the door only budged an inch. Some of its eucalyptus grey/green paint - a common feature of Cotswold buildings - flaked off and blew away on the breeze.

Doug stepped closer to examine the portal. "Must have swollen with the moisture. This area is quite damp."

"That's typical of these river valleys. Part and parcel." Elizabeth tried pushing harder. No response.

"Oh shame, we can't get in. Time to go home then?" Rebecca said.

Her mother scowled at her while Doug put his shoulder into his own attempt to gain entry.

With a rubbing noise of wood on stone, the door juddered open.

The Ashbournes filed into the hallway. Through a doorway to their right, sat a comfortable lounge. Faded and worn cream carpet lay illuminated by light from triple aspect windows. A large inglenook occupied the remaining wall. Its copper hood flowed down over the hearth of an open fire, now cold but still containing unswept ashes. Two threadbare armchairs and a sofa were all the furnishings the room contained. One of the chairs positioned close to the fire, appeared to be the most worn.

Elizabeth's eyes moistened, and she touched her chest. She thought of Grandpa sitting there all alone, eating a meagre meal before a fading fire. The mental image caused a lump to rise in her throat.

"What on *earth* is that?" Rebecca's voice rang more with contempt than curiosity from another room across the hall.

The rest of her family shuffled in to find a large country kitchen that opened out onto a conservatory.

The teenager stood pointing at a massive, cast iron beast of an object.

"That's a cooking range." Doug strode up to the green monstrosity and opened one of the oven doors by way of demonstration. "Hey Lizzie, did your Grandpa have a back boiler on this?"

"Yes. It heated all the water and everything else. The fireplaces only provided some extra warmth."

"Guess they shut it off after he... Anyway, how was it fed?"

"Oil fired. A tank in the garden. No wonder it's so cold in here." Elizabeth watched their breath hang on the air in small clouds.

Joshua wandered through a door in the rear kitchen wall. It opened into a comfortable dining room, also featuring a fireplace. This one contained a wood-burning stove, its glass window sooted up. The room was devoid of table, chairs or anything else in the furnishing line. A couple of old prints hung either side of the fire. Another door connected to a utility/boot room with rear external door. The utility also led back into the hallway alongside the stairs.

"How about a look at the bedrooms?" Doug's eyes widened, and he leaned over to grin at his youngest daughter.

Bethany could barely contain herself and ran to the stairs with a skip and a bounce.

"Are you sure she's eleven? I'm certain I was more mature than that at her age." Rebecca's lidded eyes followed the younger girl out of the room. Her head shook in minute movements.

"Will you stop?" Elizabeth brushed passed the eighteen-year-old without making eye contact. They ascended the creaking staircase. The woman walked to the kitchen end of the house. It was the place where her grandparent's master bedroom had been situated.

Doug opened one of the dirty windows. He latched a wrought iron lever in place to let some fresh air into the upstairs space. A thick-legged spider scurried into a crack in the sill. "This is a nice size. Lovely view across the gardens. I reckon we could put a small en-suite with loo and shower at the back there, if you fancy?"

"Sounds like you're warming to the place." Elizabeth joined him at the window.

"I think your notion is an inspired idea."

"What on earth is that smell?" Rebecca demanded in disgust from one of the other rooms.

Her parents emerged into a medium sized bedroom at the opposite end. Elizabeth knew it had once belonged to her Auntie Amy.

Doug sniffed and ran his hands down a patch of mould stuck to one wall. It was moist to the touch. "Only some damp, Becky. I imagine the roof needs a look."

"Isn't that unhealthy or dangerous?" Rebecca examined every wall surface closer. She acted like a detective on the hunt for some mass murderer.

"Only if we were to make you sleep in here before it's fixed." Doug accompanied her inspection tour.

"It's so dark." The girl didn't appear encouraged.

"Well, that's the advantage of having a room under a pitched roof. We can put an extra skylight window in."

Elizabeth walked over. "Yes. That way you can lay in bed and look up at the stars. The night sky is great around here. Not much light pollution."

"You've got the wrong Ashbourne for crap like that," the girl crossed her arms. "Anyway, my phone only has one signal bar. And even that has dropped to no signal once or twice. What's wrong with this place?"

Bethany streamed into the room. She seemed oblivious to the pungent odour and her big sister's objections. "Mum, Dad, this house is amazing. Oh, when can we move in? Christmas would be so wonderful here."

Elizabeth grinned at her husband before looking back to the excitable eleven-year-old. "Well, not this Christmas at least. But we should be in and well settled by the next one, if everything else goes okay."

"I'm going to head back to the lounge and imagine where our Christmas tree could go near the fireplace." The girl turned and ran back downstairs. Her feet thudded on every step at the pace and enthusiasm of her descent.

Doug moved to the door. He paused to regard his

wife on the way out. "I'll find Josh and see if he wants to inspect the outbuildings with me."

"You do that, Hun. As for me: it's time I had a little chat with our teenage daughter."

"This is a reasonable space. Hold that end of the tape measure, would you Son?" Doug passed a metal clip into Joshua's fingers. The clip attached to the end of his extending pocket measuring device.

"Sure thing, Dad. Do you think there will be enough room without building extra?"

They stood in one of three long, low, single storey, pitched roof stone structures. It must once have been a piggery, dairy or served some other such purpose. Something agricultural, down through the centuries of the property. The floor was dirty, with corroded garden implements scattered here and there. An old Belfast sink rested against one wall. Above, a rusty-looking tap protruded through the stonework.

Doug noted down his reading into a small, leather diary where he had drawn a rough floor plan sketch with a pen. "Well, we could get a good three, small business sized stainless steel conical fermenters in here. Water and power connections will be easy enough. We'd better check the drainage situation. I reckon we could move storage tanks around on pallets after racking the must. That way we can mature it in the other buildings. They're close together and all on the same level, with decent sized double doors. A hand-pumped pallet truck should do the job. Means I can keep things flexible. Less upfront costs if I haven't got to plumb rigid pipework in." He paused from writing to look at his son. "So how was your room?"

"Great. I like this place. So much better than London. Do you think the move is a go?"

Doug thought for a moment then nodded. "I'm not sure what would be worse: Becky's moaning if we *do* move here, or Bethany's moaning if we *don't*."

Joshua chuckled, clenching his teeth. "Good luck making Becky happy about anything."

Doug retracted the tape measure and placed it back in his pocket. "Mmm. Well, your mother is hammering a few home truths into her as we speak, unless I'm very much mistaken. Don't say anything though, will you? I know your big sister can be a pain at times, but we're all going to have to pull together and get along to make this thing work. Can you do that for me, Josh?"

"No worries, Dad."

"Good man." Doug clapped him on the shoulder and they walked back into the grey, misty morning air.

4

Points West

Tyres splashed through a puddle. The water had been coloured a dull beige from the claggy Cotswold soil. Doug turned downhill at the lane leading away from Pennycress Cottage. The Subaru descended past a twelfth century church on their left. Several impressive seventeenth and eighteenth century table tombs adorned the greensward. They stood out amidst the regular stone markers.

"They're funny graves." Bethany pointed and leaned across her brother for a closer look.

"Built by the emerging middle classes. St. Mark's is quite a nice church. Shame we haven't got time to stop today," Elizabeth said.

"Are they for showing off?" The eleven-year-old continued her line of inquiry.

Doug glanced at her in the mirror. "Something like that. A way for people to go from saying, *'look how successful my life is,'* to *'look how successful my death is.'* Consistent."

His wife prodded the man's leg and shook her head. "Cheeky monkey."

Coln Abbots was a minor village built into a gentle

hill on the banks of the River Coln. It sat midway between Winson and Ablington. By way of services it had a small, volunteer run local shop and post office. Also a pub and the church they had already passed. A variety of quaint, chocolate-box cottages poked up between patches of trees. Local farms occupied a couple of overlooking hilltops. The river snaked throughout the whole. Its volume increased here and there, courtesy of small tributary channels. Sparkling little watercourses that flowed down from the rounded hills.

"The Woolpack Inn. Do you think we can get lunch here, or is it still a bit early for you?" Doug noticed the pub getting closer. It was a two-storey structure with an attractive porch, hemmed in by a low stone wall.

"Too early. I promised Becky we'd pop into Ciren for a look at a decent sized local town. We'll do Cheltenham another time, of course. Don't want to play all my cards at once," Elizabeth said. She bent her neck to notice Rebecca staring out one of the rear vehicle windows. The girl didn't comment.

"Ciren? Oh, you mean Cirencester. Hark at you with all the local lingo." Doug rocked his head from side to side in a teasing fashion.

"We'll find a nice pub or something for lunch on the way back through, I'm sure."

"Okay, Ciren it is."

Their late Sunday morning perambulation around Cirencester, assuaged some of Rebecca's anguish. The ancient market town proved a pleasant surprise. Familiar high street chains and tasteful, bespoke shops all falling over one another. Their proximity to Coln Abbots made the world feel a little less like it was about to end.

As the day wore on, the Subaru came to a halt in the car park of a smart looking pub. A swinging sign declared it to be 'The Fosse Arms.' It sat in a tiny hamlet off the A429 Fosse Way. The car park was crammed with shiny Range Rovers, executive Land Rovers and other upmarket vehicles. Most gleamed with a spotless sheen and evidenced very little mud. Alongside the area where patrons sometimes dined alfresco, stood a collection of hitching rails. A glossy notice read: 'Horse Parking.' On this particular day, nobody had stowed their equine transport there.

Inside the bar and restaurant, the place appeared spotless. Its polished wooden floor - blemish free. Not a hint of dust, dirt or grime could be found anywhere. The wall ornaments seemed (to Doug and his wife at least) rather tacky, fake and stereotypical. The menu consisted of traditional-sounding fare like 'Steak and Ale Pie.' But, the arriving wood or slate platters displayed fussy foam and arty-farty squirts of sauce. A hint of sculpted veg, if you were lucky. Not exactly honest pub grub. The place was a gastro joint for the chattering classes. It played at being a 'proper local' for those who wouldn't be caught dead in a real one.

"Did you want to eat here, or try somewhere else?" Doug read his wife's mixed facial expressions. She seemed to be thinking the same type of things.

"On a Sunday we'll be lucky to get in anywhere without booking. Let's see if they've got a table. If they have we'll take it, otherwise the decision has already been made for us."

"Good call."

'The Fosse Arms' had fortunately received a cancellation from a party of six. So, the family of five settled down to a well presented (if somewhat fussy and overpriced) meal.

Doug paid at the till as a beaten-up, old green Land Rover Defender chugged into the car park. Its driver staggered out and made several attempts to close the vehicle door before it took. Mud caked the wheel arches and knobby tyres. The panels were scraped and dented, windows about ready to fall out.

Further along the bar, a boisterous group of the elite roared with laughter. All wore designer label polo sweaters and tailored shirts. They sneered at the portly but not over-fat figure ambling towards the pub entrance.

"Whatever *is* he driving?" one bellowed and slammed his palm down alongside a half-empty beer glass.

"Go away, Farmer Giles. This isn't a place for the likes of you," said another. A fresh round of mirth rippled through his friends.

The pub door opened to allow access to a white-haired man in his mid-sixties with a circle beard. His threadbare tweed jacket and holey green jumper spoke of old-school character. A perfect match for the dirty beige work trousers and nondescript black wellies he also wore. The chap was thick set, of medium height with rosy cheeks - no doubt obtained from a life working outdoors.

"What do you call that vehicle of yours then, a tractor?" one of the well-to-do barflies shouted. He tried to deliver a Gloucestershire accent with his clipped Eatonian one. The attempt was a complete failure.

Doug was getting more than a little fed up. "It's a Land Rover. The original Land Rover, in fact," the former project manager said. He shot the crowd an annoyed frown.

"Looks old enough to be," one of the men laughed.

Another of his friends raised a set of car keys and pressed the plip. Outside, lights flashed on an immaculate 'Chelsea Tractor.' A vehicle that cost more than Liz and Doug's first house. He pressed it again and cleared his throat, nose pointing in the air. "No, old boy. That's a Land Rover."

The roughly attired new arrival scanned down one of the menus. His eyes studied what people were being served. His head shook, and he wheeled on the spot. Only a faint muttering accompanied his exit. The Ashbournes weren't far behind.

"What a rude bunch," Doug said loud enough for the retreating old man to hear, once they were all outside.

The scruffy local stopped to regard the family walking up behind him.

"Bloody toffs and incomers. They've destroyed the

Cotswolds. Turned it into a sodding theme park and ruined all the good pubs by making them like this. Don't even get me started on what it's done to house prices. When my grandson finishes at university in Hereford, there's no way he'll be able to live where he grew up. Fat chance of him going into dairy farming round 'ere with his dad and granddad."

"Dairy farming? That's a tough gig these days." Doug was warming to this guy already.

"It wouldn't be, if the supermarkets gave us a decent price for our milk. So many of my friends have gone under. Costing more to produce the stuff than we can sell it for."

Elizabeth's eyebrows gathered in, a pained expression crossing her countenance. "Is your farm close by? You seem familiar."

"Washburn Hill Farm."

"At Coln Abbots? No wonder. I must have seen you around when I spent my summer holidays there as a youngster."

"You know the village?" the man's shoulders slackened.

"Yes. Oh, I grew up in Berkshire. But, my folks often dropped me off in Coln Abbots at Pennycress Cottage to stay with my grandparents."

The stout farmer placed both hands on his belly. "Well glory be. You're Alan and Charlotte Boardman's granddaughter? From which child: Jim, Amy or Sandra?"

"Jim. He still lives in Berkshire."

The man stomped over and extended his hand first

to Elizabeth and then Doug. He nodded to their children and beamed, then looked back at their mother. "I'm Bob Faringdon. I used to go to school with your dad and aunts when we were all kids. How are Jim and the rest these days? I always knew him and his sisters wouldn't stick around here. Everyone said those three were going places. Shame for Alan and Charlotte though."

"We're the Ashbournes. I'm Elizabeth. This is Doug, Becky, Josh and Bethany. Mum, Dad and both my aunts are all fine. Thank you for asking. They haven't been back here for years, except for Grandpa's funeral. I couldn't get away for it, unfortunately. That tore me up. I loved him so much."

The farmer's face lowered. "Wish I could have been there too. I got laid up in bed with a virus myself. So have you been up to the cottage?"

"Yes, we were there this morning. Actually, we're planning to move in and start a local business."

"Well there's a turn out for the books. Doing what exactly?"

"My husband makes meads, melomels and country wines. I'm a beekeeper like Grandpa. We're hoping to sell our home in London and try to make a go of it here."

Doug raised one hand in a delicate defensive posture of submission. "Though what my wife hasn't said, is that we're sorry about being incomers ourselves. We promise not to be anywhere near as rude as that lot." He nodded back in the direction of the pub.

Bob laughed. "You seem alright to me. What with

standing up to those toffee-nosed pillocks and all."

"I bet this used to be a great local." Doug lowered his hand again.

"You're not wrong there, old son. Bill and Mandy Porter ran 'The Fosse Arms' for over forty years. It was a proper pub then. Sausage and mash to eat, a dartboard on the wall, pickled eggs in a jar. Also cheap local ale, plus peanuts and crisps behind the bar. Bill didn't always manage to clean the lines - especially when he got older - so the beer was sometimes a bit stale. No bugger cared, though. The place was full of local farmers, trades and craftsmen. All good folk sharing the latest gossip about our community. That's before the 'money' came in and sucked all the life out of the place. Most of the old crowd's original houses have either been knocked together into bigger properties, or bought as second homes. They sit empty for when weekend visitors come down from the smoke to grace us with their presence. Like that lot inside. I thought I'd pop in today for a bite to eat and see what it was like now. After one look, I'm glad I didn't stay. Thank goodness 'The Woolpack' in Coln Abbots hasn't gone the same way yet. Only a matter of time, I suppose."

"It's a shame." Elizabeth sighed.

"So, you make country wines, eh?" The farmer eyed Doug. "I make a pretty mean blackcurrant wine from my own bushes myself. As good as any bogey-lay, as far as I'm concerned."

Elizabeth and Doug fought down a laugh at his bastardised reference to Beaujolais.

The farmer continued. "Anyway, if you're Alan's granddaughter, you're not exactly foreigners now, are you? That lovely old boy would be completely made up to know you're taking over Pennycress and keeping bees. He always teased me about having more livestock than I did."

Elizabeth rocked back and forth. She placed hands beneath her chin and imagined her grandfather having a good old laugh at his clever comment. "Well, legally speaking bees *are* livestock, so I suppose he was correct."

"Oh I'm not knocking it. He made great honey."

"Well, if you enjoy honey, fruit wine, or a glass of the alcoholic honey variety, I'm sure we'll be happy to hook you up." Doug offered his hand again. Time was pressing on and he knew they still needed to get back to London.

"Likewise. If you need milk, machinery or an extra pair of hands or two settling in, my boy Mike and I will be happy to pop over. Whenever we can spare a moment away from the girls, that is."

By 'girls' Doug correctly guessed him to be referring to his herd of dairy cows. "Well, if you can sell me some cuttings from your blackcurrant bushes, that might be nice. I didn't see any at the cottage while we were up there."

"Done. But no selling necessary. You can have a few plants, I've got plenty. No charge. So, when are you moving in?"

Doug and Elizabeth exchanged glances. They hadn't discussed it as a couple yet. But, everything about this stay had pretty much settled matters, and they both knew it.

Elizabeth spoke. "We need to get some workmen in for a spot of maintenance on the place first. Just the major bits, you understand. Everything else we can sort out after we arrive. Doug's old job recently finished, so I imagine he'll pop up and down to project manage things along the way."

Doug grinned at Elizabeth's suggestion. It was exactly what he had been thinking. "I reckon we'll be in around spring. Early summer at the latest."

"Then I'll see you again soon." Bob Faringdon raised a finger with a flourish. "Merry Christmas, folks."

"You too." The family watched him hop in and start the old Land Rover with a cloud of smoke and fumes. It lurched away down the country lane and disappeared into the fading light of a December afternoon.

* * *

Christmas came and went back in London, much like many others. In the Ashbourne household, there was definitely something extra bubbling away beneath the surface. An excitement not limited to the children of number twenty-eight; even if the eldest of those presented an image of mourning at the idea of leaving 'civilisation' behind. Doug and Elizabeth also felt like a couple of youngsters. A heady mix of joy and nerves. But, with the faintest hint of potential disaster hanging over their heads like *The Sword of Damocles*. Overall though, the feelings were of positivity, possibilities, and a new beginning.

"That's a good job sorted." Doug closed one of several new, fitted skylights in the - now leak free - roof. He completed his inspection of the latest work for the day. "You guys have done a great job throughout." He was speaking to a father and son team of local builders. One he and Elizabeth had managed to recruit for the initial general maintenance at Pennycress Cottage.

"We'll take a look at the structural work on your outbuildings next week," the elder of the two builders said. He was a man in his early fifties.

Doug was keen to make the cottage ship-shape, so he could focus on the meadery/winery setup. Shortly after Christmas, the Ashbournes had got an agreed sale on their London home. But Pennycress needed to be liveable before the family moved up from the city. Thus Doug had used a mixture of his redundancy money and some savings to pay for the building work to date. Released equity from the house sale would provide the extra finance required to finish the cottage. Also to set up in business and keep the proverbial wolf from the door until money started coming in again. While she remained in London, Elizabeth was still working as an office manager. At least one of them was earning. Doug couldn't wait to start bringing home the bacon again. He knew they were shooting for a new goal. But, his self-esteem still took a beating from being a man of leisure. Or at least as much of a man of leisure as someone like Douglas Ashbourne could be. Sitting still and doing nothing wasn't his forte. The guy always had to have at least one project on the go.

"Are you off back to the city in the morning?" Adam Compton, the landlord at 'The Woolpack' in Coln Abbots asked. He placed a simple fry-up down on a table where Doug sat before a crackling, smoky fire. The black Labrador pub dog, Jess, padded over and sat next to him. She licked her chops and watched him with unblinking, shiny eyes. A look as if to say *'you're not going to eat all that yourself, are you?'*

"Yep, back to town on the morrow. Thanks." Doug acknowledged receipt of the hot meal and took another pull on his pint of bitter.

Over the last three months, the incomer had been a regular feature at the pub. A place to lay one's head on his many trips back and forth during the renovation work. The pub had a few basic rooms - all en-suite. Doug liked the old-fashioned, unpretentious atmosphere of the ancient inn. No TV in the rooms. No WIFI or tea and coffee facilities. A simple bed, wardrobe and nightstand with clock. Plus, a shower, toilet and hand basin placed behind a dividing wall. A feature that made the space compact but comfortable. It was all he needed, the price was good, and he could even reach Pennycress Cottage on foot. If he fancied a stroll halfway up the hill, that is. Once the family finally moved in, he intended to frequent this hostelry.

Use it or lose it, as they say. He'd even talked with the landlord about supplying his goods to the pub. Once he got his made-wine production duty and sale licences sorted for the business, of course. Doug knew this wasn't the kind of establishment that would likely sell a lot of mead or country wine by the glass. It was more a gesture of support, and the owner appeared to appreciate it.

Doug ate his evening meal in peace, acknowledging the odd local when they popped in for a swift half. Jess started to dribble and received a chunk of sausage for her trouble. *The Oscar for best play-acting hungry dog goes to...* The diner grinned to himself while she wolfed down the treat.

Evening turned to night and Doug finished his time in the public space of the bar with a glass of cognac. The chest of a fat and grateful canine moved up and down like a pair of bellows, where she lay curled up at his feet. The dog stirred to look up at him as he gave her a pat and turned in for a rest.

Coln Abbots was always quiet at night. 'The Woolpack Inn' sat on the main thoroughfare through the village. But this was such a minor road that it could be thirty minutes between cars passing. Even then, they contained locals travelling to and from home. So, the night watches remained as still as the grave.

Doug's eyes opened. In the pitch-black room, an orange glow flickered through the street-facing window. A commotion of angry male voices assaulted the tired man's ears with indistinct phrases.

Doug peered at the bedside clock. It was well after midnight. *What on earth is going on?*

He swung his legs over the side of the mattress and staggered upwards. From the locked-up bar down below, Jess whined. Already the din from the street sounded like it was moving on. He reached the window and peered out in time to catch what looked like a rather disorganised torchlight procession. They marched with determined strides along the lane away from the pub. *Pretty strange time for a festival. Odd that the barman didn't mention it.* With peace and quiet resuming, he slipped back under the duvet and was soon in a deep sleep once more.

"What was the festival about last night?" Doug resumed his spot from the evening before to take breakfast. Jess wandered over in search of a pat and a tummy rub.

"Festival?" the landlord tugged on an ear, a blank expression written across his face.

"Yeah. Sometime after midnight. A bunch of blokes with proper, old-school torches. There might have been some lanterns too, I'm not sure. I was rather groggy. It's amazing 'Health and Safety' let you get away with that these days. They've been stopping unguarded real flame torches at town carnivals, all over. Didn't sound like Jess enjoyed it much, either. I heard her whine."

The soppy dog nuzzled his leg.

The landlord shrugged. He grabbed the falling glass he had been wiping, right before it almost smashed into the bar. He fidgeted and rolled his neck. "I must have slept through it. Probably some club on a midnight hike. We get all kinds of stuff like that going on round here."

Is he sweating? Doug regarded the grimace on the landlord's normally affable face. *Wonder if he was supplying booze after hours on the quiet to them for something? I'd better not push.*

After breakfast he settled his bill and shook hands with the landlord. A brief goodbye and he climbed back into the rental car. It was a vehicle he usually hired for these multi-day Cotswold progress excursions. The Subaru had been left with Elizabeth. It wouldn't be long now before their family estate made a one-way trip to the village. A trip to settle in the whole Ashbourne clan at their new home.

* * *

"Wave goodbye to the twenty-first century, Becky." Joshua couldn't resist at least one teasing comment. His elder sister stood in the middle of her now-empty London bedroom, mobile phone clutched to one ear.

"Shut up, wimp face." The girl twisted away from where her brother leaned around the doorway. She returned her attention to the call. "Just my lame brother. Oh my God, Kate, I can't believe this is it. We're heading off into the Gloucestershire wilderness like a family of hermits."

"How can you have a *family* of hermits?" Joshua said with a sarcastic groan.

The bedroom door slammed in his face.

The boy descended the stairs into the hallway. Bethany was fidgeting and flitting about like a coffee addict on a fix.

Elizabeth appeared from the kitchen and caught sight of her son. "Is Becky almost ready?"

"Relaying her last will and testament on the phone to Kate, or so I gather."

"Play nice," Doug stifled a laugh. He moved from the living room past the crowd in the hallway. Moments later he spoke with the removal men making their final checks outside.

Elizabeth touched her youngest child under the chin. "Have you said goodbye to number twenty-eight, then?"

"Yes Mum. When are we going?"

"Any minute now, Darling." She angled her head to call up the stairs. "Becky?"

No response.

"Rebecca Charlotte Ashbourne." The tone came sterner, voice louder this time.

A door opened above.

"Okay, okay, I'm coming." The teenage girl stomped down the stairs, banging her feet like a child having a sulk.

"And you're eighteen, are you? Do try not to be such a sourpuss." Elizabeth sighed. "Some people dream of living in the Cotswolds their whole life and never actually get the chance."

"They can have my slot if they want," Rebecca said,

face sullen.

It was the Easter break. The Ashbournes decided this would be the opportune time for their move to Pennycress Cottage. The children were given permission to study at home for their respective exams. An easier deal than commencing new schools during the short summer term. Bethany would start at a Cotswold secondary in the autumn. Joshua was looking at a similar move for his A-Level studies. Rebecca had possible options from two different universities, depending on her results.

The silver Subaru pulled away behind a large blue Pantechnicon. The removal lorry contained the majority of the family's worldly possessions. On his last few trips over to Coln Abbots, Doug had already delivered a lot of stuff: Memorabilia, knick-knacks and other items not essential for day-to-day life in London. He deposited these in various rooms throughout the cottage. Rooms finally in a fit state for habitation. Damp had been removed from the bedrooms - now freshly painted and with thick, plush fitted carpets. The master had a nice en-suite, although the main family bathroom still needed a refit. The parents showed their kids some sample images from the work so far, captured on Doug's phone camera. They promised Rebecca she could use their shower until they completed the other washing space. Joshua and Bethany weren't particularly bothered.

Elizabeth's bee hives were closed off with fly wire and transported to Gloucestershire earlier in the week. She rented a large van for that one and managed to take a quick look herself at the present state of play. Since the couple had to be there and back in a day, the woman was now more eager than ever to return to the Cotswolds. It had been such a tantalising taster.

Doug also emptied the basement of his precious hobby fermentation equipment. It had already gone to Gloucestershire with his collection of home vintages. While the outbuildings at Pennycress still had plenty more work required, they were dry and secure now. Suitable enough to hold such valuable cargo, which barely occupied one third of a single hut. It put things in perspective for Doug. The space showed how much extra scope he now had. Room for developing his beloved pastime into a stable income stream. A lot of work to be sure, but then Douglas Ashbourne was no shirker. He lived for challenges like that.

"Coln Abbots, Coln Abbots!" Bethany pointed at a road sign and bounced in her seat. "I can't wait to sleep the first night in my new bedroom."

It had been a slow journey, keeping the removal lorry close behind them.

A swell of pride rippled through Doug's body as they passed 'The Woolpack Inn' and drove up the hill. "Any minute now." He signalled left. The wheels rumbled over the loose stones of the drive leading to Pennycress Cottage. It looked as quaint as ever. But now fresh paint gleamed on the woodwork. Its windows sparkled and an array of brand new skylights adorned sections of the roof.

"Good job, Dad," Joshua leaned forward and put a

hand on his father's shoulder.

"Thanks Son. Our builders have been excellent. More to do yet, like the kitchen and family bathroom. But, now your mother and I are getting access to cash from the London house sale, we can get those jobs booked."

"At this rate the cottage will be appearing in one of those country lifestyle magazine spreads," Elizabeth said.

Her husband could tell she was very pleased.

"Well if they come round for a photo shoot, you're not making me wear wellies. Not even designer ones." Rebecca's voice was still adamant, but more subdued and less combative than when they first left the city. She wasn't about to admit it to her family, but the cottage appeared welcoming and picturesque. Spending a summer here before heading off to uni, might not be quite such a chore after all.

The estate car rolled to a halt. Doug dropped a set of polished house keys into his wife's palm and gave her a kiss. "I'm so glad you suggested this, Lizzie. It's turned a massive minus into an incredible plus. I know there's a lot of work to do but-"

"But we'll get there." Elizabeth gazed around with determination.

5
Settling in the Valley

"Can we go for a look round the village today?" Bethany asked. She plonked down at a pine table in the old kitchen. The room was still rough, beaten and in need of a refit. Joshua passed her a box of cereal, between crunching on mouthfuls of his own. Rebecca waved her mobile phone around. She fought to maintain enough of a signal to relay her adventures back to Kate in London. Doug sat hunched over his own phone. He was busy keying new figures into a revised business spreadsheet. In front of him, a neglected cup of coffee cooled.

"I should think so. I'm sure we could all use a break from unpacking," Elizabeth said. She sat down with a steaming herbal tea and nodded at her husband's mug. "That'll get cold if you don't watch out."

"Huh? Oh, yeah. Sorry." He took a long gulp of the dark liquid, eyes never leaving the columns of figures.

"There isn't that much to see, is there?" Rebecca gave up on the phone and looked at her mother.

"True enough. But some fresh air and a spot of exercise might be nice. I'll show you the church and then we can have a look at the village shop and post office."

"Thrilling," Rebecca rolled her eyes. "I bet we'll have to stand in line for that one."

Elizabeth ignored her. The woman was no fool. She knew the late teenage strop and bravado ran skin deep at worst.

It was a warm and sunny morning as the family left the cottage behind. They strode down the steep hill towards the village church. The incline was deceptive. Not as gentle on the legs as it first appeared.

They studied a wooden notice board. It stuck up behind a limestone wall that skirted the graveyard.

"St. Mark's" Bethany read the name aloud.

The church was a modest structure. Its Norman south door featured scalloped capitals and billeted hood moulding. The majority of burials appeared to be on this side of the building. As they entered the porch, Doug found an information panel and read aloud.

"St. Mark's is a twelfth century church, with a later addition of this porch in the following century. Note the carving of votive crosses into the stonework by pilgrims."

"You mean they even had graffiti back then?" Joshua said.

Doug continued. "In the medieval period, it was believed that the north door of a church belonged to the devil. Evil always came from the north. So, the superstitious villagers of Coln Abbots blocked up that entrance. Consequently, most people didn't wish to be buried on that side of the building either. A fact represented by the distribution of graves outside. The graveyard features several rare, seventeenth and eighteenth century table tombs. These are indicative of the wealth that once came here on the back of the wool trade. Inside, you will find a Victorian stained glass window. This depicts an angel with scales, weighing the souls of the dead. There is also a fine example of a Norman chancel arch. In the mid-twelfth century, St. Mark's was given - along with Bibury and all its chapels - to Osney Abbey near Oxford, by John of Pagham, Bishop of Worcester. Coln Abbots remained in the hands of the abbey until the Dissolution of the Monasteries."

The church was cool inside. Doug, Joshua and Bethany studied the Victorian window while Rebecca sat in a pew. Her phone was actually registering two signal strength bars in here, so she wasn't about to waste it. Elizabeth found a large visitor's book laid open and read the last couple of entries. One written by an old couple on holiday from Yorkshire. The previous - a family vacationing from New Zealand. She picked up the pen and scribbled an inscription of her own: *'So good to be back in the village where I spent my happiest summer holidays. This time I intend to stay.'*

"No 'intend' about it. We're going to rock this," Doug whispered in her ear.

The woman hadn't noticed his subtle approach behind. She looked up, reading his aspect of projected confidence. Her teeth unclenched and her eyes softened. "Indeed we are."

"Hello there. You must be our new arrivals," a podgy, red-faced woman called to the family. She finished facing-up some tins of veg on one of the few shelves adorning the village shop and post office. "I've seen this gentleman pass on some of his trips and, well… news moves quickly in a small village."

"Elizabeth Ashbourne. The 'gentleman' is Doug, and these are our children Rebecca, Joshua and Bethany."

"Jane Cowley, postmistress and shop volunteer coordinator." The figure waddled over behind a counter. "And how are you settling in, up at Pennycress Cottage? Dear old Alan Boardman used to come in here for his paper every single day. Said the walk up and downhill kept him young and fit, God rest his soul."

"He was my grandfather."

Jane's demeanour had been pleasant from the outset. At the news their recent arrivals had a genuine family connection to the village, this warmed to full-on friendly. "Is that so? I hadn't heard that. How wonderful. Well, I hope we'll be seeing a lot more of you around here."

"Meeting some new customers?" a playful, feminine voice with a hint of cheekiness called from the doorstep.

The Ashbournes turned to find a slim woman, about the same age as Elizabeth. She stood around six feet tall with layered, light brown hair below her shoulders. Piercing bright blue eyes, thin eyebrows and a long, slender nose adorned her oval face. Wide pink lips spread into a subtle, upturned smile. She wore a sky blue, low cut top that matched her eyes, and cream trousers almost the same hue as her flawless skin. In one long, elegant hand the woman clutched a traditional wicker shopping basket.

"Hello Nancy," Jane Cowley called across the heads of the family. "This is-"

"The Ashbournes. Yes, I heard. Thank you." The woman directed her attention to Elizabeth. "I'm Nancy Robbins. We've not long moved here ourselves. October, in fact. Oh, by 'we' I mean my husband and daughter." She shook hands with each member of the family.

"How old is your daughter?" Doug asked.

"Eighteen going on nineteen. She finished her A-Levels last summer, but has no idea what she wants to do next. I don't think university is quite her bag. Moira couldn't wait to get out of formal education. Now she's done with school, Howard - that's my husband - and I decided it would be a good time for us to move to the country."

"Have you come far?" Elizabeth asked.

"No. Not at all. We're from Cheltenham. Once part of the 'Chelts' scene and everything that goes with it." She rolled her eyes and chuckled in a semi-mocking tone. It made Elizabeth think she might be more genuine and less of a snob than some who fit into that grouping. This endeared her immediately.

Nancy glanced from Doug to Elizabeth and back again. "So, do you mind if I ask what you do? I don't mean to be nosey, of course-"

"Oh, no no," Elizabeth interrupted. "We came up from London. Doug's project management job ended, and the city is almost unrecognisable to us now. It's become quite violent, too. So, we decided to sell up and try to turn our hobbies into some sort of income. For starters, at least. Becky is going to uni in the autumn. Josh should start a new school to begin studying for his A-Levels. Bethany will be attending 'big school' for the first time in September."

"How marvellous." Nancy wrinkled her nose in an exaggerated and friendly manner at Bethany. The youngster swayed from side to side with pleasure. Nancy went on. "Which hobbies were you describing, by the way?"

"Ah. Sorry. I keep bees and produce honey and beeswax related products like candles and soaps. Doug is a keen maker of meads and country fruit wines. He's done it for years. Quite accomplished, actually."

"I'm sure he is. It's exciting. Well, if either of you need a hand with your taxes or finances, Howard is a freelance accountant. It's one reason we were able to move out here. He conducts most of his work from an office at home."

"That's good to know," Doug nodded.

"And you've moved into your grandfather's cottage?"

"Yes, Pennycress Cottage, up the hill," Elizabeth waved a hand in the general direction.

"Splendid. We're almost neighbours, in country terms at least. Our place is 'Box Cottage.' It's at the foot of the hill alongside the stream that feeds into the Coln."

"I know it well. Never been inside. But, I used to play hereabouts while staying with my grandparents. Childhood summer holidays and all that."

Nancy's brows raised, warm lines appearing round the edges of her eyes. "Well, then it's time you *did* go inside. Howard, Moira and I would love to have you all over for a welcome dinner, if you're not too busy, that is?"

"We'd like that, wouldn't we Doug?"

"Sounds marvellous. We'd also enjoy returning the offer, but you might want to wait until we've had our new kitchen fitted. That's next on the agenda."

"Excellent. Well, how about Friday evening around seven?"

"That will be great, thank you," Elizabeth and Nancy shook hands again.

"Did you need anything while we're in here, Lizzie?" Doug asked.

Elizabeth glanced around. "Not right now. But, it's good to know what's available, should I find I'm short."

The Ashbournes passed Nancy. She squeezed past further into the little store to begin her shopping.

"Well, that was a worthwhile visit," Doug said while they walked along the lane towards the pub. He looked at Rebecca. "Maybe you and this Moira will get along?"

The girl thought for a moment. "Well, at least her mother seems normal, and they *have* come from the civilised world."

"Knock off the rebel nonsense. It's getting old," Joshua said.

Rebecca didn't bite back but caught the look of slight disappointment on her mother's face. "Sorry Mum. Nancy seems like a nice lady. Moira could be cool too."

"Better. Much better," Doug said with an even tone. "Hey, why don't we pop into 'The Woolpack' so I can introduce you to the landlord? He's been looking forward to meeting you all."

As they approached the pub, a loud and friendly bark erupted from inside. Jess came bounding out of the porch and jumped up at Doug, licking his hands.

"Friend of yours?" Rebecca asked, leaning away.

"Ah, so this is the other woman, Jess, who you've been carrying on with during your visits?" Elizabeth grinned and patted the shiny black dog. The playful animal circled the Ashbournes, tail wagging at a furious rate of knots.

"Oh she's lovely, Dad," Bethany grabbed hold of the Labrador's back. It was an action that almost ended with her riding the animal like a horse.

"Come on girl," Doug motioned at the building. The dog barked again and ran inside ahead of them.

"Well, my goodness and here they are." Bob Faringdon looked up from where he had been leaning on the bar chatting to the landlord. Alongside him stood a younger man around forty-two years of age.

He had watery, pale blue eyes, and a thin straight mouth with lips so pale as to almost appear non-existent. His rectangular face was clean-shaven. A firm jaw complemented the well-built six foot one frame and buzz cut of receding brown hair. Bob motioned to the man. "This is my boy, Mike. Mike, these are them Ashbournes I was telling you about. Elizabeth 'ere was Alan Boardman's granddaughter. I went to school with her father and aunts."

"Pleased to meet you." Mike examined each member of the family. "Dad said you were moving in to Pennycress."

"Doug is going to make meads, country wines, and what were them other things?" Bob scratched his head, broad Gloucestershire accent in full effect.

"Melomels. Mead with fruit in. While you're here Bob, I've got three new stainless steel fermenters on order now. Should be arriving in the next week or so. I don't know how you're fixed, but some extra muscle moving them into position might be useful."

Bob looked at Mike. "I reckon we can spare a bit of time for that. How long do you figure, Doug?"

"Shouldn't be more than an hour or so, after they're delivered. A bit of heavy lifting, that's all. Once the conicals are in the rough spot I need them, I can take things from there: cleaning, sterilising, connecting up valves and so on. Josh and I might be able to manage, but I don't want to do either of us a mischief."

"Say no more." The dairy farmer held up one hand. "You give us a shout up at Washburn Hill Farm when you need us, and we'll be along directly."

"Cheers. I appreciate it. Can I get you fellas a drink?"

Bob's face broadened into a satisfied expression like the cat that got the cream. "Well now, we *were* going to head back to the girls, but I guess an extra twenty minutes or so won't hurt any. What do you say, Mike?"

"Two pints of bitter would go down pretty sweet. Thanks Doug." The younger Faringdon waved at the barman.

* * *

"Must you?" Elizabeth scowled at her eldest.

Rebecca slouched in the kitchen, arms folded, chewing a piece of gum with accentuated slurps.

"Come on Josh, save your game and get down here. We don't want to be late over at the Robbins' house. That would be downright rude," the mother called upstairs.

"Uh," a sound of frustration echoed along the landing by way of reply. "Coming Mum."

"You might be mistaken for one of Mr Faringdon's cows if you keep chewing like that," Bethany giggled at her big sister.

"Lose the gum, Becky." Doug walked in the front door, clutching a couple of bottles from his previous vintages. He placed them in an attractive box. His wife had already added a candle, some soaps and two jars of her homemade honey.

"Yeah, lose the gum, Becky." Bethany stamped her feet with mock annoyance. She examined the box.

Rebecca frowned at the little squirt. Her lips curled into a minute grin. She pulled the sticky, pink blob from her mouth and attached it to the back of Bethany's head. *That'll teach you, Madam.* Bethany didn't notice.

"Josh," Doug called up the stairs with an authoritative tone.

"I'm here," the boy hurried down two steps at a time into the hallway.

"Right then." Doug turned to his wife. "I guess you'd better lead on."

"Did anyone bring a torch?" Elizabeth asked.

Her family exchanged blank expressions.

"Good job I did then." The woman retrieved a tiny, battery operated LED flashlight from her skirt pocket. She clicked the blue/white beam on for a second, then switched it off and stowed the item again.

"I should have thought about it after all those trips earlier in the year," Doug slapped his forehead. "No street lights in the country and it will be dark when we come home."

"You're so prepared, Mum," Joshua said.

"You'll get used to it round here soon enough." Elizabeth twisted for the box.

"Oh hey, let me get that. You be trail guide." Doug reached over and lifted the container of goodies with both hands.

'Box Cottage' was a classic example of an ancient, Cotswold limestone house. One that had been added to over the centuries. Building work at least quadrupling its size. It sat tucked into the base of the main hill. A shallow, singing stream bubbled right past near its side door. The two storey structure also featured the archetypal stone mullions and eucalyptus grey/green paint on its woodwork. Thick, wonky walls plus stone tiled roof laden with moss, completed the picture. Welcoming light streamed out from behind lowered blinds. With help from a coach lantern fixed on the corner, the family found their way to a recently constructed sun porch at the front.

"Hello hello, how lovely to see you. Come on in," Nancy Robbins opened the door and kissed Elizabeth on the cheek.

She ushered the family into a smart, flagstone floored entryway.

A six foot tall man of medium build walked out of another room behind. His curly, dark brown hair was brushed back from a high brow. It receded round the temples and flowed down to sideburns showing not one hint of grey. Surprising for a man two years Doug's junior.

I wonder if he colours it? The former project manager shook the pointless thought aside.

The fellow's triangular face featured a short, fat nose; wide, brown happy eyes that appeared half open, and low, broad eyebrows. A carefree smile emerged from the middle of his designer stubble. It made Doug think of a model in an aftershave commercial. The thick neck and pronounced Adam's apple further dispelled images of your average accountant.

"I'm Howard Robbins. You must be Doug." He extended a hand.

Doug passed the box into his wife's hands. "Doug Ashbourne. Pleased to meet you."

"We've brought you a few samples of our wares as a gift," Elizabeth tilted the box so Nancy could see in.

"Oh you shouldn't have done that. How lovely."

Doug whipped the bottles out to show Howard. "A medium mead and my signature blackcurrant wine."

Howard admired the labels. "We'll have to give these a jolly good sampling. Nancy said you were setting up some sort of country wine business. Excellent. I won't keep pushing my services - because that's crass and annoying - but feel free to give me a shout if you need any tax advice and so on."

"Thanks Howard. I'll do that."

Elizabeth continued. "There's also a beeswax candle, a couple of soaps and two jars of our honey."

A shapely, five foot six, broad-shouldered natural blonde with hair dyed shocking pink sauntered into the hallway. Her locks flowed straight down to her mid back, side parted and diagonally obscuring half her face. That face had full, pouting lips with bright red lipstick. Her narrow mouth sat beneath a long, rounded nose. Blue eyes scanned the new arrivals from beneath dark, wispy brows. She was slim but with a well-rounded figure. A shapely bottom and strong, prominent thigh and calf muscles spoke of athleticism. These were on display thanks to her Gothic dress hitched up between muscular - if feminine - legs. A pair of large, firm, plump breasts spilt over the edge of a scant, black lacy top.

Joshua's head felt hot as the girl's gaze lingered on him with a cold, wicked, yet coy and seductive stare.

Nancy swivelled to introduce her daughter. "And this is our Moira. Moira, meet Rebecca, Joshua and Bethany."

"Hi," the coolness melted from the teenager's gaze. She gave them a nondescript but welcoming wave.

"Rebecca Ashbourne!" Elizabeth caught sight of the back of Bethany's head. "How could you?" She reached up to touch the sticky gum, now wrapped in light brown hair. "Oh no, it's stuck firm."

Bethany shrieked. "What, Mum? What's stuck? What's Becky done?"

"She's put her chewing gum in your hair. Becky, that's so spiteful. Not to mention embarrassing. Bethany, hold still. You'll make it worse." The woman flushed and looked at Nancy. "I apologise for the immaturity of my eldest daughter. You wouldn't happen to have a small pair of scissors handy, would you?"

"Yes of course. Hold on a moment." She went into the kitchen.

Rebecca flushed. This hadn't quite worked out as hoped, and now she felt like a child in front of their new neighbours. She caught the slightest hint of a playful grin from Moira. It spoke of everything being okay between them. Rebecca had never been into the Gothic scene. But she could tell from the outset that this girl had a strong and independent personality. Having looks like that, she'd be a good person to pull boys with. Rebecca even felt a hint of jealousy over that ample bust. Something Joshua could hardly keep his eyes off.

"Here we go," Nancy handed a petite, shiny pair of nail scissors to Elizabeth.

"Thank you, Nancy. Right then Bethany, hold still." There were a couple of snips. "There. No long term damage done. Though your father and I will have a thing or two to say to your sister later." Elizabeth pulled the sticky glob between awkward fingers.

"Oh here, let me," Nancy reached over.

"I'll dispose of it, Mum," Moira intercepted the exchange. She saved her mother the hassle of getting her fingers gunged up.

"Thank you, Darling."

"Yes. Thank you, Moira," Elizabeth added. "It's nice to see at least one young lady around here is polite and responsible."

Rebecca let out a subtle sigh.

They dined in the kitchen at a large farmhouse table. Nancy proved to be quite the hostess. But then with the woman's 'Chelts' social background, Elizabeth wasn't surprised. When the Ashbournes returned the favour, she knew she would have to pull out all the stops. A time to up her culinary game and keep score in this friendly domestic rivalry.

Afterwards, Bethany remained with Nancy and her mother at table. Doug, Joshua and Howard adjourned to the living room. Moira took Rebecca upstairs to her own personal sanctuary.

"So, have you done it yet?" Moira's first question took the Ashbourne girl quite by surprise.

Rebecca flushed. "Do you always start conversations with new people this way?"

Moira grinned and sat down on the bed, signalling the girl to join her. "Nothing to be ashamed of if you haven't. Just asking."

Rebecca lowered her head. "No. Not yet."

"Well, there's not much choice round here. I caught sight of Mike Faringdon's son while he was back from uni at Christmas. Not bad. Wouldn't mind some of that. Not worth hanging around for if a better option comes up though. Hey, your younger brother is pretty cute."

"Josh?" Rebecca was incredulous, eyes wide, mouth dropping open.

"So what's he into?"

"Nerd stuff, mostly. Fantasy games. Wizards and Elves. Anything except growing up and getting himself a girlfriend." Rebecca realised she would sound like a dreadful hypocrite if Moira asked about boyfriends back in London. She didn't have one. Should she lie? This girl would never know, unless another member of the family blabbed.

"Hey that's not so bad. I like some of that scene myself."

Rebecca glanced around at pictures of mythical creatures hung on her walls. There was a faint hint of sandalwood incense hanging in the air. She was most intrigued by what appeared to be a large crystal ball positioned on the nightstand. "Is that real, or some kind of Goth themed decoration?"

"It's real. But not everyone can use them."

"Can you?"

"I'm getting better."

"You're joking?" Rebecca didn't know whether to scoff or feel intrigued. "Is it like turning on a TV?"

"Not quite. More internal images and feelings to begin with. Have you ever dabbled?"

"Dabbled?"

"Yeah, you know: The occult, magic, witchcraft and so on."

"Err, no. And I'm pretty sure my mother would either disown me or take me to an exorcist or something if I did. What about yours? She seems pretty laid back."

"Mum is free and easy. I guess she thinks it's a phase I'll grow out of, so she lets me get on with it."

"She's cool. I wish mine was a bit less strict and stressy sometimes."

"Well hey, if you hang out with me now and again, you can have a reprieve. While the warden's away, the inmates can get up to whatever they jolly well please."

Rebecca giggled. Her shoulders released stored tension and lowered. The girl's tummy stiffened, and she placed a hand on it.

Moira glanced at the simultaneous wince on her new friend's face. "You okay?"

"Yeah. Time of the month. Would it be alright if I use your loo?"

"Of course. Straight down the hall."

"Thanks." Rebecca stood and made for the door.

"Becky?"

"Yeah?"

"There's a special bin for Mum and I in there. Feel free... Well, you know."

"Thanks," Rebecca grimaced and left the room.

"And what sort of things are you into, Joshua?" Howard asked.

The boy wriggled and fidgeted. "Oh, normal teenage guy stuff, I guess."

"You mean girls?" Howard thought back to the way his eyes lit up when he first saw Moira.

"More like fantasy role-playing games, painted wargame miniatures and consoles." Doug grinned at the accountant and slapped both palms against his upper legs.

"Oh? That's very interesting. Do you like Tolkien?"

"Does he? Josh has devoured his work ever since he was a kid," Doug replied before his son could respond.

Howard moved to fetch a large volume from a floor-to-ceiling bookcase. "Well then, you might enjoy having a quick look at this." He handed the book to Joshua.

The teenager perched on the edge of an armchair and opened the book to the first few pages. His eyes widened, and he gazed upward, open-mouthed. "A first, single edition of *'The Lord of the Rings.'* And signed!" He showed the book to his father.

"Now that's a bit special," Doug gasped.

"My late father was an Oxford man - English Language and Literature. He was a student during Tolkien's final year teaching at Merton College in 1959. Dad picked up that first, single edition after it was published in 1968. He was due to have lunch with his old professor and some friends, back under the dreaming spires. 'The Eastgate Hotel,' I believe. Anyway, Tolkien signed it for him."

"I'm sorry about your Dad," Doug's voice was calm.

"He didn't father me until he was in his late thirties. Dad was always a workaholic. It's what did for him in the end. One of the reasons I was keen to move out here and slow down after Moira finished school, I guess."

"Yeah. I've seen a few folk carried off in ambulances from the city over the years. More to life."

"That there is, Doug." Howard clapped him on the back and retrieved the book from Joshua.

"Thank you again for a lovely evening." Elizabeth wandered from the kitchen into the hallway, Bethany and Nancy by her side. Moira and Rebecca appeared at the foot of the stairs. Doug, Joshua and Howard emerged from the living room.

"We look forward to having you all over to our place, soon." Doug added. He switched attention to focus on Howard. "Anytime you develop an interest in the making of meads, melomels and country wines, feel free to pop round. It's an open invitation. No appointment necessary."

"I might do that. Thanks Doug. And hey, Josh?"

The boy stopped in his tracks.

"You keep reading Tolkien. That's epic literature, right there."

"I will. Thank you. And thanks for showing me that book."

"What book?" Rebecca asked.

Joshua blanked her. "You wouldn't be interested in hearing about it."

Doug gritted his teeth. "Besides, she'll have a few other things to listen to when we get home."

Moira squeezed Rebecca's hand in subtle solidarity. Rebecca felt strengthened to know she had found a new kindred spirit - of sorts - out here. She stepped towards the front door. "Thank you for having me, Mr and Mrs Robbins."

Nancy touched the teenager's arm. "You're welcome here anytime. I'm sure Moira will see you soon."

Elizabeth fished out her pocket torch and clicked on the light.

The Ashbournes walked out into the night. They climbed back up the hill to Pennycress Cottage in silence.

6

A Walk in the Woods

"Okay, over a bit. A little more. Hold it there and lower." Doug Ashbourne's voice strained and puffed. The physical effort from lifting a large, stainless steel conical fermenter left him quite out of breath. Attempts to gauge its positioning added to the effort. The first two hadn't been so bad. But, by the time they lowered the third into place, he was starting to notice the effect of his exertions.

"Looks great, Dad." Joshua glanced up and down the back wall. The long, low building was now filled with his father's shiny new fermentation equipment.

"Very smart, eh Mike?" Bob Faringdon caught his own breath.

"Haven't done this much lifting since we installed the new milkers," the younger farmer replied. "When are you planning to start production, Doug?"

"As soon as possible. Lizzie's grandfather had a store of honey I can tap into. That's the nice thing about the product: it doesn't go off. They found edible honey in Tutankhamen's tomb, if you can believe it. Forget the dates you see on supermarket products. Stuff and nonsense. Companies going through the grocery motions and procedures. Anyway, with the combined hives we have now, it means there'll be enough to get us started." He pointed at some of his old home brew equipment resting on the floor at the far end. Alongside an empty glass demijohn, stood six bottles of golden liquid. "While I was over on my supervisory trips during the renovation, I made a test batch. Regular mead with Alan Boardman's honey and spring water from Pennycress. I wanted to get an idea what the final product might be like round here. Normally you wouldn't drink mead less than a year old, although you can. It varies a lot during those early months. One day it can seem passable, and the next taste like jet fuel. But, at four months old, the samples I tested during secondary racking were pretty special. Should be nice once it's aged and smoothed out a little."

Mike listened and rubbed his chin. "Well, there are a few other locals around here who produce honey. So if you run short while you're getting off the ground, they might be able to supply you. Would eat into your bottom line though."

"Yeah. As long as I can get it for three quid a pound or thereabouts, we'd still be moving in the right general direction. Slower, of course. Better if we can produce as much of the honey ourselves. Thanks for the thought, Mike."

"We brought a load of blackcurrant bushes over in the Landy." Bob jerked a thumb in the direction of his battered off-roader. "If you need more plants or extra fruit, let us know."

"Fab. Thanks. Once the season starts in July, I'll tie up one of these stainless steel beauties with a decent batch of fruit wine. Now we're into May, I can already harvest and source as many raspberries as possible for a rudamel."

"Rudamel?" Mike tilted his head and frowned.

"Raspberry melomel. A mead made with honey and raspberries. Light and refreshing with a delicate, perfumed taste. Goes with a lot of things. I'll also make a regular batch of medium mead."

Bob eyed the sample bottles and licked his lips. "Shame we'll have to wait a year. I'm rather looking forward to sampling some mead made with dear old Alan's honey."

"Well goodness, help yourself to a couple of those bottles. It's the least I can do for all your help. Like I said, they're only four months old. But, you'll get some idea what to expect in the end."

Bob ambled over and picked up two bottles of test mead.

Doug looked between him and Mike. "Once we bottle the fruit wines and others, you are welcome to a case."

Bob leaned back against the door frame. His kindly old eyes studied their handiwork one last time. "Well, we'd best unload the plants and get back to the farm."

"Josh and I will give you a hand."

The four made a move for the vehicle. A ripping sound emanated from behind Bob.

"Darn. Caught my shirt on a loose nail." The old farmer lifted his untucked blue and white checked shirt tail. A small piece of the fabric had been torn away. It clung to a rusty hand-forged nail hanging out of the ancient doorway.

"Oh Bob, I'm sorry. I'd better hammer that down." Doug flicked the offending item, jaw clenched.

"Not to worry. My dear misses used to say that she never ran out of ideas for Christmas presents. I always needed a new shirt or two. When she couldn't fix the ragged old ones, that is." He raised his eyes skyward. "Bet she's up there now, darning the Angels' garments as we speak."

Mike bowed his head at the comment. Without a further word he began fishing blackcurrant plants out the back of the Defender.

A few minutes later, the four of them had lined up an impressive array of fruit shrubbery. They stood beneath the exterior overhanging eaves of the mead production room. Mike and Bob climbed into their vehicle and rumbled off with a wave.

Doug looked at his son. "We'll get these in as soon as possible. Further installation work on the fermenters can wait for now."

"Okay Dad. I'll carry them over to the beds we earmarked."

"Great. I'll fetch a hammer and sort out that nail before someone does themselves a serious mischief on it. Then we'll get planting."

Joshua made multiple trips back and forth, carrying one blackcurrant plant at a time. Doug returned from his tool shed with a hammer, as the boy re-appeared to fetch another bush.

"Did you pull out that shirt fabric?" the man pointed his tool at the claw-like nail, now hanging empty.

"Nope."

"That's odd. Guess Bob took it with him after all."

"No he didn't. It was still there a minute or two ago."

"Blown away on the breeze then. Ah well. This won't take long. Be with you in a tick."

"Sure Dad." The boy picked up another blackcurrant plant and lumbered off.

Doug squatted by the frame and walloped the iron nail head with a series of precise strikes. Its point twisted over and embedded into the frame. The work was hardly strenuous, so it came as something of a surprise when his head flushed. The man's pulse quickened. There was a sudden, overwhelming sense of being observed. He eased himself up and glanced around. Across a hedge at the far end of the building, stood a woman in her mid to late sixties. She was tall and thin, with grey hair evidencing a curious hint of mauve in volume curls. High cheekbones and pencil-thin arched eyebrows combined with her triangular face. Together they presented an almost haughty aspect. Even at this range the sunlight illuminated her hazel eyes. They regarded the man with emotionless curiosity. The hedge was low and formed part of the freehold at Pennycress Cottage. A public footpath ran across the land, on which the observer now stood.

"Hi, Mr Ashbourne," a young, feminine voice rang out behind Doug, causing him to jump. "Oh, gosh.

Sorry. Didn't mean to startle you." Moira Robbins placed one hand at the base of her neck in surprise at his reaction.

Doug laughed. "I was a million miles away. Hey, do you know that woma..." His voice trailed away as he turned back to the hedge. There was no-one in sight.

"Huh?" the teenager peered at where he was staring.

"Never mind. Are you here to see Becky?"

"Yeah. Well actually, I wondered if she might like a walk in the woods. It's a nice day. What with all the spring flowers out and all, it should be pleasant."

"That sounds fine. She's up at the house."

"Err, Mr Ashbourne?"

"Yes?"

"Do you think Josh would like to come too?"

Doug almost dropped his hammer while fighting down the surprise. Her statement caught him off guard. He knew his teenage son had taken a shine to this buxom, Gothic beauty. But he had no idea there might be any hint of reciprocal interest. "I should think so. Look, we're about to dig in a few blackcurrant bushes. Why don't you go and have a cuppa with Becky for a spell or something, then pop back?"

"Sure. Catch you later."

Doug watched her wiggle away. Joshua returned from depositing the last of the shrubs. He caught sight of the wry smile on his father's face.

"What?" the boy shrugged.

"Come on in, Moira. Becky's upstairs studying. I'll

give her a shout." Elizabeth went to the foot of the staircase and leaned forward to call out. "Becky? You have a guest down here."

The Robbins girl stood watching Bethany sit hunched over, drawing a picture at the table. The youngster's face creased in concentration. She gripped a colour pencil in one hand.

A minute later Rebecca appeared in the kitchen. "Hey Moira. Whatcha doing?"

"Wondered if you fancied a walk? If you're busy studying though, we can do it another time."

"No. I'm done. Pretty sure I've got everything down for now. Guess we'll know, shortly. Do you want to come up for a minute?"

"Sure."

The girls adjourned to Rebecca's room.

Moira looked around the upstairs space. It was neat and well-organised. For all Rebecca's playing at being a rebel, she seemed quite straight-laced and studious.

"So, I asked your Dad if Josh would like to come out with us. Hope you don't mind?"

"Josh? Please tell me you're not planning to get jiggy with my little brother? I don't know quite how I'd handle that."

Moira snorted. "Nah. But he'd be fun to flirt with a bit. No harm done. You should try it sometime. Give you a chance to experience your own feminine power. It's a real confidence booster, I can tell ya."

"Try it with my own brother?"

"Well NO, I didn't mean that. Duh! But try flirting

with a stranger, without any intention of things going anywhere."

"Don't break his heart, okay? Josh might be a pain in the arse and a hopeless nerd, but he's still my brother."

"Cross my heart," Moira swept fingers above her ample chest in a promissory gesture.

"Okay. Well, I guess he can come along. Where are we going again?"

"A stroll in the woods on the hill overlooking the village. It's nice and peaceful up there."

"Should do me good. I'm getting cabin fever in here, anyway. Haven't been anywhere much for a couple of weeks. It's not like London. There I could hop on the tube and go shopping if I needed a change of scene."

"You have to be a bit more creative with your free time in the country, that's all. I found it a little difficult for the first couple of months. But you know what?"

"What?"

"It makes you look deep down inside yourself. After a while, you realise all those other activities are distractions from introspection."

"Why?"

"Because it can feel a little uncomfortable at first. Pondering the deeper issues, I mean."

Rebecca raised one eyebrow. "What are you, the guru of teenage country life or something?"

"I promise we'll arrange some girlie shopping trips to Ciren and Chelts sooner or later. But Coln Abbots has more about it than you might realise at first."

"If you're going to suggest we join a bridge club or sewing circle, I'll eject you from this room." Rebecca plonked herself down on the bed, arms crossed.

"Don't panic. I'm not sure you're wild enough for some of it. Not yet, anyway."

"Huh?"

"You'll see. Stick with me, Becky. I'll show you things you never even dreamt about." Moira stood to her full height and arched her back, pushing her chest out.

"Are you going to show my brother what he has almost certainly dreamt about?" Rebecca examined the gesture, narrowing her eyes and raising one corner of her mouth.

"Josh likes my tits, doesn't he?"

"And how. Think he's quite partial to your bum as well. I woke up the other night and could swear I heard him beating off. Pretty sure I know who he was thinking about, too. Unless it was a picture of some pretty elf maiden from one of his geeky games."

"Don't you find it a turn-on to think of a guy having a wank, while dreaming of getting it on with you? God it gets me wet."

"Moira!" Rebecca's face turned crimson.

"Hey girl, he's sixteen now. Age of consent-"

"Enough. I thought you weren't going down that road with him? Please Moira, no."

Moira flicked her lashes and shook back the pink mane. "Okay, okay. A bit of titillation and harmless teasing then."

"Or TITTY-lation in your case." Rebecca shook her head and stood up. "So, expedition leader: Which way to the jungle?"

"Here they are." Doug stood a spade against the exterior wall of the fermentation building. He and Joshua had just returned from planting the blackcurrant bushes.

"Hey Mr Ashbourne," Moira said. "Hey Josh." Her words lingered on the pronunciation of the boy's name. She accentuated the sibilance of the 'sh' sound. Her lips moistened to mimic other parts of feminine anatomy. The effect wasn't wasted on the teenage boy. He straightened up and took a deep breath.

Rebecca peered round the doorway of the outbuilding. "Are the fermenters in? Hey wow, check those. It looks like a real professional outfit, Dad."

"That's the goal, albeit on a small scale to begin with." Doug poked his head alongside his daughter's. "Not too shabby. So Moira's taking you and Josh for a walk in the woods?"

"Yeah."

"Is Bethany going too?"

"No. Still working on a picture she's been drawing of the cottage. She took a photo on her phone this morning and is trying to recreate it with colour pencils. It's actually pretty good for an eleven-year-old."

"I'll have to get a look at that later."

"Oh. Mum told you not to overdo it."

Doug grinned. "Did she now? Bless. Well, we're done with the heavy lifting for the day. I've only got to sterilise the sampling ports, racking arms and dump valves. Then connect them up to each conical and perform a water test. A bit of washing kit, greasing some O-rings, fitting lid seals, attaching tri-clamps and the like. Nothing too strenuous."

"Cool. Well, have a good day, Dad."

"Will do. You guys enjoy yourselves."

"Whoa," Joshua jumped.

"What is it?" Doug turned.

"Err, nothing."

Moira pursed her lips and moved away from where she had been standing right in the boy's personal space.

Joshua could still feel the cheeky pinch of the girl's fingers on his relaxing buttocks.

Rebecca glared at her friend and mouthed a single word in silence. "Behave."

Doug lingered to watch the three teenagers. They wandered off along the footpath; the one where he had observed that curious woman studying him earlier. The trio turned left and ascended the steeper part of the hill. The trail disappeared into a thick canopy of trees.

* * *

Doug appeared in the kitchen for a midday bite.

"I've made you a round of ham sandwiches." Elizabeth indicated a plate stacked high with doorstep-sized bread snacks. "I imagine you're a bit peckish after all that humping."

The man kissed his wife on the cheek and whispered

in her ear. "How come you don't normally fix me sarnies after a good humping?"

"Naughty," Elizabeth's eyes flashed. "So how did it go?"

"Excellent. The three conicals are in and I've cleaned, sterilised and fitted the attachments. Water test went okay. All the ports and valves worked fine. No leaks."

"Bet you were glad of Bob and Mike's help."

"No question about it. This would have been a tough job without them. They also brought a load of blackcurrant plants over from the farm. We've dug them in already."

"That's nice of them. A successful morning's work, then. Where's Josh?"

"He went for a walk with Becky and Moira."

Elizabeth slipped one coy hand onto her hip. "Did he now?"

"Moira asked him, actually."

Elizabeth whistled. "I knew our boy had a bit of a thing for her. Thought it was teenage hormones. I had no idea she liked him back."

Doug placed a curled finger on his top lip and rocked on his heels. "I reckon it's the fantasy stuff, you know. Nerds are cool. I was one once, if you recall?"

Elizabeth gagged and shuddered at the memory. "Don't I know it? I thought you were so into your prog rock music you were never going to notice me. Let alone ask me out."

Doug picked the plate of sandwiches up off the side. "You should have asked me for a walk in the woods."

"We did enough of those while we were courting, or

don't you remember?" A mischievous light flashed in Elizabeth's grey eyes.

"Did enough of what?" Bethany turned in her seat and placed a colouring pencil back in the box alongside many others.

"Nothing of interest," her mother said.

"Oh?" Doug wagged his head.

Elizabeth shot him a warning glance and turned back to her youngest. "How is your picture coming along?"

"All done. Come and see."

Doug and Elizabeth wandered over to examine the artwork.

"Bethany, that's excellent. What do you think, Lizzie?"

Elizabeth wiped a hint of moisture away from her face, disguising the gesture by rubbing her nose. The picture showed a stylised image of Pennycress Cottage. Clearly an image drawn by someone who loved the subject in question. "Your Great Grandfather would have adored that. This place meant so much to him. Are you happy here, Darling?"

Bethany nodded and closed her pencil box. "I'm going to fix it on my bedroom wall then go outside to play. Where are Becky and Josh?"

"They went for a walk with Moira. You were so engrossed in your drawing that they didn't want to disturb you."

"Oh, okay. I'll be in the garden."

Drawing secured fast to her bedroom wall, Bethany went outside. It was a warm, May afternoon. She meandered to and fro between the various plant beds. The youngster's eyes squinted. She imagined all manner of fantastic creatures flitting between the stems and flower heads. Clusters of tiny white blooms adorned many narrow stalks. Each led down to an array of waxy grey-green leaves. These non-competitive perfoliate plants weren't much to look at. But, the girl had formed a strong bond with the species from which her new home took its name.

A short distance away, the line of bee hives were busy with buzzing workers darting in and out. Her mother often said she had more employees than many major corporations, and she didn't even pay them.

A bee whizzed out of the flower beds and bumped into Bethany's forehead.

"Oh, poor thing. Dozy bee." The girl looked around but couldn't see if it lay stunned anywhere.

Another bee bumped into her right arm. The eleven-year-old knew better than to swat it away or flap her limbs. Elizabeth always told her that bees generally left people alone, unless something was very wrong. Shooing bees away didn't scare them off. It made them consider you a threat. One which they might call upon further help to deal with.

Several more bees bumped into her face, arms and legs.

This isn't normal. What is going on? While her thoughts might have sounded calm, the eleven-year-old's heart was starting to race. She had grown up around bees. Their behaviour today was very odd.

The sound of a gentle breeze became interrupted by a growing hum. The girl turned and was immediately struck by a dozen or more angry workers. Across the lawn, she caught sight of a stream of the tiny creatures pouring out of the hives in her direction.

"Mum!" She let out a scream. Two bees darted into her mouth. Their furry bodies bounced on her tongue and struck her palate. The youngster coughed and spat them out. The cloud drew nearer and the advance guard settled on her exposed skin. Seconds later, the first searing heat of sting venom pumped through the girl's penetrated flesh.

Bethany ran as quickly as her legs could carry her, back towards the cottage.

If bees start to swarm or attack, run as fast as you can and get indoors. It was advice that her mother had taught her since she was old enough to understand.

The sacrificial suicide weapons of her assailants, continued to ooze toxins into her bloodstream. Their tiny abdomen sacks still clung to the girl's swelling skin.

A roaring, pulsing cloud of the insects overtook the terrified fugitive on either side. Whimpering in panic, Bethany saw them form up in front of the cottage and charge right at her. She cried out again and altered direction. Her feet stumbled on the uneven ground. The pain was getting worse. Bethany knew this was the cumulative effect of the venom sacs continuing to deliver their chemical payload. Her hands swiped across face and opposite arms. She attempted to dislodge any of the tiny offensive devices with frantic movements. There was no time to stop. The buzzing clouds were gaining in mass and ferocity.

She made another turn, this time in the direction of the family's outbuildings. Again a forward cohort of angry bees headed her off.

Beyond, the garden met the steeper slopes of the hill that led up to the woods. Bethany plunged into the undergrowth. She knew bees could chase you half a mile or more, without issue. The only hope now seemed to be losing them amongst the trees and hoping they gave up the pursuit.

Streams of angry, buzzing insects ripped through the leafy canopy like rounds from a machine gun. But these were intelligent bullets that locked onto their target and followed it. There was going to be no easy escape.

Pulse pounding, the girl's breathing became laboured. Whether through shock to her system from the poison, the exertions of the steep climb, abject fear or all three; she shook with each slowing step. The effort of placing one leg in front of the other became a task of gargantuan proportions. A short distance beyond the crest of the hill, the trees opened into a clearing. There sat a large, murky woodland pond. Choked with weeds and covered in all manner of vegetation, it offered her only chance to shake the pursuers. In her numbing mind, the child could hear her mother saying that diving into water was no solution to a bee attack. An urban myth. Sooner or later you had to come up for air. But what else could she do?

"That's a wicked view of the valley and village. I'm glad we did this, Moira." Rebecca shielded her eyes from the sunlight and scanned across the bucolic vista.

"What do you think, Josh?" Moira studied the winded teenage lad. Both he and his sister had yet to get used to climbing Cotswold hills. The Robbins girl was now pretty adept at the task. She had honed her physiology and fitness level since the move up from Cheltenham.

"It's great, isn't it?" The young man let out a satisfied sigh.

"Like *The Shire*?" Moira asked.

Joshua nodded. "Something like that." *God this girl's hot and she likes Tolkien.*

The pink-haired Goth brushed past him. She pressed her backside into his crotch with a deliberate rub.

Joshua pushed down the arousal. He caught sight of his big sister shaking her head in small movements.

Moira pointed down a spongy woodland trail. "We'll do a circuit of the hilltop, then I'll show you an ancient pond the village used to execute witches in."

Rebecca sauntered up to her new friend. "Probably good for you they still don't." The words came out in a subdued voice.

Moira ignored the quip and started walking.

Bluebells nodded in a calm breeze and the air bore a sweet fragrance of new life in bloom. The restrained perfume wafted into the trio's nostrils like expensive incense. It was as they crested a rise overlooking a large woodland pond that they heard the screams. A young girl staggered through the undergrowth from down below on their left. She was being pelted by a mass of black dots. From behind her, a seething cloud burst out of the bushes and flew straight at the fugitive. A second scream was cut short by a splash. The figure dived into the murky waters and disappeared from view.

"Are they bees?" Moira asked. Her mouth hung open.

"Josh, that's Bethany," Rebecca clapped hands either side of her face.

"Oh shit!" Joshua raced headlong down the steep incline, slipping and sliding on old leaf mulch.

The cloud of bees gathered together. They melted back into the undergrowth and disappeared the moment the boy's body hit the water. Joshua swam for all he was worth. His arms pulled the rest of his torso along in a desperate front crawl. He crossed the pond to where ripples from Bethany's impact faded towards stillness. No sign of her. He twisted round, head bobbing.

"Bethany? Bethany!"

No response either.

He took a rapid breath. Lungs filled with air, the boy dived downward. His eyes attempted to penetrate the inky blackness. On the horizon of visible sight, he could make out two tiny hands waving in a frenzy.

Bethany whipped her arms back and forth, struggling in a blind panic. Dirty water attempted to force its way into her mouth and nose. Try as she might, her kicking legs brought the tiny circle of light representing the pond's surface no nearer. Something grabbed hold of her ankles and held the youngster firm. In one last effort to free herself, the girl looked down. Several rigid human faces stared unblinking at her from the depths. Hands clasped her legs and pulled relentlessly in the direction of those terrifying visages. Bethany let out an underwater cry, the vile pond liquid racing into her mouth. Then her wrists were tugged in the opposite direction. The wavy brown hair flicked as she glanced back towards the light. Joshua was attempting to rescue her.

The teenage boy couldn't lift his sister. Something held her like a vice. He pushed himself further down and located a mass of underwater plants wrapped like tendrils around her ankles. Much ripping and kicking later, the pernicious weeds relinquished their hold. The siblings rocketed to the surface.

Bethany and Joshua broke free of the depths with a unified gasp for air. Rebecca and Moira watched from the bank, bodies tensed, brows furrowed. The girls reached out to help the swimmers onto the slippery bank.

Bethany coughed and choked. Her face looked pale. An angry collection of reddening welts covered both countenance and limbs. The girl's eyes rolled back into her head and she passed out.

"Josh. Josh, I don't think she's breathing!" Rebecca screamed.

"Should we do CPR or something?" Moira asked.

Joshua rolled over and crawled towards his youngest sister on the ground. He placed his ear close to her mouth. "She's breathing. But her breaths are faint and erratic." He pushed himself off the woodland floor and scooped the eleven-year-old girl into his arms. "Quick Becky, run down the hill and have Mum or Dad call an ambulance. I'll be as close behind you as I can manage."

"*We'll* be close behind. Let me help," Moira said.

"Thanks." Joshua welcomed the steadying eighteen-year-old's hands on his shoulders.

Rebecca tore through the undergrowth. She almost tumbled head over heels in her rapid descent to Pennycress Cottage.

7
Some Relief

"We'd like to keep her in overnight for observation," a balding male doctor from the Clinical Decision Unit at Cirencester Hospital declared. He addressed Bethany's anxious family by her bedside. The girl lay unconscious. "She's lucky to be alive. With the cumulative effect of that many bee stings, there's no way she would have been able to free herself from the pond. Not without your son's help. You did a good job, young man. Are you okay in yourself?"

Joshua shrugged. "Yeah. The water tasted rank, but no harm done. Bethany's legs got caught in some weeds. Once I freed them, we popped right out."

Rebecca put an appreciative arm around her brother's shoulders. Elizabeth had accompanied Bethany in the ambulance. Doug, Rebecca and Joshua followed along by car.

"I can't understand why she didn't run into the house." Elizabeth stooped over the sleeping girl with a pained and watery gaze. "She knows better than to dive into water during a bee attack."

"Has she ever suffered one before?" The doctor blinked.

"No. Thankfully not. Such occurrences are very rare with ordinary, docile European bees. Until we have a chance to speak to her, I guess we won't know exactly what happened. But Bethany has grown up around bee hives. I don't believe for one minute that she did anything stupid or reckless to antagonise the colonies. They would have to get pretty riled or consider someone a serious threat to chase them like that."

"Are the hives close to your house?"

"A safe distance, why?"

The doctor coughed. "I'm not questioning your expertise or competence, Mrs Ashbourne. I only ask because young Bethany has suffered a very traumatic experience. All I'm saying is that she could evidence signs of anxiety, if made to go too close to the hives for a while. Panic attacks are a common response to mental associations with the cause of such trauma. Close proximity may act as a trigger. Something to think about."

Doug squeezed his wife. "Thank you, Doctor. We'll be sure to keep that in mind."

"Okay. Well, I'll look in on her again in the morning and see you before she goes home. Don't worry, the nurses will attend to her throughout the night if she needs anything."

Doug shook the man's hand.

Back at Pennycress Cottage, Elizabeth donned her white beekeepers bee suit. She visited each hive in turn. The mother of three had to know what had occurred to provoke such an uncharacteristic attack. But all appeared in order and her miniature livestock as content as ever.

"Maybe it's some freak, one-off incident." Doug sat with her in the kitchen afterwards, over a calming glass of wine.

Elizabeth's frown almost caused her to form a unibrow, the muscle contractions were so pronounced. "What if the doctor's right and she's terrified of bees afterwards, Doug? We've built our home and both our businesses on beekeeping. I can't watch her suffer panic and distress - day in, day out."

"Hush now. Listen. You know better than I what a bizarre - and unusual - thing happened today. I've seen panic attacks before with guys in the city who suffered burnout. One couldn't even go near a computer for a couple of months afterwards. But, with some Cognitive Behavioural Therapy, he conquered that trigger to his stress response. It's all about graded, measured exposure. If Bethany has a tough time at first, the worst thing we can do is try to shield her from bees. The girl won't thank us later once the fear becomes an impossible monolith in her life, I can assure you. We'll need to re-introduce her to them at a pace which minimises her discomfort. That's all."

"Getting back in the saddle, so to speak? I hope you're right."

"Let's get her home first and then take things one step at a time, okay?"

"Okay."

The Ashbournes were heartened when they first arrived back at the hospital that following morning. Bethany was awake and enjoying some breakfast. While Elizabeth felt desperate to hear the full story, there was an ache inside. One thing she definitely did not want to do: Stir up her daughter's distress and halt any positive progress in her recovery. Thus she avoided the subject for the time being.

"Make sure she gets plenty of rest. Apply hydrocortisone cream or calamine lotion to help reduce the redness, itching and swelling." The doctor looked from Elizabeth and Doug down to Bethany. "Now, you take it easy, do you hear?"

Bethany nodded in silence, her face unsure.

The Subaru rumbled down the drive in Coln Abbots. Elizabeth glanced over her shoulder to the rear seat. Any minute now, Bethany would catch sight of their bee hives. How would she respond?

The eleven-year-old shuddered and pulled away, squishing into her brother's shoulder. Elizabeth's face fell.

"Easy." Doug placed a reassuring hand on his wife's leg. "It's the first sight, that's all. Give it time, Lizzie."

As they opened the front door, the Ashbournes became aware of two figures strolling onto their property. They turned and caught sight of Nancy and Moira walking down the driveway. Nancy carried a pretty basket of flowers.

"Hello there," Elizabeth greeted them.

Nancy licked her lips. "Moira told me what happened. How is Bethany?"

Elizabeth tapped her subdued youngest daughter. "A bit sore and itchy, but still with us, thank God."

"I hear Joshua was quite the hero."

"Yes, we're very proud of him. Proud and thankful. Moira also helped bring Bethany back down the hill. In the commotion I didn't have a chance to thank her. It means the world to us, Moira. Thank you."

"You're welcome," the pink-haired Goth said. "I hope you feel all better soon, Bethany. Mum and I brought you something."

Nancy handed the basket to the young girl. "A simple spray of flowers and some chocolate. A neighbourly 'get well soon' gift to cheer you up."

A bee landed on one of the blooms. It almost caused Bethany to drop the present. She flinched and took a deep breath. The insect buzzed off.

"What do you say to Mrs Robbins?" Doug placed a hand on the girl's shoulder.

"Thank you." The words were meek and soft.

"You're very welcome, my dear."

"Did you want to come in for a cuppa?" Doug looked at the gift-bearers.

"Well, a quick one might be nice. As long as we're not intruding. You *have* just got Bethany home, after all."

"It's no trouble." Elizabeth ushered them into the

hallway.

"Whatever possessed the child to jump into that pond?" Nancy whispered. She stood by the kitchen sink watching Elizabeth pour out the tea.

Elizabeth raised her shoulders. "It beats me. I haven't had the heart to ask her for the full story yet."

Bethany looked across at them with empty eyes. "There were people in the water."

"What, Darling?" Elizabeth twisted around. These were almost the first words the girl had spoken since they arrived home.

"There were people in the water, dragging me down."

Doug pulled up a chair alongside the eleven-year-old and put on his best wannabe counsellors face. "I'm sure it must have felt like it, what with the shock and the effects of those bee stings. But Joshua said your feet were caught in some weeds. Stressful situations play tricks on the strongest of minds, you know."

"But there were people," Bethany insisted.

"Think about it," her father went on. "How could there be people in the water? How would they breathe - for starters? It's a hallucination, Poppet. Nothing to worry about."

"Nevermere *is* supposed to be haunted," Moira declared with a deadpan expression. "They executed witches in there almost four hundred years ago."

"Don't start with the witchcraft nonsense, Moira." Nancy went to stamp her foot, face like thunder. "I'm getting a little fed up with hearing about it."

Elizabeth touched a delicate hand against her neighbour's arm. "It's okay, Nancy. I've heard those stories ever since I used to come here as a kid. Grandpa always warned me to stay away from Nevermere. It's got quite a reputation in village folklore. I reckon he was more concerned about me getting stuck in the weeds like my daughter, than anything else." She looked at Moira. "But I'm sure the only thing holding Bethany down were weeds. Not people, ghosts or anything else, wouldn't you say?"

"Sorry," Moira muttered.

Elizabeth went to sit with the frightened youngster. "Do you want to tell us what happened?"

Bethany clenched her fists and summoned up the memory. "I was in the garden looking at the flowers when bees started bumping into me. I knew that wasn't right."

Her mother drew a sharp breath. She recognised the precursor action of bumping. It was indicative of bees dealing with the first stages of a perceived threat. "Go on, Darling."

"When I turned, bees were pouring out of the hives in clouds. They started hitting my face, landing on my arms and legs. Then the stinging began. It burned so hot." Bethany rubbed the welts on her arms.

Elizabeth's mouth dropped open. "How can that be? They aren't swarming and you were nowhere near the hives?" It was more a question to herself, which she put aside for another time. "I'm sorry. Please continue. Why didn't you run into the cottage? How many times have I told you to get indoors as fast as possible, if bees attack?"

Bethany sobbed. "I know, Mum, but the bees wouldn't let me."

"Wouldn't let you?" Doug scratched his short beard.

"Every time I tried to make for the house, they formed a bigger cloud and dived straight at me." Tears slid down her flushing cheeks. "I tried to run to Dad's outbuildings instead, but the same thing happened. The only path left open was a dash into the woods." Her cries became more heart-rending. "I know I'm not supposed to jump into water to get away, but when I saw the pond, I didn't know what else to do."

"Oh Darling," Elizabeth hugged her tight and kissed the girl on the head. "Shh, now. You did the best thing you could in the circumstances."

When the girl settled down, Rebecca reached out a hand to her. "How about coming upstairs with me? Reginald has been missing you and getting rather worried. Why, when I got up this morning, he was wandering up and down in quite a state."

Bethany broke into a welcome grin. She took her big sister's hand and walked towards the hallway. At the door, Rebecca glanced back in time to catch her mother mouth the words "Thank you." The girl looked at her brother. "While I'm settling Bethany in, why don't you take Moira up to your room and show her some of your fantasy stuff?"

Joshua's eyes bulged. He turned to the buxom eighteen-year-old. "Would you like that?"

"Hell yeah." Moira delivered a sultry wink. "I want to know what turns you on and makes you tick."

"What do you make of that then, Lizzie? Bees forming co-ordinated attack patterns and steering their victim." Doug sat back and sipped his tea after the children had left.

Elizabeth shook her head. "I've never heard anything like it."

Nancy joined them at the table. "Could she have imagined the clouds forming up to stop her getting indoors?"

Doug juggled imaginary balls with his hands, weighing up the possibility. "With the panic and effect of the stings, I guess that's possible. Seems odd though."

Elizabeth stared into space. "I've never known bees to behave like that before. It doesn't make any sense."

"I'm sure it was a fluke, albeit a terrible one," Nancy said. "Sorry about Moira and her witch nonsense. Rather makes you think about the supernatural, given Bethany's description I suppose. But there must be a logical explanation for what happened. Even if we are at something of a loss to discover it."

"Kids will be kids. I know Moira doesn't quite fit that label. But, even adults drop clangers from time to time. Think nothing of it." Doug waved the offence away. "Yeah, it's bizarre. We'll keep a careful eye on Bethany. She's likely to struggle with being around bees for a time."

"I should think so, poor dear. Well, I've intruded enough on your day. Send Moira home whenever you want to be rid of her." Nancy stood up to leave, then paused. "Oh, we have a semi-regular social evening at Box Cottage with some of the Chelts set. Got another coming up on Friday. Howard and I wondered if you might like to attend? Nothing spectacular. Cheese, nibbles, wine and socialite gossip."

"Are you sure we're posh enough?" Elizabeth asked.

Nancy rolled her eyes. "Don't even get me started. They're a decent enough bunch, but most of them are Howard's wealthy clients and their partners. More of a networking event, I suppose. My reason for asking isn't entirely altruistic, if I'm honest. It would give me a bit of solidarity to know I've got a couple of decent faces there. People who are something more than mere professional acquaintances, if you catch my drift?"

Elizabeth exchanged amused glances with her husband. "Sure. Thanks, Nancy. We'd be happy to come along."

"Great. Show up anytime you like. The cars usually start pulling in around seven."

"Do you want any help with the catering?" Elizabeth asked.

Nancy clapped her hands together. "Now isn't that a great idea? Well, if you want to pop down an hour or two early, you can help me set things out. That would be a real bonus."

"Count on it. Thanks again for bringing that flower basket and chocolate up for Bethany."

"You're welcome. 'til Friday then."

Nancy let herself out. The sound of her shoes crunching on gravel drifted through the open kitchen window. It faded away, replaced by valley birdsong.

* * *

"Some of Dad's old prog rock albums have great cover artwork. That's something we miss out on with small CD wallets. Even more so with music downloads. Back in those days, the packaging was all part of the mystique and presentation. Several of these sleeves are proper works of art. Almost as iconic as the music recorded on the vinyl inside." Joshua held up *'The Ancient Realms of Yore'* by a group called *'Wanderer,'* for Moira to examine the cover. "Dad has an amazing collection that he lets me play on this old turntable." The boy patted a dated, wooden-sided record deck that once belonged to his father.

Moira sat on his bed. She leafed through the illustrated pages of a hardback fantasy role-playing game rulebook. "Why don't you put something on?"

"Sure. Anything in particular you fancy? Do you know much about this stuff?"

"Have you got *'Elysium Ascendant'* over there?"

"Duh! Wouldn't be much of a collection without that." He flicked through several sleeves. "Here we go. I've got Cry Heaven's third studio album with it on right here."

"I once heard the song originated at a spiritual retreat in Scotland. Chuck Hulbert and Billy Ronson were hanging out there after a concert tour of

America."

"You know your stuff. Dad would be impressed." Joshua lowered the stylus onto the spinning record. A static pop sounded on a pair of matching speakers. They had come with the deck and its associated amplifier.

"Isn't he a little young to be into music from 1971?"

"Dad was a bit of a geek like me, I guess. Anyway, the crowd he hung out with at school loved all that stuff. I suppose it was a culture thing. Like a tribe."

"I'm not criticising, it's timeless music. I love it." The girl's fingers stroked one of the pages in the book on her lap. "She's pretty."

Joshua moved closer. Moira rubbed the picture of a buxom female elf warrior sporting long, flowing blonde hair. The Goth patted the mattress alongside her.

Joshua sat down. His stomach tensed and filled with butterflies.

The classic rock track started to play. A finger-picked mandolin and Renaissance style flute opened the song. Their dreamy tones drifted from the old stereo.

"Yeah. She *is* a bit special."

"Nice tits, hey?"

Joshua flushed.

Moira licked her lips. "What's wrong? It's a natural observation. Guys stare at my tits all the time and I love it."

"It doesn't annoy you?"

The Goth laughed at the wide-eyed look of shock burning on that shy lad's face. She flicked back the mop of pink hair that ordinarily half covered her face. Arms folded across her chest and pulled the short top over her head. The action exposed a black lacy bra that struggled to restrain its contents. Her blue eyes never broke contact with Joshua's. She reached around to unfasten the undergarment. Its material fell away. This exposed the full glorious reality of the boy's erotic night-time fantasies.

Joshua drew a sharp breath. His head felt hot, and he folded hands across his lap. He was desperate to conceal the stretching material of his trousers. A response to the arousing vision before him.

Moira leaned closer. "Don't be nervous." She picked up his hands and cupped them around her mammaries. "Let yourself play a little. Don't panic, we're not going to do it - even though we could at your age. But why shouldn't you have a little treat? I was so impressed with your heroic actions at the pond."

Joshua gulped. "She's my sister. What else could I do?" His voice came out with a squeak at first until he cleared his throat mid-sentence. He was anything but smooth and confident around girls.

Moira squeezed his fingers together into a massaging motion. She breathed into his ear, her voice husky. "Don't you like me?"

"Of course I do."

"Then work these puppies, will you? Come on, Josh. Don't hold back." The girl released her own hands and let out a deep and gratifying sigh as the boy kept fondling of his own free will. She draped one gentle hand across his crotch and stroked the bulge. Her blue eyes moved right into the boy's field of vision. "Can I touch it?"

Joshua felt unable to speak. All he could do was pant and nod.

The quieter first movement of *'Elysium Ascendant'* changed into an analogue synthesiser stage. It was accompanied by the sound of the boy's fly unzipping. The tempo and volume of the music rose. Moira grabbed hold of the Ashbourne boy's throbbing salute and started to tug.

"You don't have to pretend Reginald is a real person for me." Bethany picked up the bear from her bedside and gave him a quick cuddle.

Rebecca sat down at her younger sister's dinky dressing table. She examined the eleven-year-old with sad eyes. "I'm sorry I've given you such a hard time lately."

"You're in the upper end of those difficult teenage years." Bethany parroted a phrase she had heard their mother utter on several occasions.

Rebecca put one hand up to her mouth and laughed. Her face shone. "If the truth be known, you're a lot more mature than I was at your age. Don't give up on your imaginary world too soon, Bethany. The alternative isn't so great. Maybe it took this move and my kid sister to wake me up to the fact."

Bethany waved the bear at the teenager as if he were speaking and put on a funny voice. "If you'd listened to me, you'd have realised that a lot sooner."

Rebecca wrinkled her nose. She adopted a mock serious and penitent air. "You're so right, Reginald." Her warm gaze moved to the puppeteer. "I love you, Kiddo."

"I love you too."

Rebecca joined her sister on the bed. She hugged her furiously until the girl squealed with delight.

From the room across the hall, the sound of seventies rock music reverberated through the walls.

Rebecca listened and shook her head. "Sounds like Josh couldn't contain himself any longer."

In Joshua's bedroom the music track was reaching its third and final crescendo. Billy Ronson hammered away on his electric guitar. Moira hammered away with skilful fingers of her own. The slapping sound of flesh yanking flesh and her exaggerated breathing kept time with the beat. She felt the boy's muscles tighten. The Gothic temptress glanced into his eyes to let out a sultry pant. She reached over and whipped a couple of wizard-themed tissues from a box on the nightstand.

Chuck Hulbert drew out the final words: *'And the angels all fly back to Elysium.'*

Joshua let go with a series of grunting spurts in the general direction of that heavenly locale.

Moira's pouting lips twisted into a coy smile. Her hands mopped up his ecstatic produce. She followed on by delivering one long, lingering kiss on the boy's breathless mouth. When the moment was over, the girl pulled away and winked at him. "Perhaps we'll take this further sometime."

* * *

"Why don't you pop up to the bathroom and take a look?" Doug ducked into the living room where Rebecca and Bethany were playing a board game. The sisters had been inseparable in the two days since the younger one came home from hospital.

"Is it finished, Dad?" Rebecca bobbed on her sofa cushion.

Doug grinned. "Oh yeah. No more showers in your parents' room for you."

Rebecca swept her folded legs down to the floor and dashed out the door. A moment later she poked her head back round the frame. "Are you coming, Bethany?"

The other Ashbourne girl beamed and followed her out. Already her sting marks were beginning to subside. She had found a new confidence and zest after the incident with the bees and woodland pond. This was thanks in no small part to Rebecca. Together they ascended the staircase to the family bathroom.

Rebecca's shriek of delight echoed down into the hallway below, a few moments later. "O-M-G! Oh wow, Dad. A quadrant, hydro-massage shower?"

Doug appeared in the doorway behind his daughters. "Yep. Six hydro-massage jets, built in FM radio with LCD control panel, and internal mood lighting. Not to mention overhead monsoon rain shower plus hand shower. It even has a flip down seat and sliding doors. I'm a bit worried we won't get you out of here now."

Bethany eyed the shower cabinet with interest, then looked at her sister. "You'll turn into a prune if you stay in there too long."

"That I will. Can't wait to try it first thing tomorrow, though."

Joshua and Elizabeth arrived on the scene. The lad cleared his throat. "What's all the shrieking about?" He caught sight of the shower. "Hey. Awesome, Dad."

"It *is* pretty awesome," Elizabeth nudged her husband. "Makes our en-suite power shower seem a little tame."

"I'm sure the kids will let you try it out."

Bethany, Rebecca and Joshua exchanged unsure glances.

Doug folded his arms. "Hey, it's not only for you lot, you know."

Rebecca walked past, prodded her brother and drew him aside. "What are you so happy about lately? Ever since Moira went up to your room, you've been walking on air. Dare I ask?"

Joshua bit his lip.

Rebecca changed tack. "Did she like your junk?"

"I guess that's one way of putting it, yeah."

Rebecca closed the door of the new, fitted bathroom next morning with a satisfied sigh. She slid the bolt across to ensure privacy and hung her white bathrobe on a brass hook. This was the moment she had been looking forward to all night long.

The sliding shower panels gave her easy access. Before closing them and activating the water programs, she pressed a button to bring in the radio. Chart music rang out of quality audio panels, producing a full and rich bass.

"Yes," the last letter of the word stretched into an elongated hiss of pleasure.

The massage jets and rain shower were invigorating and stimulating. She was amazed at how much residual tension seemed to wash away down the drain as her muscles relaxed. Her head swayed in time with the music. She twisted to expose more of her body to the tingling jets and sang along with the pop song.

A burst of static interrupted the music a few moments later. Rebecca frowned but continued to enjoy the tactile water sensations. The song came back for half a verse and then the static crackled again. The girl banged her fist against the rear panel. She hoped to dislodge whatever issue might be causing the problem.

"Don't say the radio has a fault."

Her feet became heavy and caused the girl to look down. Water had stopped draining away, and the cabinet was now ankle-deep.

"Shit." She punched the off switch to kill the massage jets and rain shower. The drain failed to admit any more waste water. "I knew this was too good to be true. Dad *must* have tested it. He's so thorough." The girl pulled down the seat and plonked her naked backside on it. She poked fingers into the drain cover to provoke at least a little movement. The radio static fizzed again. Rebecca thumped the off switch and let out a frustrated grunt.

The massage jets and overhead shower both erupted back into life.

"What the fuck?" The girl pressed the 'off' buttons. No response. The water around her ankles rose to touch her calf muscles. She hurried back to her feet and pressed the buttons again. The shower died. *What am I going to do now? I'd better not slide open the panels, or the new landing and stair carpet will turn into a waterfall.* She eyed the bathroom door with the bolt she had engaged to be left alone. *Mum and Dad can hardly get in and help. I'd better call and see if Dad can check the drainage from outside. This water must flow away on its own, eventually.* "Dad?" The words sounded muffled by the time her enquiring voice breached both the shower cabinet and bathroom doors.

The shower burst back into action. All jets fired at full power and the monsoon rain shower lived up to its name. The rising water soon reached the girl's knees. She screamed. "Dad!" The pitch of her voice climbed at an exponential rate. One that exceeded that of the filling torrent. The radio crackled back to life on a different station. *'Elysium Ascendant'* thundered at full volume from the speakers. It drowned out the girl's frantic screams. The water reached her tummy and self-preservation kicked in. Rebecca knew her parents couldn't care less about the state of their decor. Not if the life of their eldest daughter was on the line. Her frantic fingers tugged at the sliding doors, but the panels wouldn't budge. "Mum! Dad!" She screamed at the top of her lungs. Her throat already felt hoarse.

The water rose to lift her bosom, and the radio crackled with static again. The liquid reached the base of her neck. Rebecca pulled as hard as she could at the resistant door handles. A silvery female voice whispered out of the speakers. "Seven souls are required." The timbre hung thick with mockery. Deafening laughter caused the cabinet to shake.

"Josh, will you *please* turn that music down? It's great that you love Cry Heaven and all, but..." Doug banged on his son's bedroom door.

The portal flew open a second later. Joshua stood in his pyjamas attempting to hide some morning wood. He rubbed sleep from his eyes and waved a hand back inside his room. "As you can hear, it's coming from next door."

Doug shook the woolly feeling from his head. The thundering strains of *'Elysium Ascendant'* had instinctively brought him to his son's door. Now his awakening ears attuned to the correct source of the racket.

Rebecca's screams - followed by a loud coughing - rose to challenge the competing noise.

"Oh my God. Becky?" Doug ran to the bathroom entrance. "Becky?" He tried the handle and found the door bolted.

Elizabeth climbed the stairs with a tray of tea and biscuits for them to enjoy in bed. She winced at the pounding noise from inside the bathroom. Her eyes caught sight of her husband's expression of anguish. "What's wrong?"

Another scream and a cough from inside the room.

Elizabeth almost dropped the tray. "Doug?"

Doug slammed his shoulder into the door. It shuddered but held firm. Inside, the ratio of screaming to coughing and choking altered in favour of the latter. With every spluttering noise, Doug ran and threw himself into the door with renewed vigour. Finally the barrier gave way with a crash and the man tumbled inside, tripping over into the bath.

Elizabeth saw her eldest daughter inside the shower cabinet. She was almost completely immersed, like a specimen creature in a bottle.

"Becky!" she wailed and ran to tug at the sliding doors.

Joshua had been drawn in by the noise and now raced downstairs to the fuse panel below. Seconds later he located the trip for the bathroom and threw it.

The shower jets and radio died. This left Rebecca fighting to keep her head above a now stationary water level. She had already taken a lot of fluid in and gagged for air with a reddening face.

Doug joined his wife and forced the sliding doors open. The wave of water gushing forth from the resulting gap, almost knocked them both off their feet. It splashed down the stairs, causing Joshua to grab hold of the railings to steady himself on his way back up. Rebecca fell into her parents' arms. Elizabeth wrapped a towel around her. Bethany appeared at the door and screamed. She ran to stroke her sister's hair.

"Is she okay?"

"I think so," Doug patted the girl's arm and led her aside.

Rebecca curled up on the bathroom floor and coughed up some more water.

Doug frowned. "How could this have happened?"

Elizabeth wept. Her eldest daughter opened her eyelids. Bare skin pressed against the cold, saturated floor tiles.

"Thanks Mum. Thanks Dad." The faint words came out between fits of shaking and choking.

8
Echoes of the Past

"So, have you been back in the shower since?" Moira ran a jerky hand through her dyed pink hair.

Rebecca winced. "Yeah. But I leave the door unlocked these days. I'd rather have Josh spy my naked bod than risk another episode like that one."

The girls meandered up the hill from the village at a lazy pace. The afternoon sun poked through an overlapping canopy of trees in occasional fingers of light.

Rebecca flushed. "To be honest, it did take me a couple of days before I would trust the thing again. I used my folk's en-suite until Dad took a few showers in the bathroom himself to show that all was well. It's not the shower so much I'm worried about though."

"Has something else happened?"

"No, it's this weird voice I heard while the water was rising."

"How do you mean?"

"The radio kept playing up. Okay, that could be a wiring or component fault. The shower switching on? Possibly some kind of other electrical issue. But nothing can explain that voice."

"Did the radio change station? You know, like catching a talk show or something?"

"I've tried telling myself that. But it said 'seven souls are required.' Bit odd for a talk show."

"Book reading or review?"

"Possible, but I don't believe so. Its owner was actually present in that room with me somehow."

"Have you told your parents?"

"Yeah."

"And?"

"And Dad said it must have been some kind of cookery programme speaking about fish."

"Fish?"

"He reckons it wasn't souls but soles, like Dover Sole. Seven soles are required. They must be preparing a frickin' royal banquet to need that many."

Moira paused and studied Rebecca's strained features. "You don't seem convinced by his explanation."

"Ya think? The whole shower cabinet shook with what I can only describe as cruel laughter. It was some chilling woman's voice, Moira. That voice sounded evil. Pure evil. It bloody well freaked me out."

"Could your mind have exaggerated things during the panic? I know I'd be bricking myself if something like that happened to me. No way I'd think straight."

Rebecca wrung her hands and looked down at the tarmac. "I don't think so. What with that and the weird situation with Bethany and the bees…"

"You're starting to wonder if something sinister is afoot in Coln Abbots?"

Rebecca raised her eyes to lock faces with her companion. "Bethany still claims there were people in that pond pulling her under. She is adamant. Mum and Dad are having none of it, of course. And Josh said he could only see weeds wrapped around her feet and ankles."

"But now you believe she might be telling the truth?"

"My kid sister likes to live in an imaginary world. She's in no hurry to grow up. That's not news to anybody. But it's an escape. I know she can tell the difference between fantasy and reality when it comes down to it. She's so frustrated that our folks don't believe her. I've heard the story in private many times over now. My mind can't shake the certainty in her voice. She insists on her portrayal of events being absolute truth. The girl might only be eleven, but she's no attention seeker."

Moira pursed her rouge lips and studied the rays of sunlight. After a moment she swivelled to look back down the lane to the village. "How would you like to see something freaky?"

"Such as?"

"Do you remember I mentioned wild things going on round here?"

"Sure."

"Well, why don't I show you one? If you can survive a situation like your ordeal in the shower, I reckon you're up to it. Bloody hell, Becky, that must have been scary."

"You're not wrong there. So, what is it you want to

show me?"

"Ghosts."

Rebecca frowned. "Be serious."

"I am serious. A whole procession of them, in fact."

"Where?"

"Right where we're standing."

The Ashbourne girl scanned the high wooded banks of the lane. Was Moira aware of some spectre standing there watching them that she hadn't noticed? "I don't see anything."

"Not now, silly. Why don't you come down to Box Cottage for a sleepover tonight? I'll let Mum know we're popping out for a midnight stroll. I sometimes take them, so she won't think it odd."

"You go for walks at midnight?"

"Hey, this is the country, Becky. As long as you're watchful for traffic on the lanes, it's relatively safe. Not too many rapists and murderers lurking amongst the hedges of Coln Abbots. Something to be thankful for."

"Okay. Make a believer out of me then."

Moira's eyes half closed. "You won't be disappointed. But please promise me you won't start screaming."

Rebecca sneered. "Yeah, yeah. Big it up, why don't you? We'll see."

"Indeed we will."

Moira and Rebecca slipped out of the Goth's bedroom. The house was still. Nancy and Howard had already retired for the evening. They left a downstairs light on for the girls to find their way. Moira halted at the top of the stairs and held up a hand. Rebecca almost collided with her and sent them both tumbling forwards. But, she caught herself in time and grabbed hold of the girl in front for stability.

The mop of pink hair flicked around like a cracking whip. "Listen." That rosy red, lipstick adorned mouth curled open. Her eyes twinkled.

Rebecca gulped. She wondered if the cottage was haunted too. Her ears strained for any noise.

At first all seemed quiet. Then, from down the hall came a rhythmic creaking. A male grunt followed a few seconds later. Finally, a wanton female moan rose to cut through the stillness. "Oh God yeah. Oh fuck that feels good. So good."

Moira giggled. "Mum and Dad are going at it like a couple of pistons."

Rebecca's cheeks reddened. Her voice came in a harsh whisper. "Jeez, Moira. I've never even heard my own folks having sex. How am I going to look either of your parents in the eye now?"

"Perhaps your mum lays there like a sack of potatoes. Mine is pretty vocal as you can hear. Anyway, don't be such a square. It's normal and natural."

"Is it natural for us to stand here listening to it also?"

Moira descended the staircase with Rebecca close in tow. A faint glow pulsed in the fading embers of the living room fireplace.

Rebecca pulled a compact torch from her pocket. She had learnt her lesson from Elizabeth well.

Moira slipped on a pair of shoes and indicated the flashlight with her forehead. "Try to keep that for emergencies only, hey?"

Rebecca snorted. "Why, will it scare the ghosts away?"

"No. But we don't want to arouse unnecessary suspicions, if we can help it. This place is a regular gossip factory."

"What *is* the procession exactly?"

"It's a replay from the civil war. Witch hunters - or so the stories go. I've only caught a glimpse of it once before."

"How did you hear about it?"

"Coln Abbots is a small village. Not too many secrets around here. Country folk love their local stories and legends too. Doesn't take much persuading to have them tell you a few."

"How do you know we'll see this procession tonight?"

"It's supposed to happen on a full moon. Or at least, it's always been a full moon when others have seen it. It was on my first time."

"Weren't you scared?"

"A little. I was actually higher up the hill, so the figures were faint and far enough away for me not to feel threatened."

Rebecca fidgeted. "If they're witch hunters, you could be in a world of hurt."

Moira smirked. "Nah. These ghosts aren't aware of the living around them. We're not going to be in any danger. Do you think I'd put us both in harm's way?"

"I guess not." Rebecca donned her own shoes.

Moira jangled house keys in her pocket for reassurance and opened the front door. "Okay, let's go."

It took several minutes until their vision adjusted to the darkness. The silvery luminance of a full moon in a cloudless sky, provided adequate perceptual help. The girls walked down the lane from Box Cottage in the direction of the village. Further along the stream that ran past Moira's house, a much smaller limestone cottage hugged the bank. It was squat and higgledy-piggledy, but solid. Although the time was after midnight, a faint light flickered through the glass of a downstairs mullioned window.

"Shall we take a look in?" the Goth motioned at the building.

"I don't want to *see* people having sex, Moira. Hearing it was quite enough. Thanks anyway."

"No chance of that here. This is Wendy Simpson's place."

"Who's Wendy Simpson?"

"Some dried up old spinster who lives with a cat. The kind of person you're going to turn into, if you don't learn to relax and lighten up a bit."

"Thanks a lot."

"I'm kidding. There are all kinds of stories floating around that she's a witch or something. She lives alone and makes herbal remedies and cosmetics for a small income. I imagine that has something to do with it."

"And then there's the cat."

Moira snickered. "Yeah. Do you know what this place is called?"

"Enlighten me."

"Gingerbread Cottage."

"Get off. You're making that up."

"Check the gate if you don't believe me."

Rebecca hunched over and crept closer to the building. The front gate was far enough away from the downstairs window to fire up her torch unnoticed. Its beam flashed across a neat, carved wooden property name: 'Gingerbread Cottage.' The girl sucked in a laugh and covered her mouth.

Moira sidled up to her. "Told you so."

"That's so funny. Like Hansel and Gretel."

"Best not let your sister Bethany near here, in case Wendy eats children."

"Oh, Bethany would want to go inside. Her mind would be conjuring up all kinds of fantastic images."

"Aren't you even a bit curious?" Moira edged along the side of the house towards the window.

"Moira." Rebecca felt a shiver run down her spine. It was a curious mixture of fear and excitement. She followed her friend to where the girl stood poking her nose round the thick, deep-set window frame.

A heavy drape had been drawn across the pane, but enough of a crack left for the girls to peek inside.

A large, flat cross section of tree trunk rested against the far wall of a small room. On it sat a fist-sized smooth stone that must have come from the river. Next to that stood a clay bowl of earth and another of water.

A fat candle burned in a glass holder. What appeared to be sage incense smoke rose from a smudge stick. A dried flower and old hairbrush completed the curious collection of items.

Rebecca whispered in Moira's ear. "What *is* that?"

"Witch's altar, I should say."

"You mean you don't know?"

"Hey, I'm a dabbler, remember?"

"This is weird. Let's get out of here."

"Hang on a minute, someone's coming."

The girls froze. Both held their breath.

A tall, thin woman with mauve tinted grey hair in volume curls entered the room. High cheekbones and immaculate skin spoke of a lady in her mid-sixties. One who had taken care of her appearance; even if that appearance was a little eccentric. Rebecca felt a tightness in her chest. It seemed rather sad to find this curious creature all alone. Her sadness turned to shock a moment later. The blade of a short dagger emerged from the woman's dress. Metal flashed in the reflected candlelight. Back turned to the window, the homeowner knelt at the altar. She clutched the knife between slender hands.

Rebecca let out an involuntary squeak. There was a flurry of motion inside, followed by a feline wail. A tabby cat with almost luminous green eyes flew onto the windowsill. The girls ducked down. They pressed themselves flat against the rough Cotswold limestone of the cottage walls.

"What is it, Tink? Do we have company?" A smooth, calm female voice sounded on the other side of the glass.

Moira and Rebecca could feel the blood pumping in their jugulars. Their hot bodies cooled in the roadside grass.

The voice inside spoke again. "Must have been a fox."

When the figure at the window finally appeared to have lost interest, the girls crept back onto the lane.

It seemed to Rebecca that she didn't draw breath until Gingerbread Cottage was behind them. Moira however, seemed thrilled by their encounter.

"Can you believe it, Becky? Wow, so she is a witch after all. How cool is that?"

"It's bloody freaky. Don't tell me you're going to try and get to know her now."

"Nah. I'll do my own thing. There are certain aspects of her life I definitely don't want tuition in."

"Like the fact she lives all alone? Speaking of which, what on earth did you do to my brother? He was bouncing around like a nutter after your visit to his bedroom. Now he's getting all responsible; taking an interest in sensible things like Dad's business. Please tell me you didn't shag him."

"No. Nothing like that. Well, almost nothing."

"Almost?"

"Let's say I helped him engage with the natural flow of his sexual energy. A lot of occult and new age practises involve that. Harnessing, channelling and directing our energies. Master that and you master your life."

"Well you must have directed him in *some* fashion. I mean, he was always willing to lend Dad a hand. But now my old man thinks he's going to develop a passion for wine making and the like."

"Maybe he will."

"True. I hope it doesn't wear off. It's kinda cool to see Dad brimming over with familial pride, you know?"

"Yeah. That's nice. Glad I could help." Moira raised a finger to point in front. "There's 'The Woolpack Inn.' The witch hunt procession starts from there and heads back up the lane this way. Or so I'm told."

"So where do we watch from?"

"How about those bushes on the bank?"

"Okay. God, I'm glad it's been dry lately. I don't fancy squatting in wet foliage waiting for these ghosts of yours to appear."

The girls clambered up the grass verge. They settled down amidst a collection of undergrowth parallel to the thoroughfare. Now it was only a matter of time and patience.

* * *

Adam Compton glanced at the wall calendar behind the bar. Along with common holidays, the month-to-view article also included lunar cycles. Helpful moon phase symbols indicated these on different days. Tonight was a full moon. The old landlord shuddered. He loved 'The Woolpack Inn,' but full moons were a difficult time for him. When that nice Ashbourne fella had stayed during the renovation of Pennycress Cottage, he'd downplayed events. Claiming ignorance might have dealt with the concerns of a visiting patron, but Adam knew the truth. He couldn't wait to close up the pub after last orders. The sooner he got everything cleared away, the sooner he could leave the barroom and tuck himself safely away in bed. He wasn't exactly scared. After living here all his life and with many years as landlord, Adam knew he wasn't in any real danger. That didn't make the supernatural manifestations any easier to cope with. He always tried to avoid encountering the apparitions that appeared on those nights.

Jess dosed by the diminishing embers of the open fire. The shiny black Lab yawned and lifted her square head to regard her master for one brief moment. Satisfied all was in order, she rested it back down between two outstretched front paws.

Adam switched off an under counter cooler. His kitchen help had called in sick earlier that day. It meant he didn't get the full two-and-a-half hours required to clean the lines. Instead, the landlord ended up doing a partial job before peeling spuds that required his attention. He hoped the local bitter keg - whose line he hadn't cleaned - would not let his reputation down. Not before he finally sorted it, at least. This was the first free moment of time in his day. Being a fastidious sort, Adam knew he couldn't leave the line dirty until morning. *"Never go to bed with a job half done,"* his old father had always said.

The man disappeared through the kitchen door, propped open the beer cellar entrance and flicked on the light. He stuck a large, red plastic bucket in the sink. A pair of PVC gloves and bottle of cleaning fluid solution were retrieved from a cupboard underneath. Some solution squirted into the bucket, he turned on the hot tap to fill the receptacle. Legs and back aching from another day on his feet, Adam descended the steps. He clutched the sloshing bucket in one of his gloved hands. The keg couplers were first to be removed and cleaned in the solution. He washed down the sockets and boards with a cloth. The landlord re-inserted the couplers into their cleaning sockets - gas turned off. The pumps themselves stayed on. After bleeding air/gas bubbles through the main into a cleaning container, he climbed back up the steps.

Jess watched motionless as her master re-emerged from the kitchen. Adam popped a long, yellow plastic container under the bar taps. He flushed any residual beer through the offending line until the cleaning mix followed suit.

A chill wind blew down the chimney. The dog's ears raised, haunches tensing. She let out a low whine.

Adam looked up from the bar. In the stillness of the common room, hazy figures began to take shape like an emerging fog bank. At first one might confuse the manifestations with the action of subdued light and a flickering fireplace on dust-heavy air. Shadowy silhouettes materialised from the curious mist to become partial solids. Their appearance was that of rough male labourers clad in old smocks of yesteryear.

It wasn't the first time the landlord had witnessed this replay. But, he usually liked to be out of the room when it happened. Always on a full moon for some reason. *Damn that kitchen help.* It had been a rotten day. Not only was he left to fend for himself, but he had lost a handkerchief. Not any old handkerchief, though. It was the special one his late wife had embroidered with his initials. He'd definitely pegged it out on the line with the rest of the washing. But when he returned, the item must have blown away. Sure, it was only a piece of cloth, but the sentimental value to the old publican was tremendous.

Out in the culinary preparation area, both sink taps twisted open. Water gushed into the stainless steel unit with a din. A cloth slid along the flat draining board of its own accord, dropped into the basin and stopped up the plughole. The water volume soon overwhelmed the kitchen feature. It flowed over the side and washed across the floor in waves.

A red-faced, ghostly apparition stood at the bar with his back to the landlord. Adam found him translucent enough to spy the fellow's compatriots eyeing him beyond. Their pale countenances seemed transfixed on this man, as if he were some kind of ring leader.

"You heard her curse Goody Parsons. She extended her hand and called for endless suffering and torment," the spirit bellowed. He slammed down a pewter tankard on the bar. Beer splashed over the edge but disappeared, leaving the worktop dry.

"And don't forget her charge that Margaret should remain barren," added a meeker tone from one side.

"Aye, there's that too," roared the first. "How much longer are we to allow the Blackwood daughters license to persist? Daughters of darkness foisting their evil curses upon our God-fearing community. One has met her judgement, but the other still remains. What say you?"

Shouts erupted around the room. Their owners may not have appeared solid to the eyes of the living, but the sounds cut loud and strong.

Adam caught a flash of movement out the corner of his eye. From one of the street-facing windows, a pale old woman's face turned. She shuffled away into the night.

Jess whined and stared at her master. The whites of the dog's eyes were showing. She trembled but remained frozen to her spot by the fire.

The spectral gathering walked towards the door and passed straight through it. From the lane outside, flickering torchlight cast an orange glow against the front of the old pub.

Adam's pulse pounded, and he leaned against the bar for support. The yellow container almost full, he shut off the tap. His hands trembled. "Shit, I could do without seeing that again." He walked back into the kitchen and his feet almost went out from underneath him on the flooded tiles. The sink was still sending a cascade of water over its edge, both taps on full stream. "What on earth?" The landlord caught hold of a food preparation table to steady himself. He attempted to reach the sink without slipping over. At last he was able to shut off the water. His hand plunged into the deep sink and he tugged the cloth out of the plughole. The water level began to recede at a ponderous pace. "What a day." He let loose a heavy, drawn-out sigh and turned to face the open cellar door. "I suppose it's going to need mopping up down there now, too."

From behind, two unseen forceful hands delivered a sharp shove, square on his shoulder blades. The landlord staggered and slid forwards. His legs almost did the splits. He struggled to retain his footing on the slippery surface. The cellar door came closer. The hands struck his back again. This time Adam tumbled forwards and fell headlong down the staircase. The pain of impact caused the man to yell. His cry was cut short on the next bounce. Inertia tumbled him head over heels, joints smashing into each step with a series of sickening, bone-crunching snaps.

Up in the bar, Jess raised her head and looked towards the kitchen door. The Lab knew something was wrong. But, obedience kept her from entering the room she had been trained to avoid.

At the bottom of the cellar steps, Adam Compton's paralysed gaze stared up at cobwebs on the joists above. His mouth hung open in a silent scream, limbs folded back in odd directions abnormal to healthy ranges of movement. Residual water from the kitchen flood trickled down the staircase. It pooled around his broken, rag doll body. The man could only move his eyes. Pain surged through his anatomy. Pain he was unable to express.

Up in the kitchen, the cloth flopped back into the sink and the taps returned to an open position. It wasn't long before a cascade of water came flowing down the cellar steps. It began to fill the tanked, subterranean chamber. The flood rose underneath Adam's body. It washed up around his ears and soon overwhelmed them. In a perverse twist of fate, all he could do was cry and add saltwater to the fatal volume filling the makeshift cistern. The level passed his cheeks and eyes. Frantically flaring nostrils - like a manic snorkel - were the last visible sign of the landlord to disappear beneath the artificial lake. For a moment or two, bubbles rose to the surface. Finally, all was calm.

In the kitchen above, the taps shut themselves off. From the bar beyond, a dog whimpered.

* * *

"Oh my God, what is *that*?" Rebecca froze to the spot.

"This is it." Moira moistened a pair of dry lips with her tongue.

Below them and a little further down the lane, The Woolpack was all closed up for the night. One tiny porch lantern cast a courtesy light a few feet from the front door. A number of subdued bulbs remained aglow from inside the bar. The proprietor was most likely cleaning up. Now the exterior, artificial electric lantern was joined by the sudden, natural shimmer of flickering flame. Orange tongues of fire sputtered in the night atop torches carried by a rough-looking group of men. The figures were pale, like smoky vapour and semi-transparent. Yet still their illuminations reflected off the side of the old pub.

"Fuck, I can't believe you talked me into this." Rebecca dug her nails into the palms of her hand, voice cracking.

Moira panted and caught her breath. "We're okay. It's going to be okay."

"Are you saying that to me, or trying to reassure yourself?"

"Oh man, this is amazing."

Rebecca's whisper became shrill. "They're coming this way." The girl wanted to shut her eyes, but couldn't force herself to look aside. Instead she held hands with Moira. Their gaping jaws never moved.

The gang of men marched up the lane - purpose in their steps, determination written across cloud-like visages. Every now and then one yelled a word of encouragement which turned into a shared chant. At their head, a red-faced individual led the mob.

Behind him another shouted, "Tell it how it is, Jethro."

The leader bellowed at the top of his spectral lungs. "Thou shalt not suffer a witch to live." His voice sounded half-cut from too much ale. The unified hollering of "Aye" in agreement following his utterance, wasn't far removed from the same state.

Rebecca and Moira studied their appearance as the crowd strode by. The clothing appeared to be a mid-seventeenth century style. That worn by farm labourers and other working men. The gang continued apace and a minute later passed from sight. They disappeared up the incline in the direction from which the girls had arrived, shortly before.

Rebecca let go of her companion, placed her palms on the cool grass and breathed in a series of slow pants.

"So what do you think about ghosts now?" Moira went pale and her voice trembled a little.

"I wouldn't have believed it if I hadn't seen it for myself. Nobody in my family will accept it. Well, not my parents anyway." Rebecca rested back in a squatting position.

"I told you there were some pretty wild things going on in Coln Abbots. What with this and Wendy Simpson, it's been a brilliant night. Spooky though." She shivered.

"What do you suppose she was doing?"

"Casting, I imagine."

"What, you mean spells?"

"Well she wasn't casting a fishing net now, was she?"

"Okay, okay. Well, I've had quite enough excitement for one evening. I guess the mob have sufficient head start for us not to run into them. Can we go and get some sleep now?"

Moira helped her up. "Yeah. If we do this again sometime, we can find out where they went. How cool would it be to discover who the group were after?"

"I'm not sure I want to see someone accused of witchcraft and attacked by an angry, half-drunken mob. Even if they *are* only ghosts."

"You've got a point. Alright, let's head back then."

* * *

The air was damp and heavy with characteristic morning valley mist. Rebecca climbed up the hill after breakfast at the Robbins household. She knew the moisture-filled atmosphere would soon clear to reveal another fine day. At the end of the drive leading up to Pennycress Cottage, Bob Faringdon's beaten up Land Rover stood - more abandoned than parked - at a jaunty angle. Bethany leaned over the rear tailgate. She clutched something in her hands that moved with hesitant jerks. Outside the cottage door, her mother, father and brother chatted with the old dairy farmer. Their discussion appeared quite animated. Even from this distance, the girl could tell her family appeared upset. Joshua caught sight of his sister and sprinted down to meet her.

"What's wrong, Josh?" the words were out of Rebecca's mouth before the lad even had time to stop.

"Adam Compton - the landlord at The Woolpack - died last night."

The girl's face went ashen. "How?"

"It seems he slipped on some water in the pub kitchen and fell down the beer cellar steps. Broke pretty much everything, from what Bob Faringdon told us. The kitchen helper rocked up first thing this morning and found him. He was lying submerged at the bottom of the stairs in a twisted mess."

"Submerged?"

"The room flooded a couple of feet deep, from the kitchen sink above. Looks like he left the taps running while he was away doing other things. Must have realised his mistake and shut them off before going below, then had an accident on the way down. The fire brigade had to pump out the cellar this morning."

A flash of heat rippled through the girl's body. She continued walking with her brother at her side. Now it became clear that the moving object in Bethany's hands was the head of the black Labrador who lived at the pub.

"Oh Dad, can we please keep her?" The eleven-year-old held the dog's head up to touch noses with it. The forlorn-looking animal gazed back with mourning eyes.

Rebecca and Joshua reached the vehicle. They each took turns petting the unresponsive animal. The eldest daughter thought back to the night before. She wondered if Mr Compton had lost his life while she and Moira had been only a few feet away outside. The girl shivered and gulped.

Bob Faringdon approached with Doug and Elizabeth.

Bethany twisted the dog's head to point it at her mother. "Look Mum, she's heart-broken. Please can we look after her?"

Elizabeth glanced at her husband. He shrugged. "Your call, Lizzie."

"Oh, thanks a bunch. So if I said 'no,' it's me that

would be the ogre then."

"Look, we've got room now. A dog might do us all some good." He looked at Bob and stroked the animal. "She's well trained and behaved, I'll bet."

"None better. Poor creature's an institution around the village. Everyone knows her. I was going to take her back to Washburn Hill and see how she got along with our dogs. But, if you want to take her on, you'll not find a more loyal and well behaved animal."

"Except when you are trying to eat a fry up?" Elizabeth raised an eyebrow at Doug. She remembered his tales from those renovation trips to the pub.

Bob grunted. "That's a dog for you, Elizabeth."

Bethany stuck out her bottom lip and slanted her eyes downward.

Elizabeth tried to hold in the laughter. "Oh alright then, we'll take her in."

"Yay!" Bethany dragged the startled animal out the back of the Land Rover.

Doug kissed his wife. "Thanks, Love. Jess is a sweetheart. You'll adore her, I promise."

"Make sure everyone takes their turn walking and cleaning up after the creature, okay?" Elizabeth moved her stare from husband to each of her children. "Don't leave it all to your mother."

"Come on, Girl." Bethany ran a short distance towards the cottage, spun back and slapped both her legs. The dog seemed a little unsure at first. Then she trotted over and received another hug and rub to her ears.

Bob raised the tailgate on his vehicle. "It'll take her a

time to settle in. Poor old girl was devoted to Adam. Must be confusing for the animal. But, I'm sure she'll come around." He picked a dog lead and bowls out the back, secured the canvas flap and handed them over to Doug.

"Thanks, Bob."

"No problem, old son. Oh yes, Mike and I tried one of those sample bottles of mead last night. Right good stuff, too. Being a generous lad, he's going to let me have the other one all to myself. Perks of old age and seniority. Or so he tells me."

Doug dropped the canine accoutrements down on the grass and shook the farmer's hand. "That's good to know. If you like the sample, then you should enjoy some of the aged stuff when we get it bottled."

"I look forward to it." Bob straightened his worn tweed jacket and made for the driver's door. "See you again soon, Ashbournes."

A minute later, the four-wheeled mechanical cloud factory chugged away down the drive and turned up the lane.

9
Cheese and Wine

"Did you want me to get started on the smoked salmon and cream cheese canapés?" Elizabeth nudged a kitchen tap open with one elbow. Water hissed into the Belfast sink at Box Cottage, enabling her to rinse a pair of sticky hands.

Nancy studied her neighbour's work on the hors d'oeuvre spread taking shape on the large wooden table. "Yes please. I've got some prawn vol-au-vents to attend. I appreciate the help, Elizabeth."

"You're welcome. I hope Doug and Howard haven't polished off all the wine before your guests arrive."

"As long as they stay out of our hair, I'm not too fussed. The Chelts set usually bring some pretty nice plonk with them. Another way to engage in a bit of one-upmanship, it seems."

"Keeping up with the Joneses?"

"Exactly. Or the Poncenby-Smythes, at least."

"Oh, hey..." Elizabeth swiped a tea towel from a hook near the sink and leaned across the table. Nancy took the hint and bent forward to meet her. The neighbour wiped a spot of flour from her nose. An action that demonstrated almost motherly care and attention.

"Thanks for that. We'll have an opportunity to pop upstairs and smarten ourselves before the well-heeled throng descends. Don't worry."

Elizabeth turned her attention to the canapés. "Anyone I need to avoid in particular?"

"Well, you'll get cornered by Ralph and Daphne Tremayne. No question about it. I swear if I hear another play-by-play account of choosing wallpaper for their Million Pound Montpellier Regency town house, I'll scream. At least you'll be getting your ear bent for the first time about it."

"Delightful. Anyone else?"

"Chelsea Worthington will attempt to sign you up for one of her tea dances at the Pittville Pump Room. By all means go for it, if you wish."

"But?"

"But, unless you like watching someone with two left feet swanning around like a debutante... I'd make any excuse you can about being tied up with your business."

"Shouldn't be difficult. I won't have to lie."

"Splendid. How are the children settling in now?"

"Pretty well, all things considered. Bethany still insists there were people in the pond. Other than that, she seems to have recovered from her ordeal. Bees don't phase her as much as we worried they might."

"What it is to have a young imagination." Nancy pulled an oven door open a crack to take a better look at the contents. "And what of Rebecca? Moira said she had the most awful experience with your new shower."

"Oh gosh, that gave us all a scare."

"What happened?"

"Doug wanted to make the family bathroom a bit special. So, he sold some equities he'd been hanging onto in the city. Used the extra cash to splurge on one of those massaging quadrant showers with music and lights."

"All singing, all dancing?"

Elizabeth stopped dead and blew out her cheeks. "Or all *speaking*, if Becky can be believed."

Nancy frowned and tilted her head.

Elizabeth rested her backside against the sink. "She was trying out the new shower. At first everything went well. The jets were functioning, and the radio was on. Then she looked down and noticed water filling the cabinet and not draining away."

"Oh my God." Nancy touched one long, feminine hand to the base of her own neck.

"Yeah. She turned off the unit. Then it switched itself back on and wouldn't disengage."

"Did she try to get out?"

"Once the water started getting higher, yes. But the sliding doors wouldn't budge. Then - and get this if you will - she claims an eerie female voice said *'Seven souls are required'* and laughed at her."

"Seven souls?"

"Doug thinks the radio switched over to a cookery show, or something. Soles, like fish." She waved her hand at the smoked salmon. "The radio was playing up and crackling with static right before."

"What happened next?"

"Next thing the shower started playing that old rock song, *'Elysium Ascendant'* at full volume. Doug got up to go and have a pop at Josh, before he realised where the music was actually coming from. It was then he heard Becky's screams."

"Thank goodness you got her out."

"In the nick of time, too. She'd locked herself in the bathroom like a typical teenager. Doug broke down the door. Josh had the presence of mind to kill the power on the downstairs fuse panel."

"He's quite the gallant champion, that boy of yours. So, you managed to get her free of the shower cabinet."

"The new landing and stairway carpets got an unexpected bath, but Doug and I were able to force the sliding doors." Elizabeth's eyes watered and her voice trembled. "My baby almost drowned in there."

Nancy hurried over and placed an arm around the woman's shoulders. "Goodness, Elizabeth. I'm so sorry. How thoughtless of me. I didn't realise it was quite so serious."

Elizabeth patted her hand. "That's okay. It's a mixture of stress and general pressure from our lifestyle change. Not to mention two near misses with the kids, I suppose. I'll be fine. Don't worry, I won't blub in front of your guests."

Nancy flicked her hand in the air with a carefree gesture. "Blub all you want. These shallow toffs might benefit from a hard dose of reality." Her voice softened. "On a more serious note though, Elizabeth?"

"Yes?"

"If it all gets too much this evening, drop out and go. Don't worry about coming to find Howard or myself. We'll not take offence."

"Thanks. I understand Moira is going to hang out at Pennycress this evening?"

"Indeed. Not sleeping over. She'll be back before too late. These little soirees aren't her thing. She *is* only eighteen going on nineteen, after all. Plus, the Chelts set tend to examine her like some curio - what with the Gothic clothing and so forth."

"She and Becky seem to have formed quite a bond."

"Mmm. We couldn't be more delighted around here. I'm hoping your normal daughter will tame some of her wilder nonsense. Especially the occult fixation. That drives me bonkers. I'm rather glad Moira doesn't have a steady boyfriend yet. Dread to think what sort of guy she'd bring home. There were a few when we were still living in Cheltenham…"

"Not ideal?"

Nancy shook her head.

Elizabeth smiled. "Pickings around here seem a little slim. Not something I thought about during summer holidays in the village as a youngster."

"Pretty much true. An ageing population, for the most part. Moira's taken a bit of a shine to your Joshua, though. Don't think they're an item, but your handsome lad has turned her head."

"Puppy love and hormones. Thank goodness those years are behind us."

Nancy smirked. The oven timer alarm beeped, and she opened the door to retrieve her pastry casings.

"You won't believe our Moira's latest story."

"What's that?"

"When Rebecca stayed over, they went for a midnight walk. Our girl enjoys odd things like that. At least there's not much mischief for her to get into round here."

"So what's the story?"

"First she claimed that our neighbour along the lane, Wendy Simpson, was some sort of witch." Nancy rolled her eyes. "More of her occult nonsense. I imagine they caught the shy old biddy sweeping the floor with a besom broom or something."

"It sounds like there's more?"

"There is. Once before, our girl swore blind she'd seen a procession of ghosts on the lane. They are supposed to emerge at the pub and walk northward. Anyway, Moira tells me she and Becky got so close, they even heard them speak."

"Becky hasn't said anything about that."

"She didn't say much at breakfast next morning to Howard or me, either. Something appears to have made her uncomfortable. She could still be in shock from that episode with the shower."

"True. Doug and I need to listen to her a little closer, maybe. She seemed a might peeved about our refusal to believe that eerie voice tale. I would hate to think our daughter felt she could no longer confide in us."

"Teenagers." Nancy removed a pair of oven gloves and hung them up. "Anyway, they must have been right outside the pub, the night the landlord died."

Elizabeth's brow furrowed and her mouth

straightened. "Oh, wasn't that awful? The poor man slipped and tumbled down his own beer cellar."

"I spoke with someone I know in Pathology at the hospital. They reckon he wasn't killed outright. The flood from the taps upstairs finished him off by drowning."

"No! Can you imagine lying there in the dark and wet; life seeping away, bones broken, knowing nobody will hear you cry out, even if you could? And then the water seeping into your lungs like..." Her voice trailed away for a moment. "Bob Faringdon brought us the news the following day that he'd fallen down and smashed himself up. We assumed he'd been killed outright."

Nancy blinked. "Your imagination is quite Shakespearean. Mr Faringdon brought the dog too, as I understand it."

"Well yes, sort of. That is, he brought the dog along with him and Bethany begged us to keep her instead."

"Sounds like the little one could twist you around her pinkie."

"Mmm. You're right there. My last baby. I don't want her to grow up, if I'm honest. I guess that's why we indulge her so."

"Have you ever had a dog before?"

"No, but Grandpa kept one at the cottage when I was a kid. He'd approve of Jess. Plus, she's so well trained. The animal is almost better behaved than our children."

Doug's voice rumbled from the kitchen doorway. "You might change your tune if the kids squatted and took a dump in the garden."

"Douglas!" Elizabeth flushed. "I'm so sorry, Nancy. Please excuse my crude husband."

Howard prodded the man in his ribs. "Sounds like you're in trouble there."

Doug nodded. "Yup. Got the full name: 'Douglas.' That's never a good sign with Lizzie."

"Are you two blotto yet?" Nancy folded her arms and studied the men with a suspicious, raised eyebrow.

Howard pretended to sway. "No, but let's say the journey has begun."

"Well, make sure you don't slur if you answer the door to our guests while Elizabeth and I are freshening up." She grabbed the other woman's arm. "Come on, fellow domestic goddess. Let's leave these Neanderthals to their rough speech, fire-making and alcohol."

The women pushed past and made for the stairs.

Howard beat his chest like an ape and spoke like a caveman. "Men make fire."

The hallway, kitchen and living room buzzed with the hum of conversation. Elizabeth and Nancy descended the stairs with graceful poise. They found Howard and Doug acting the part of charming, well behaved hosts.

It didn't take more than a minute after introductions with the Tremaynes, for Elizabeth to experience tales of upmarket interior decoration. Their swanky pad in the trendy Gloucestershire town nestling below the Cotswold escarpment, proved all they seemed able to talk about. Elizabeth wondered what the couple might discuss, were their home a two bed terrace in Stroud. The farmers' market instead?

Chelsea Worthington grabbed her arm and stuck like a barnacle on a trawler bottom. Only after Elizabeth explained her schedule didn't allow for tea dances, did the preening lady finally free her captive.

"Elizabeth. Over here. There's someone I'd like you to meet." Nancy waved across a sea of bobbing heads.

Elizabeth took a long sip on her glass of wine. No wonder her neighbour wanted some moral support during this soiree. What kind of diamond encrusted monster was she going to have to put up with now?

Large, shadowed eyes watched her from beneath a perm of red hair. They at least appeared friendly. The lady was a little shorter than Nancy and Elizabeth, but around the same age.

"Elizabeth, this is Katie Benson. She runs an excellent boutique in Broadway. I showed her the candle and soaps you brought over. She'd like a little chat." Nancy wafted between the women. The new acquaintances shook hands. Nancy winked. "Jolly good. Now, if you'll excuse me, I mustn't neglect our other guests."

"So you have a shop in Broadway?" Elizabeth took a more demure taste of her wine this time. "My Grandfather sometimes took me for picnics on the hill by the tower."

Katie twisted her lips at the word 'shop.' It was as if the term bore distasteful, working class connotations. Her minor frown soon passed and faded away. "My boutique purveys all manner of handmade, quality items from local producers and craftspeople. Nancy tells me you sell most of your products via an on-line store."

"That's right. I've never thought of my stock as smart enough to approach a London outlet. Plus, I've only ever done it as a hobby until now, so range and volume are both limited. There's a website-"

"Yes," Katie interrupted. "We had a look on my phone. I like the fact you've used your own name: Elizabeth Ashbourne. That conveys confidence and has a nice sound to it. A definite USP when marketing to the more discerning customer. The only thing is, your prices are a little low."

"I've always thought of them as reasonable."

Katie almost spat. "Quite. Well, you're in The Cotswolds now. People round here - the well-heeled incomers at least - will pay a hundred pounds for a small cheese knife. Assuming it's sold and presented well, that is. The *'Cotswold'* name sells. And when we combine *'Elizabeth Ashbourne'* with *'Cotswold Producer,'* you'll almost be able to write your own salary. If I'm going be a purveyor of your stock, we can bump the prices up at least four hundred percent."

Elizabeth tried not to spray her drink in the woman's face. She coughed and regained her composure. "I'm sorry, please excuse me. But what about my customers further afield?"

"If you still want to sell to them, fine. But we would need to downplay your website at my establishment. That is, if there are going to be two very different pricing structures. To be honest, many of our customers are visiting tourists. They go back to America and Japan (and goodness knows where else), then show off their treasures acquired here. If you have a website, don't be surprised to find people who will pay the same prices their friends did, to get some of your wares."

Elizabeth pondered her words for a moment. "I'll need to mull it over and have a chat with my husband."

"Of course, of course. Look, here's what I propose: How about I put up a small, temporary display with some of your items at a price I know the market will bear around here? If they sell well and we're both happy, we can go forward on that basis."

"That sounds fair. Thank you."

"Good. Here, I'll give you my card. You can always contact me through Nancy, anyway. I understand your husband produces mead and fruit wines?"

"Yes. It's been a hobby of his for years. Now he's hoping to make a go of it on a professional basis."

"I'd say he's chosen a good spot. We have all manner of micro-breweries, wineries and distilleries around here. There's even a local Cotswold whisky, if you can believe it. Good stuff, or so I'm told."

"I'd heard that."

"You and your husband are quite an enterprising couple. I wish you well."

"Thank you. And thanks again for the selling opportunity."

"Pleasure." Katie caught the eye of someone she knew across the room and excused herself.

"How's the mingling?" Doug's voice sounded in Elizabeth's right ear.

"I'm tired. How about you?"

"They're an interesting and mixed bunch. I get the feeling Howard and Nancy are actually friends with some. But the others are professional acquaintances they tolerate."

"That was my assessment too."

"Who were you chatting with?"

"Katie Benson. She runs a Broadway boutique. Offered to stock my products on a trial at four times the current on-line price."

"Get out. Did you bite her arm off? That's amazing, Lizzie."

"Not exactly. I know it's a great opportunity, but I don't like the idea of ripping people off."

"Even people like this? A fool and his money are soon parted, you know."

"I know. But with all the love I put into my products... I'm not sure the deal reflects my values. Anyway, she's offered to put some soaps and candles on display for a trial. A lot of tourists buy that sort of thing."

"Elizabeth Ashbourne, global entrepreneur?"

"Don't start. I agreed to that, at least. Can we go home, Doug?"

Her husband frowned.

Elizabeth kissed him on the cheek. "Not to London, silly. I mean, back up the hill. You know, while I've still got enough energy to misbehave before bedtime."

Doug coughed and took her empty glass away. "Well now, since you put it that way."

"I'll say goodbye to Howard and Nancy. See you in the hall."

* * *

It was sometime in the small hours when Elizabeth rolled over in bed. By her side, Doug's chest rose and fell. An occasional group of snores commenced and then ceased. The waning moon still shone bright. Silvery fingers poked between a gap in the bedroom curtains. From somewhere in the trees behind the cottage, an owl hooted. The woman turned back to her own side of the mattress. She shut her eyes, but sleep wouldn't come. Her lashes flicked open again. Luminous hands on a small bedside travel clock indicated three AM. She lay there a moment longer, allowing her vision to adjust. The outline of their wardrobe and chest of drawers emerged from the gloom. Elizabeth slid her legs from beneath the duvet. Her feet found their way into a pair of slippers on the carpet. She turned back to examine her husband, fast asleep. Tender fingers reached out to stroke his short hair. It felt almost as fine as silk. Elizabeth leaned over and kissed him on the cheek.

The door creaked for one brief moment, causing her

to wince. The resuming rhythmic whine of Doug's snores reassured her that she hadn't disturbed him. The woman let herself out onto the upstairs landing. She paused in the darkness and clicked on the palm-sized torch she always kept handy.

From the other side of a door opposite, a series of panting gasps rose in volume and desperation. Elizabeth closed her eyes, mouth turning up at the corners. A helpless, feminine moan broke through the stillness in a series of repeated exclamations. "Oh! Oh! Oh, oh, oh..." The last few outbursts trailed away into a sigh. Rebecca was masturbating. Elizabeth remembered her own teenage years. The thrill of waking in the small hours to find sexual release away from curious familial ears. Her firstborn was becoming a woman. She thought back to those initial weeks after she had met Doug at university. Would Becky find herself a nice young man in the autumn? Would Doug ever leave the guy alone, if their daughter brought him home for the holidays? She might have to remind him that he too was once a horny teenager. In fact, he hadn't changed much by his mid-forties.

Elizabeth crept to the top of the stairs. She was anxious not to embarrass Rebecca by making her presence known. Even now the girl would be enjoying a few aftershocks. Not to mention that delicious sense of wellbeing. The one that waves of orgasm wrapped around a woman like a warm blanket.

Jess lifted her head out of her basket when Elizabeth opened the kitchen door. The room was big enough that the family allowed the dog to sleep in there. Doug had been right, she was as good as gold. "It's alright, girl. Only me." She knew this was a redundant turn of phrase. First, the dog couldn't understand a word she said. Second, Jess would know who it was by her scent, long before she uttered the statement.

The black Lab got up and wagged her tail.

Elizabeth retrieved a glass tumbler from an overhead cupboard. She ran the tap, swishing her hands through the torrent to test for temperature. She filled the glass and sat down at the table. The animal approached, and the woman rubbed its furry black ears. With her free hand she took a sip of water.

Across the hallway, a dull thud caused the midnight companions to start. Jess froze. Elizabeth swallowed hard and put down her glass. Silence. She got up and walked to the living room door. With quivering fingers, she reached out and twisted the handle. Inside all appeared in order, except for a large, heavy, hardback book that had tumbled off a shelf onto the floor. Elizabeth crouched to pick it up. It was her comprehensive guide to beekeeping. "How...?" her question bounced off the walls, unanswered. She lifted the weighty tome and slid it back into place. The shelf appeared level and secure. *Could one of the kids have pulled it out while reaching for another book? They might, and then left it balanced in a precarious manner.* Jess padded into the room and nuzzled her leg. The dog walked back towards the hallway and turned to face her mistress again.

"I suppose you want to go out for a wee, now I've roused you?" Elizabeth regarded the big, almond-shaped shiny eyes staring back at her. "Okay. My fault for waking you, I guess." She rubbed her face, yawned and passed through the utility room to open the back door. Jess trotted out into the darkness. A wall-mounted security lantern detected the animal's presence and clicked on.

After five minutes had passed, the dog still hadn't returned.

"Where can she have got to?"

The light extinguished, so Elizabeth leaned outside and waved her hand to bring it back on. There was no sign of Jess. "Come on, girl," she called to the blackness beyond the limited range of electrical illumination. No response. From partway up the wooded bank, there came a series of sharp barks.

"Got to be trouble with a bloody fox." Elizabeth hurried to the hallway, retrieved a coat to slip over her nightwear and popped on some outdoor shoes. She activated her torch again and trudged through the long, wet grass behind the cottage. "Yuck. Why did I ever get up?" The barking started again. It must be near the top of the hill now. The woman grumbled and winced as her feet squelched on a patch of mud. She huffed and commenced the ascent to where the sound of the dog appeared to have stopped moving.

"Jess?" her voice was almost the only noise floating around the velvety blackness.

An owl hooted back its response from a tree branch above. Elizabeth jumped and tapped her chest. Her breath steamed in the moonlight, creating tiny clouds of vapour. *Where is that dog?* Somehow thoughts seemed less troublesome than calling out into the cloak of darkness. It was a silly idea, but she was approaching Nevermere. That had always been an uneasy place. Even now her grandfather's warnings to stay away from the water, echoed through her brain.

A small, sappy branch scraped against the woman's face. She pushed it aside and stepped out into a clearing. The moon shone up from the still waters of that ancient woodland pond, a perfect mirror of the night sky above it.

A rustling in the undergrowth caused her pulse to raise. A series of undulating leaves - disturbed by the passage of some approaching creature - rose like an arboreal wave before her. Elizabeth drew in a sharp breath and took a hesitant step backwards.

Jess bounded out of the bushes and ran around behind her legs, whining and shaking.

"What is it, girl?"

No other movement could be seen or heard in the clearing.

A sudden ripple expanded out across the membrane-like surface of the water, disrupting the heavenly reflections. Elizabeth scanned around. She wondered if there might be amphibians abroad, enjoying a night-time swim. The rippling motion subsided, and the moon became visible once more in the natural mirror. The observing woman flinched. In the reflecting waters, she noticed something surveying her from the bank above. Elizabeth jerked her head up and found it to be no trick of the light. There atop a steep rise across the pond, stood a tall, dark figure. The sinister shape was clad in a full-length cloak which included a copious, raised hood. No face could be seen from such a distance. But, hairs rising on the back of the woman's neck left her in no doubt that she was being watched.

Jess whined again.

Elizabeth forced herself to turn her back on the silent sentinel. She twisted forty-five degrees and her eyes fell on an identical figure. It stood near the water's edge, thirty feet from her position. The shape watched her in motionless silence. Could the intimidating apparition behind, have disappeared and re-materialised close by?

Elizabeth's legs felt like jelly. She pushed one foot in front of the other and ran down the hill. Jess scampered along at her side, darting left and right. The dog crossed the woman's path and caused her to stumble into a patch of bracken. She picked herself up, daring to risk one furtive glance back the way she had come. On the brow of the hill, a robed figure watched. Was it a ghost? A demon? All Elizabeth knew was that her body shook with almost uncontrollable fear. She hurried on. Relief caused her to emit a breathless gasp, the moment the rear security light blazed into life. Jess jumped up, as desperate to get inside and find sanctuary as she. The door opened, the pair darted through and the woman slammed it shut behind them. She double-locked the portal and shot bolts across top and bottom. Jess spun in circles on the spot. Elizabeth pulled the small utility room window curtain aside. No figures were visible in the light. A second later, the timer caused the lamp to extinguish. She let the drapes fall and rested her back against the door. Heart still pounding in her ears, she sank down to sit on the back door mat. A trembling Labrador's head came to rest in her lap.

"Lizzie?" Doug's voice called out from the stairs.

"Yes. It's me."

Her husband appeared in the hallway. The moment he caught sight of his wife and their pet huddled together, his wits sharpened.

"Good Lord, whatever happened? Are you okay?"

"There's something out there, Doug."

"SomeTHING? You mean a prowler?"

Elizabeth shook her head. "A hooded figure or figures. I don't know."

Doug strode to the darkened window. "Are they still there? Do you want me to call the police?"

"No. No, it's okay. It scared me, that's all." She patted the dog's head. "Scared us, I should say."

"What were you doing out there at this time of the morning, anyway?"

"I couldn't sleep. Got up for a drink of water and then Jess needed to pee. She didn't come back. When I heard her barking, I went to investigate. I thought it was a fox or something. Anyway, she'd made it all the way up to Nevermere and was in a right state when I found her."

"Nevermere. You mean that pond Bethany jumped into?"

"Yeah."

"So what happened then?"

"I looked up to find a robed, hooded figure staring at

us. It gave me the creeps and Jess started whining. When I turned, it was closer. That, or another figure appeared. I can't be certain. So, we ran back downhill as fast as we could."

"Look at you, you're both trembling. Anyone would think you'd seen a ghost." Doug crouched to touch his wife on the shoulder and pat the dog.

"I'm not being silly or making it up, Doug."

"I believe you, Darling. Whoever they were, they can't have been up to any good. Just as well to get away from them. We'd better have a word with Becky about not going out for more of her midnight walks with Moira at present. If there are criminal types or weirdos lurking around here, the girls could be at risk. Might be poachers or scumbags targeting farms and rural properties for burglary. But, you never know."

"Yeah. That's good. God, I was so scared." Elizabeth swept a cold hand back through her dishevelled hair.

"Since we're up, I'll put the kettle on. I don't suppose either of us are going to get a lot more sleep now."

10
Fallacious Fermentations

"Okay, Josh. Can you fetch the trial jar and hydrometer from the sterilisation bucket, please? That's it, right there." Doug bent to examine the sampling port on one of his stainless steel fermenters.

"Here you go, Dad."

"Thanks." The man opened the lever and allowed some cloudy golden liquid to run into a tall, plastic trial jar. He shut the valve, stood the receptacle on a bench and took the glass hydrometer from his son's hand. "Right then, let's check how this batch is coming along. When I drop the float in, see if you can tell me the reading."

Joshua moved his nose close to the jar and waited for the measuring device to settle at a constant level. "Looks like 1.012."

Doug double-checked the reading. "Very good. This is going to be a regular batch of medium mead. We opened at 1.10 and I'm aiming for a final gravity of 1.006 before stabilisation and racking. Should give us an *Alcohol by Volum*e rate of around thirteen percent."

"Great. Do you still have to siphon the must off the lees like you used to back in London?"

"Not any more. Do you see those two bigger valves, further down the inverted cone?"

"Yeah."

"The top one is for racking the must into another vessel, like the storage tanks I recently bought. But for primary racking it stays put and we flush the lees through the dump valve at the very bottom. Chuck a container underneath, open the flow until the dead yeast and junk runs clear - job done."

"Wow, that's a lot simpler."

"Oh yes. Now, let's see how the rudamel is coming along."

"Does that need a reading too?"

"Not yet. The raspberries are still in there. It's only been going for a day. But, we need to punch down the cap."

"How's that, Dad?"

"The fruit will float to the top and form a crust during the early stages of primary fermentation. At this point we actually want the must to get some oxygen to help the yeast establish itself. There's not going to be any serious competition from anything else that could cause off flavours. Not while its bubbling away like that."

"So what's the punching thing?"

"Punching down or 'punching the cap' is the act of breaking up that crust. If you don't, it causes the yeast unnecessary strain. Additional heat is produced and the organism can't thrive as it should. So, while the fruit is still in there for three of four days, we need to perform this function several times a day. After that we'll remove the dissolving husks before they rot. Otherwise gross lees can cause the melomel to taste and smell pretty rank."

"Got it."

"Great." Doug opened the lid of another fermenter and they both felt a mild wave of warmth. Inside, a brownish pink crust floated atop the surface of some liquid. Here and there the contents bubbled through. The whole container gave off a rich and sweet, fruity aroma. The man pointed to a large bucket of sterilising solution where the hydrometer had come from. "There's a beer paddle in there. If you fetch it, you can punch down the cap and aerate the must with a couple of good stirs. The developing yeast will thank you for it, and so will I."

There was a whine at the door. Doug glanced round to catch the broad head of a black Labrador poking through the jamb. Bethany's face joined it a second later.

The man held up a flat hand. "Keep her out of here please, Darling. We can't have Jess wandering into these buildings."

"Okay, Dad. I wondered what you're up to. Mr Faringdon asked if you've got a real brace or something."

"Do you mean a wheel brace?"

"Oh yes, that makes sense. His car has a flat tyre on the hill. Is that a tool?"

"Yes. I'm surprised he hasn't got one. Must have put it aside while using the Landy for other jobs. Josh, did you want to punch down the cap while I sort him out?"

The boy nodded and retrieved the long beer paddle.

His father clapped him on the back. "There's a lad. I shouldn't be long. Dissolve the cap, give the Rudamel a couple of good stirs, then close the fermenter, okay?"

"No worries."

"Right. Bethany, where exactly is Mr Faringdon?"

"Not far from the end of the drive, on the way downhill to the church."

"Good girl. Thanks for letting me know." He left the outbuilding and went to retrieve his wheel brace from the Subaru. A couple of minutes later, Doug headed off down the drive to help the farmer.

"I'm a daft old bugger. I've got a jack but forgot my bloomin' brace. Thanks for coming along so sharp, Doug." Bob Faringdon stood alongside his trusty metal workhorse. It had been pulled close in to the verge. Now the hulk stood on a semi-level passing place, right before the hill dipped into a steeper gradient.

"Not a problem. Any idea what caused it?"

"Slow puncture, I reckon. A nail or something I've picked up in the last day or so."

Doug approached the front near-side wheel and observed the sagging rubber tyre. He fitted the wheel brace over one of the nuts. His foot went on it for leverage until the nut loosened. Then he spun the item free with both hands. As he lifted his head from fitting the brace over another nut, he noticed a figure out the corner of one eye. There beyond the hedge, stood a familiar woman. The same one he caught watching him from the footpath, the day the fermenters were delivered. Her mauve tinted grey curls blew in a gentle breeze. She stared unblinking at the old farmer.

"Do you know her?" Doug stood upright and pushed his foot against the brace a second time.

"Wendy? We went to school together. Many years ago now, of course."

"Does she usually stare at people like that?"

Bob chuckled. "It's her way. She's always been a solitary sort. Lives at the cottage she grew up in with her parents. They're long gone, now. Wouldn't say boo to a goose, that one."

"Those looks give me the willies." Doug decided to loosen the rest of the nuts and then unscrew them in succession. It would be easy now he had ascertained they weren't too stiff.

Bob fixed his gaze on the woman. She flushed and hurried away into the undergrowth. "Some folk in the village don't like her. They tell all kinds of wild tales - some of them not very nice. But she's always been civil to me. On the rare occasions we've spoken, that is."

"I thought you said you went to school with her."

"True. But even then she was a loner who danced to her own tune. Quite sad, in some ways. A few of the same kids who teased and bullied her at school, are the exact ones who gossip about her now. I don't see what she's ever done to deserve it, myself."

"That's because you're a decent sort." Doug finished loosening the nuts. "Best jack this baby up before I actually remove any more."

Bob set about pumping up the Land Rover. Doug glanced around. Further down the road, a couple of cars pulled out of the drive at Box Cottage. They appeared the same vehicles from their social evening the night before. Howard Robbins waved them off. He caught sight of Doug and began a stiff climb up the lane.

"This hill never gets any easier." The accountant bent over and caught his breath after reaching them. "Anything I can do to help?"

"We're pretty good," Bob said. He took the wheel brace from his rescuer and removed the remaining nuts.

Doug fetched a spare wheel from the rear of the vehicle. He rolled it down the lane and eyed Howard. "Looks like some of your guests never made it home."

"Well, the wine was still flowing for a while after you guys left. No way were Nancy and I having that last lot get behind the wheel. Good job we have two sets of sofa beds."

"Have they sobered up yet?"

"Enough to drive. Nasty headaches, though."

Doug smirked. "The grape's revenge. Thanks again for having us over. Lizzie got an offer to trial some of her wares in Broadway."

"Yes, Nancy said she introduced her to Katie Benson. That should prove a good contact for her." He glanced back over his shoulder. "So, if you gents are fine without me, I'd better go and roll up my sleeves. Still a lot of tidying to do."

Doug handed the wheel to Bob. "Thanks Howard. See you soon."

* * *

Joshua hung around in the emerging sunshine for a while after his father left. He reasoned that he would give his dad a little time to sort the tyre. Then Doug would find him hard at work in the meadery when he returned. The boy walked back in and resolved to get cracking on the melomel. The door slammed shut behind him. From outside, a metal click indicated the heavy duty padlock snapping into place. The lad put the beer paddle back in the sanitising container and tried the door. It was secured fast. He hammered on the wood and shouted. "Becky? Moira? Hey, this isn't funny. Give it a rest, will you?"

No response.

Fuck, I'm going to have some words with that sister of mine. Wonder if Mum's got a spare key indoors? He fetched a mobile phone from his pocket and pulled up the number. Seconds after pressing the green call button, the boy yanked the phone away from his head in disgust. *No service. That's great. Oh well, best do this task for Dad and have him sort the girls out when he's done changing MrFaringdon's tyre.* He retrieved the beer paddle again and sauntered across to the open fermenter. A few seconds after thrusting the tool into the crust, the floating mass began to break up. Foamy pink liquid frothed and bubbled. A sickly sweet smell filled his nostrils. He continued to poke and prod at the brown, decomposing fruit. More of the liquid became exposed. Joshua lurched back with a start. A face peered up at him from beneath the surface. *What am I doing? It's only my reflection.* He shook his head, leaned back over and stirred the rudamel into a gentle vortex. He didn't know whether it was the heat, the smell, the swirling liquid or a combination of all three; but he soon became light-headed. A face appeared in the fermenter again. The reflection was not his own. Then another materialised alongside it. *Is that a young woman? These fumes must be getting to me.* He lifted the paddle from the bubbling rudamel, intending to stand up and clear his groggy brain. Two sets of pale, slimy arms burst out of the fermentation tank, each locking on to one of his wrists. With an irresistible tug they wrenched him off balance. Joshua tumbled over the edge of the conical. His head plunged into the warm, fizzing fruit mead. The faces were either side of his head now. They gazed into his panic-stricken countenance with empty, unfeeling eyes. He kicked his legs against the stainless steel body of the tank. Too much of his weight lay beneath the surface. Joshua was unable to counterbalance himself and pivot out. His nose and mouth filled with the heady liquid. He couldn't breathe. One flailing foot swung clear enough of the rim to catch some items on a nearby shelf. An old, glass one-gallon demijohn rattled against its neighbours. The whole collection wobbled and clattered. The final one toppled over the edge and crashed into the stone floor. The boy managed to lift his head above the surface for a moment and cough.

The hands gripped harder and pulled him back down.

"What on earth is the padlock doing on?" Doug spoke the words to nobody in particular. He looked around and poked his tongue into his cheek. *I guess Josh must have sorted the rudamel and lost interest.* The sound of smashing glass from inside forced him to place an ear to the door. A desperate coughing rasped within, followed by a gurgle and series of splashes.

Doug raced to the cottage and crashed through the front door into the hall. He pushed past Bethany in the kitchen doorway and tripped headlong over Jess. The dog yelped and barked.

"What the blazes are you playing at?" Elizabeth sat at the table. Alongside were a couple in their early forties that Doug had never seen before. The man wore a dog collar. He was squat and stocky. His side-parted, dark sandy hair showed the natural grey highlights of his years. It was pushed up and back atop a square, weathered face with short, wide nose. Behind the fellow's rectangular glasses, a pale pink complexion suggested a life of sampling a little too much communion wine on the sly. Perched demurely next to him, a tall, slender woman crossed and uncrossed a pair of shapely legs. Long, straggly, centre-parted chestnut hair flowed either side of her oblong head. The short and semi-bulbous nose appeared a bit too large for her face. Elegant, thin eyebrows lifted at the interruption. A curling tongue wiped across pale lips and white teeth that matched her spotless skin. She regarded him with watery green eyes. Those eyes didn't leave him for even the briefest of moments.

"Josh is in trouble." The man didn't stop to acknowledge Elizabeth's guests. He rummaged amongst a collection of keys that hung from curled hooks beneath a kitchen cupboard. With the spare padlock key in his grasp, he wheeled and sprinted from the room. Jess backed away into the corner, tail between her legs.

Elizabeth's open mouth shut an instant later. She was on her feet without another word.

Back at the outbuilding, Doug's hands quivered as he tried to insert the key. The circular padlock rotated backwards and came free. He ripped it from the metal plate, tugged open the door and darted inside the structure.

Elizabeth piled in behind. "Oh my God!" Her eyes caught sight of their son's trembling legs pointing towards the roof.

Doug pulled at the lad's feet, but something held him firm. Without another word he dropped to his knees. "Grab hold of something, Lizzie." The shout had barely escaped his mouth before he tugged open the dump valve. Sticky pink liquid spewed forth in a jet that collided with the nearby stone wall. Elizabeth gripped onto a table but soon lost her footing in the bubbling torrent. Shards of a broken glass demijohn floated past her.

Inside the emptying fermenter, Josh gagged and

coughed up a mouthful of the fluid. He pulled his head from where it had sunk into the collapsing fruit. The gross lees followed the rest of the contents out the bottom of the tank. Doug helped him out onto the flooded floor. Raspberry melomel waves flowed away into the yard and garden. They left nothing behind but sticky stone tiles, a pink tide mark on the walls, and a strong - if pleasant - aroma. The boy coughed again. Finally he got his breath and made eye contact with his father.

"Dad, I'm so sorry. I don't know what happened."

Doug held the boy close. "It's alright, son. How did you fall into the conical?"

"I… didn't fall-"

"Hi everyone. Jeez, what happened here?" Rebecca appeared in the doorway. "Ew, the floor's all sticky."

Doug's facial muscles went taut, and he bit his lip. The tone that erupted from his lips left no-one in any doubt about his emotional state. "Why did you lock your brother in here? He could have been killed."

Rebecca backed away and placed a hand on her right temple. "What? I didn't lock him in here."

"Do you expect me to believe it was Bethany then?"

Elizabeth looked at her husband. "Bethany has been with me since she came back from walking Jess. She even let the vicar and his wife in when they strolled past and called to say hello."

"Are we attending church now?" Doug's statement was addressed to Elizabeth but his eyes never left their eldest daughter.

Elizabeth frowned. "Calm down. Everybody lived."

"You haven't answered my question, Rebecca." Doug's face reddened.

Tears streamed down the eighteen-year-old girl's cheeks. "I didn't lock Josh in here, Dad. I swear I didn't." Her voice cracked and sobs of frustration followed.

"I don't think it was Becky," Josh said. He watched his big sister and thought about the faces and hands reaching out for him from the tank.

"Well who else could it have been?"

"You wouldn't believe me, Dad."

"Why wouldn't I?"

"You just wouldn't."

"Try me."

Joshua took a deep breath. "Okay, there were faces in the fermenter."

"What?"

"Told you."

"Josh, there comes a time when a man has to take responsibility for his mistakes. Okay, so you fell into the fermenter and we had to blow the batch. It's an expensive mistake and a setback to the business. But, at least you're still alive. Your mother and I are grateful for that. Can you imagine if you had drowned in there? We can carry the financial loss for now and make some more rudamel. There's still surplus honey in your great grandfather's store."

"Dad-"

"I'm a little disappointed to hear you using Bethany's story to excuse your clumsiness. As if there could be people hiding in the melomel. Don't you think that's a bit insulting to our intelligence?"

Joshua's shoulders sagged. He lowered his head but lifted his eyes to look at Rebecca.

"What if he's telling the truth, Dad?" the girl wiped her eyes.

"Don't you start, Becky. You're in enough trouble as it is for locking him in here. Why would you both want to lie to us? Have we been that unfair to you? Honestly, I want to know. Don't your mother and I deserve better?"

Rebecca span on her heel and stormed out of the building.

Doug shouted after her. "Don't you walk away from me, Rebecca Ashb-"

"Doug," Elizabeth interrupted. She shook her head. "Don't. Let it go for now. I'll talk with her another time when we've all calmed down." She lifted her sticky clothing. "And cleaned up. Yuck. I hope Bethany is being a good hostess while we're away. Whatever will the vicar and his wife think?"

Doug helped the woman to her feet. "What's all that about, anyway? We're not churchgoers."

"Only a social call. I did explain we're not attendees. They wanted to let us know we're always welcome. You know, a listening ear should we need it."

"Have they got any great advice about child-rearing? It seems like we could use some." He looked at his son.

"I'm sorry, Dad. I'll get a summer job and pay you back for the loss, honest."

"I'd settle for you being straight with us. Now, look me in the eye like a man and tell me you fell into the fermenter by accident. Is that so difficult?"

Joshua scowled. "I can't."

"Why not?"

The boy glanced between his parents. "Because despite what you think of us, you and Mum raised your kids not to tell lies. And we don't." He held his father's gaze for a moment then pushed past him and left.

Doug raised both his hands in a gesture of despair. "I give up."

Elizabeth shuffled her feet and swallowed. "He actually seemed to be telling the truth."

"Oh good God, not you as well." Doug wheeled about. "Lizzie, did you see any people float by after I opened the dump valve? As if they could even fit through a pipe the thickness of my arm. There's nobody in the conical. See for yourself. He's telling an insulting, bare-faced lie."

"He saw *something*, Doug. Or experienced something."

"Wha-"

"Hear me out on this. First Bethany, then Becky and now Josh? Either our kids are all on some kind of weird drug, or something very odd is going on around here. And consider the circumstances. Bethany almost drowned, Becky almost drowned, Josh almost drowned, and Mr Compton *did* drown."

"Adam Compton flooded his own cellar and fell down the steps."

"Did he? I thought you said he was very careful and particular about everything he did? Come on, Doug.

When have you ever known Josh to lie? He's screwed up before, but always come clean."

"The stakes have never been quite this high before."

"You know our son as well as I do. He's no liar. Neither are any of our kids, come to think of it."

"But the story, Lizzie. It's so ridiculous. That's why I'm upset more than anything. Shock at almost losing him, then relief at not doing so - yes. The loss of a batch of melomel - sure. But to be told a whopper like that from my own flesh and blood who I thought I knew..."

Elizabeth put her arms around his waist. "Either he's telling the truth or he *believes* he is. If there's any deception here, I'm pretty sure he didn't start it."

Doug sighed. "Okay. Well, I'd better scrub down in here. This place is going to be tacky as anything for a good while. I'll be in later. I hope we can find out what's going on before anything else goes wrong."

"Promise me you won't blow up at the kids?"

"I promise. Sorry." He kissed and held her tight.

* * *

Joshua banged open the front door of the cottage in a huff and stomped upstairs. Bethany looked up from where she was sitting at the kitchen table with the vicar and his wife. She examined the two adults. "That was my brother, Joshua."

"That's a nice Biblical name." The minister evidenced a somewhat overdone, friendly tone. It bordered on patronising and set the eleven-year-old's teeth on edge. "Do you know which famous battle

Joshua won in the Old Testament?"

Bethany shook her head.

The vicar blinked and frowned at his wife. She tapped Bethany on the arm. "Have you never been to Sunday school or learnt any Bible stories in your RE lessons?"

The girl shrugged.

The minister coughed. "Well. Joshua won the battle of Jericho during the conquest of Canaan. His army marched around the city blowing their trumpets, and the walls came tumbling down. He was a great Israelite leader."

The shower pump vibrated from upstairs.

Bethany thought for a moment. "*Our* Joshua is a good swimmer. He saved me from drowning recently."

The vicar's wife appeared taken aback. "Goodness me, child. Wherever did this happen?"

"The pond in the woods at the top of the hill. My mother's bees swarmed and chased me up there." Bethany paused. Her own parents' reactions to stories of faces in the water and tugging arms, had been scorn and derision. She thought better about including such details in her account to these stern, religious people. "Joshua dived in and helped me out."

"What a brave young man. His namesake would have been proud." The vicar's voice rang with a mixture of admiration and self-satisfaction. He appeared pleased to have steered the topic back onto things of a church nature.

"I'm so sorry." Elizabeth appeared in the kitchen

doorway. She stood dripping wet like a bedraggled dog, her clothing stained a curious pink hue. "Joshua fell headfirst into one of my husband's fermentation tanks. He couldn't pull him out, so had to dump the contents - hence the state of me."

The front door banged again. Rebecca pushed past her mother without a word, heading for the staircase.

"Becky. Please come here a minute. I'd like you to meet the Reverend David Leach and his wife Angela."

Rebecca glanced back at Elizabeth. She joined the woman in the doorway. "Hello."

David stood up and moved across to shake her by the hand. "Hello, Rebecca. How nice to meet you. My wife and I were out and about on our rounds, so we decided to pop in and welcome you to Coln Abbots. We would have been here sooner, but unfortunately I have responsibility for several parishes these days."

"How are you adjusting to life in the country?" Angela asked. "It's a bit different to London for you, I imagine."

Rebecca snorted. "That it is."

"Have you made any friends in the village?"

Elizabeth spoke for her. "She's developed a growing bond with Moira Robbins down at Box Cottage. Do you know the Robbins family?"

"Why yes. They're not church attendees either. But, I often meet Nancy in the shop. She's always so immaculately turned out and presented. Friendly too."

"Yes. Doug and I get along quite well with them."

David sat himself back at the table. "Love your neighbour as yourself. The second great commandment after loving the Lord your God."

Rebecca glared at her mother then smiled politely at their guests. "If you'll excuse me, I must be getting along."

Angela studied a clock on the wall. "I suppose we had better be getting along, too. David must be away to the church for a lunchtime appointment. In fact, he'll be late if he doesn't hurry. My goodness, Elizabeth, you didn't tell us how your son is. He went upstairs under his own steam, so I assume all is well?"

Elizabeth looked like someone chewing an imaginary toffee. Her eyes screwed up tight. "Yes. He's okay. Bit of family tension thrown in didn't help. But, we'll work it out."

"Is your husband about?"

"He's cleaning up the mess."

"Well, I'll say a quick hello on behalf of us both, if that's okay?"

"Yes, of course. I should warn you that he might be a bit of a grump, though. He's rescued our son from a near-fatal accident, lost an expensive batch of fruit mead and had a blow-up at two of our kids. Plus, church people aren't his thing."

"Oh, not to worry. That's nothing new for either of us. Where can I find him?"

"The outbuildings. Through the front door and turn left. You can't miss them."

"Oh yes, we passed those on our way down the footpath. Well, it's lovely to meet you. Coln Abbots is a small and sociable village. So, even if we don't see you at St. Mark's, I'm sure we'll bump into you elsewhere."

Elizabeth escorted them to the door. "Thank you for your visit." She stood on the step and watched the vicar amble off down the drive while his wife made for the meadery.

"Mr Ashbourne?" the voice rang with melodious charm.

Doug stopped mopping the floor tiles. His gaze followed a pair of waxed, curvaceous legs to an attractive slim body. Beneath the long brown hair, a flashing white smile opened wide at the surprised expression on his face.

"I'm Angela Leach, the vicar's wife. I wanted to drop by and greet you on behalf of us both. My husband, David, had to hurry off, I'm afraid."

Doug leaned his mop against the wall and took a deep breath. He wiped his hands on a cloth and loped over to greet the attractive woman. Every step on the sticky floor made a sound like separating Velcro. "You can call me Doug." He extended his hand. "I'm sorry about the mess. We had a bit of an accident in here."

"So I hear."

Angela didn't let go at once. She squeezed his fingers and allowed her own to slide out of his grip in a long, drawn out motion. Her pale green eyes swept across the developed pectorals traced by the man's sodden shirt. Doug could almost have sworn her tongue darted out and licked those pale lips. But so much had happened in the last half hour that he dismissed the idea out of hand. He cleared his throat. "Well, if you'll excuse me, I'm afraid I've got rather a lot to be getting on with after this morning's fiasco."

"Yes of course. I won't hold you up further."

"It was nice of you and your husband to drop by. No doubt we'll see more of each other."

Angela moved towards the door and almost leered with a seductive mouth. The man turned back to his mop and bucket. Her gaze fell on his buttocks and she tasted the salt on her lips. "Wouldn't that be nice? Cheerio for now."

Doug spun back, forehead creased. Angela had left. *Was she hitting on me? No, that's stupid. I must be right out of it.* He picked up the mop, dipped and wrung it. A long sigh followed. *It's going to take forever to get rid of this stickiness.*

11
Demon Drink

Bob Faringdon pulled off his wellies in the porch at Washburn Hill Farm. He wandered through an old oak door into a tiny room. The snug appeared barely large enough for a chair, side table and the tiny fireplace that dominated its opposite wall. The farmhouse was of sufficient size for him to have his own private hidey-hole. A place away from Mike and his family. After checking on 'the girls' each evening after milking, he always enjoyed a quiet glass or two. Something from a flask of his favourite tipple in this secluded chamber. This evening it consisted of the second bottle from Doug Ashbourne's Pennycress mead. For a rough sample it was rather good. A golden delight for the taste buds, made with dear old Alan Boardman's honey.

The armchair that formed the room's prominent feature creaked as he sat down. Worn springs in the seat cushion coiled in an uneven wave. Bob didn't care. His backside had formed an almost symbiont relationship with the item. It flexed and adjusted itself to match the curious contours of the ageing furniture. He placed a glass down on the side table, upon which the clear bottle of mead already rested. His head leaned against side panels of the armchair's wraparound threadbare headrest for the briefest of moments. He twisted it to cover the antimacassar instead. It was an almost automatic response after years of scolding from his wife. He could still hear her chiding him about making the chairs greasy with his hair. A faint smile registered more in his twinkling eyes than his weathered facial muscles. You never get over the loss of a close loved one, if the truth be told. When the well of tears runs dry, the empty void of loneliness that remains is impossible to fill with other company. Bob swallowed and pulled the stopper from the bottle of honey wine. It sparkled in the light cast by a dim wall lamp. The liquid was clear and clean, with a pleasant alcoholic honey bouquet. He held the glass beneath his nose, shut his eyes and inhaled the fragrance.

"Here's to you, Alan. And to your granddaughter's family. Health, wealth and happiness," Bob spoke the words in a whisper. He raised the drink to his lips and took a delicate sip of mead. It tasted amazing, like spring flowers, summer days, harvest time, autumn rain and winter fires all rolled into one. In short, all the things Bob cherished in his agrarian life. He drank some more and smiled. "Oh, that's right good, is that." The man let out a long and satisfied exhalation. He drained the glass and lifted the bottle to pour another. The semi-sweet wine tantalised his taste buds afresh with each new sip.

After finishing the second glass, the old farmer stood

it alongside the half-empty bottle. He leaned back on the antimacassar again and studied the remaining contents. *Seems I stirred up a little sediment Doug didn't filter out.* The thought wandered into his brain upon noticing a slight cloudiness begin to swirl inside the bottle. *Drink has gone to my head a bit.* This second musing accompanied what appeared to be images of faces appearing and disappearing. The liquid continued to move, despite his having not touched it for a couple of minutes. Bob coughed. Some mead refluxed from his gut into his mouth. He sat bolt upright and swallowed it back down. *Mike's wife must have used more garlic in her spaghetti bolognaise than my creaky old belly can handle.* His stomach lurched. Another gulp of mead rushed up into his mouth. Then another. Bob leaned forward and spat the fluid across the flagstone floor. His stomach continued to lurch. His mouth filled again and again, faster than he could spit. The farmer fought to breathe. The carbon dioxide in his bloodstream forced him to gasp. Mead raced down his windpipe, initiating a laryngospasm. He sank to his knees and attempted to cry out, but his closed vocal cords wouldn't budge. *But I've only had two glasses.* The frantic and confused thought seared through his brain. A copious volume of mead gushed under pressure like a fountain from his facial orifice. The farmer gagged and quivered. His vision narrowed to a darkening tunnel. Bob crawled towards the door. He struggled to reach up for the handle, shaking and retching, unable to take in any air. Only a couple of fingers ever touched the metal knob, before his unconscious body slumped against the door. Rivers of honey wine evacuated his system. A puddle of sticky mead formed on the flagstones around that motionless torso.

* * *

"Have you spoken with Mr Faringdon recently, Dad?" Bethany hung the dog lead up in the kitchen and patted the Labrador on her back.

Doug lowered a newspaper to the table and picked up a steaming cup of black coffee. "Bob? Not for a day or two. Why do you ask?"

"Oh, he always drives past me on the hill when I'm walking Jess in the morning. We get a smile and a wave every day."

"And you haven't seen him today?"

"Nor yesterday."

"I wonder if he's unwell. Crumbs, can you imagine that, Lizzie? If ever there was going to be a curmudgeonly patient to nurse, it would be Bob Faringdon."

Elizabeth wiped down the draining board and peered out the kitchen window. The familiar, battered old Land Rover crunched along the gravel driveway. "Panic over, he's here. Oh no, wait a minute, it's Mike."

Doug frowned and rose to his feet. He joined his wife to study the visitor loping towards the cottage. The younger farmer's face appeared strained.

"I'll let him in," Bethany raced to the door, all smiles and bounces. "Good morning, Mr Faringdon."

"Oh, hello. Good morning. Err, are your parents about?" the voice stuttered and shook.

"Yes. Please come in." Bethany's tone calmed at once. Despite her tender years, the girl could tell Mr Faringdon was upset.

"Hey Mike. God, you look awful. Whatever is the matter?" Doug asked.

Mike's eyes were red and now brimmed over with tears. One escaped his attempts to hold them back and trickled down his face. His voice cracked. "Dad's dead."

Elizabeth put both hands over her mouth, amplifying her intake of breath.

Doug pulled a chair out from the table and helped the dazed man sit down. "How? When?" He resumed his earlier seat while his wife pulled up a chair next to the distraught dairy farmer.

"Two nights ago. We didn't find him until the following morning."

"Were was this?" Doug placed both hands on the table and moved himself closer.

"In his snug at the farm. I went out for morning milking and Dad wasn't there. That's so unlike him. In all my days he's never arrived after me. So, I went to see if he was alright. His bed was made and no sign of him upstairs. It was when I tried the snug that I found the door wouldn't budge. At first I thought the damp had swollen the wood until I moved it enough to see through the crack. I found Dad slumped against it."

"Oh how awful." Elizabeth shook her head. "Was it a heart attack?"

"That's what I thought at first. Dad loved his fry-ups. My wife was always on at him to cut down on his cholesterol. He didn't care though. You know Dad."

Doug nodded. "I would have described him as fitter than many men half his age. So, what happened if it wasn't a heart attack, Mike?"

The farmer fidgeted. "According to the pathologist, he drowned."

"What?" Doug and Elizabeth spoke in perfect unison.

"I know, it sounds daft. Didn't believe it myself, at first."

Doug scratched his head. "Drowned on what? What is there to drown from in a snug?"

"Mead." The word came out with some hesitation.

"Huh?"

"He'd drunk half that other bottle of your test mead. Been looking forward to it all day and wouldn't shut up about it."

Doug slapped his brow. "Half a bottle? But that's only a couple of glasses. Did he choke and breathe it in or something?"

"That's what they couldn't work out at the hospital. His respiratory system was completely overwhelmed by it. He didn't even make it out the door. Half the bottle was still stood on the table in there when I found him. The floor was sticky and some wine had drained out of him. But there was too much residual fluid for what had come out of the bottle."

Elizabeth's heart sank at the troubled expression on her husband's face. She angled her head to make eye contact with Mike. "But that defies the laws of physics. It must be wrong. Doug only gave you the two bottles and-"

"We'd already polished off one. Wonderful stuff it was, too." Mike wiped away another tear and leaned forward. "I'm not blaming you, Doug. There's nothing wrong with your mead. None of this is your fault. I came to tell you because we're friends and Dad loved you all so. He was particularly fond of your youngest."

Elizabeth lifted her face and noticed Bethany standing immobile in the kitchen doorway, eyes wide with shock. "Yes, he always waved to her when she was out walking the dog."

Bethany burst into tears of her own and ran upstairs to her siblings.

Mike watched her go and his shoulders sank. "Bless her heart."

Doug folded his hands beneath his chin, eyes fixed in space. "Could the hospital have made some kind of mistake, like complications from choking? Or a mix up on their computer system? You'd be amazed at some stuff I've seen over the years. If it's on an official-looking computer system, ordinary, rational people will often believe pretty much anything. Data input errors are the bane of many an organisation."

Mike rubbed his stubble with a slow, faint scratching noise. "They're convinced he drowned in mead. When I told them the circumstances in which he was found, they looked at me like I was pulling their legs. They thought he'd fallen in and got trapped in a tank of the stuff."

Elizabeth exchanged an expression of sudden shock with her spouse. "Like Josh the other day."

Mike watched them, face puzzled.

Doug explained. "Josh fell into one of the fermenters while I was helping your Dad change a tyre. He got stuck, and I had to blow the dump valve to save him."

Mike jerked his head back. "Is he alright?"

"Yeah, he's fine. Gave us some cock and bull story about people in the tank holding him under. Other than that, he survived. It's a horrible irony after hearing about your dad, that's all. Mike, I'm so sorry."

"Couldn't have you wondering where he'd got to and then hear the story second-hand. I've asked my wife to say he collapsed while enjoying a glass of wine, if anyone asks how he died. It's the truth, in a roundabout fashion. The village loves rumour and gossip. You don't need anyone inflating or making up wild tales about your new business product. That would kill it before you've even begun. Like I said, there's nothing wrong with it and it's not your fault. Thought you should know the full story, though. Dad would have wanted things that way."

Elizabeth squeezed his hand. "Thank you, Mike. That means the world to us, doesn't it, Doug?"

"Quite. Will you let us know when the funeral is taking place? The whole family will be there, if that's okay?"

A gentle smile seeped across the farmer's lips. "Dad was so well known and loved around here, I imagine the whole village will be there. Of course you're welcome to come. They'll bury him in the churchyard at St. Mark's. The Cotswolds - and especially this valley - was his life. That and our cows, of course."

"How's that going?" Elizabeth asked.

"The supermarkets are squeezing us harder than ever. If I don't come up with a plan soon, it'll be the end of Washburn Hill. My boy is still at uni with no interest in farming. Can't say I blame him. Thing is, Dad worked the farm for love. As long as the bills were paid and there was food on the table, he didn't take a wage as such. I can't afford to hire proper help."

"Mr Faringdon?" Joshua appeared in the kitchen doorway. Upstairs Rebecca was trying to console her weeping sister.

Mike looked up, and the boy continued. His voice was hesitant, eyes half-shuttered.

"I could come over to help out mornings and evenings for a bit. If it's alright with my folks, and you can use me for anything."

The farmer blinked. "Well, I don't know what to say. Doesn't your dad need you around here right now?"

Doug watched his son with an admiring gaze. "No, he's okay. The actual daily work on production is minimal. More something that occurs in fits and starts. If he's willing to lend a hand and Lizzie is okay with it, let him help you out."

"Can I, Mum?" Joshua asked.

Elizabeth's eyes watered. "Of course you can."

Mike thought for a moment. "I couldn't pay you much. Even minimal wage would be a stretch. I don't know how I'll deal with the tax man."

Joshua shrugged "Then don't. Give me a few pints of

milk in kind for the family. It's only for the summer, anyway. Until you know where you stand. You helped Dad and I set up the meadery. And you brought us all those blackcurrant plants, after all."

"Well okay. Thank you, Joshua." He turned back to the couple. "My old man surely was a good judge of character. He was right about you and your family, Doug."

Doug didn't take his eyes off his son. When he eventually spoke, his calm voice sounded distant, even and reflective. "Perhaps he saw some things even *we* overlook sometimes."

Joshua stared back and gave his father a knowing nod of reassurance. The two of them were okay now. Without a further word, he went back upstairs to his sisters.

* * *

"So it seems he was having a glass of wine and keeled over." Jane Cowley rang up Nancy Robbins' shopping items on the till.

"That's terrible." Nancy placed a bag of flour and small tin of condensed milk from the counter into her basket.

Angela Leach piped up. "David has been pacing up and down for the last two nights, trying to find the right words for his eulogy. Bob was such a popular local character, he's desperate to do him justice." She retrieved a bag of dried rigatoni from one of the modestly stocked shelves and glanced along the short aisle to her right. Wendy Simpson stood in silence. Her face looked wan and troubled. She twisted and examined various jars of honey, lost in a trance.

"Good morning, everyone," Elizabeth Ashbourne entered the shop with Bethany close behind. She spied the mauve-highlighted grey-haired woman's deliberations. "I'm sure Jane has a great selection. But, if you're in the mood for something different and local, I produce honey at Pennycress Cottage. I don't sell much of it. My husband uses most for his mead production. But you're welcome to drop by and take a jar. I'm Elizabeth Ashbourne, by the way. I don't believe we've been introduced."

"Wendy Simpson." The woman's voice came out flat and devoid of emotion. "Thank you, Mrs Ashbourne."

"Please call me Elizabeth. This is my youngest, Bethany."

Wendy's hazel eyes regarded the eleven-year-old watching her with an unsure expression. "Hello."

Bethany whispered a polite, reciprocal greeting.

Across the store, Jane Cowley glared at Elizabeth. Her mouth twisted. She indicated with her head for the woman to draw near.

Elizabeth complied. "What's up? Oh, Hi Nancy, Angela."

"Good morning, Elizabeth" the other two shoppers responded.

Jane Cowley spoke in a pointless, hushed tone. Pointless because it could be heard the other end of the shop. Or did she intend it that way? "You want to be careful inviting the likes of her round."

Elizabeth looked back over her shoulder at the silent patron. "How do you mean?"

"Some people are trouble. Born wrong. If you ask me, she's one of them."

"Have you known her long?"

"Ever since school. She was always a weird one. Scuttlebutt in the village is that she's a witch."

Elizabeth snorted. "For goodness' sake."

Nancy lifted her basket off the counter and leaned close to her neighbour. "Sounds like the kind of nonsense our Moira would come out with. And here I am telling her to look at her elders as examples. Guess that's the difference between town and country folk. Superstitious twaddle."

"Scoff all you want." Jane Cowley's crimson face performed a fair impersonation of a stop light. She folded her arms. "But you don't know her like I do."

"There may be at least some credence to her tale." Angela placed the pasta and a loaf of bread on the counter.

"Well, I am surprised at you, Angela. Aren't Christians supposed to see the good in people?" Elizabeth adopted a haughty air and clipped her voice.

"Look. I'm not saying she's a bad person. But on our rounds in the villages, David and I meet all sorts of people. We also hear a wide variety of stories. Some of it is too prolific to classify as only gossip and hearsay, that's all. People have different beliefs and traditions of worship. The different and the secretive have always scared folk around here."

"You're not wrong there. Consider the history of the

pond at the top of the hill. The one in the woods behind our cottage. Let's hope we've finally consigned that kind of hysterical overreaction to the history books."

"Quite."

Jane Cowley observed the exchange and huffed. She refused to make eye contact with any of them as she keyed in the prices for Angela's shopping. "All I know is that some pretty odd things have been happening lately. First Adam Compton and now Bob Faringdon. I wouldn't be at all surprised if Wendy had something to do with it."

The sound of breaking glass caused all four women at the counter to jump. Bethany looked up from where she had been examining a selection of sweets. Wendy Simpson stared unblinking across the store at Jane Cowley. At her feet lay one of the honey jars, a broken and sticky mess. She pointed a long, bony finger at the shopkeeper. "How dare you suggest such a thing?" Her voice trembled with anger but also the telltale tremors of grief. She spoke again. "How could you think I would ever hurt Bob Faringdon?" She stormed out of the shop, eyes reddening.

"What about the breakage?" Angela opened her purse to pay.

Jane Cowley waved a hand away. "No point chasing her for it. We get any number of accidental breakages each week. I'll write it off. Not the end of the world. She'll be away home to her cauldron now."

Elizabeth frowned.

Jane caught the disapproving look and stared at her.

"You feel like judging me for my views now, Mrs Ashbourne. But be thankful nothing unusual has happened to you or your family, yet. If it does, you might change your tune."

A sudden chill from those words caused an involuntary cringe in Elizabeth's neck. Her head became hot and she exchanged a hesitant glance with Nancy. She gulped. "Right then. Back to shopping."

Nancy swung her basket in both hands. "I assume you're going to the funeral?"

Elizabeth nodded. "We wouldn't miss it. You?"

"Yes. We'll be there."

"See you then."

"Bye. Goodbye, Bethany." Nancy left the store.

"Bye." Bethany filled a small paper bag with cola bottle sweets.

A tall, well-built, sandy-haired man in his early forties strolled past the window. Angela Leach took her change and popped it back in her purse. "I'd best be going too. There's Harry Aston, one of our parishioners. See you both at the funeral." She didn't wait for a response and almost skipped out the door to intercept the fellow.

"So dedicated to her work, that one." Jane watched them walk side by side, off down the lane.

* * *

Bob Faringdon's funeral was about as traditional Gloucestershire rural as they come. No upmarket black limousine or hearse for the rosy-cheeked Cotswold farmer and his family. Instead, an old blue tractor pulled a flat-bed trailer down from Washburn Hill Farm. His coffin rested on the back, surrounded by flowers. Behind the agricultural vehicle, the cortège followed on foot: Mike, his wife and their son Jeff.

Becky stood with her family and the other villagers watching the smelly, chugging diesel vehicle approach the church. It was as honest, down-to-earth and unpretentious a sight as one could hope to see. But that was Bob Faringdon all over. The teenager moistened her lips after catching sight of the dead farmer's wavy-haired grandson. Moira had been right, he wasn't bad. Not too bad at all. In fact, she could feel the blood rising in her cheeks.

"I'll introduce you to him later, if you like," the Goth leaned in to whisper over her shoulder.

Becky averted her eyes. She mentally chastised herself for allowing her thoughts to stray on such a solemn occasion.

Several men from the village shouldered Bob's coffin to carry it into the church. Douglas Ashbourne was among them.

It was a modest service. In the end, David Leach also opted for simplicity in his address. Flowery words and purple prose were not a good match for the salt-of-the-earth man resting in that basic wooden casket. He had been a straight talker in life, and was commemorated by his vicar and peers in a similar fashion.

During the act of committal, Elizabeth noticed

Wendy Simpson standing on the periphery of mourners. Nobody had spoken to the solitary figure, or even acknowledged her. The woman only broke her concentration on the lowering coffin to deliver Jane Cowley a thousand-yard stare. Elizabeth watched the shopkeeper swat a wasp away from her face. It came back again and refused to leave her alone. Jane moved away from the graveside to seek relief from the pest. Elizabeth's thoughts returned to the assertions of the postmistress. Strange gossip about who and what she claimed the brusque, lonely spinster to be. It made her shudder. *This must all be wild superstition.* But, she couldn't get away from the near fatal misses all three of her children had experienced. And all after such a short time in Coln Abbots. *Something* wasn't right. Whether or not that reclusive, misanthropic woman had anything to do with it.

The funeral attendees adjourned from the church to the village hall. The local W.I. had laid on a fine and generous spread in memory of the old farmer.

"Hi, I'm Becky Ashbourne." Rebecca decided she didn't want Moira introducing her to Bob's handsome grandson. As such, she forced herself out of her comfort zone and sidled up to the young man.

The wavy-haired student took her hand. He studied her smoky gaze with deep-set, dark brown eyes. Rebecca felt a flutter of butterflies in her tummy. She tried not to sweat, but only made things worse.

"Jeff Faringdon. Wait a minute - Ashbourne? You

must be the brother of that nice lad who's helping Dad out with the cows for the summer?"

Rebecca wobbled her head from side to side. "Guilty." She had never been more proud of - nor delighted with - her younger brother than she was at that precise moment.

"Well, it's nice to meet you. Dad says Grandpa was very fond of your family. You have a younger sister too, correct?"

"Yes, that's right. She's over there." Rebecca pointed to where Bethany was feeding Jess a sandwich. The grateful pooch wolfed it down, licked her chops and looked with big eyes for another to arrive.

Jeff laughed. "That's a Lab alright. They're eating machines. Great dogs though."

"We like her."

"She was Adam Compton's until recently. I remember when Jess was still a puppy, making a mess all over the pub floor."

"Yes. I'm sure she was adorable."

Jeff switched back to make eye contact with Rebecca again. "It's strange. I go off to university in Hereford from a village where nothing ever happens. Then while I'm away, two men (both local heroes) pass away in short order. Go figure."

"It was a shock to everyone round here."

"Should give them something new to natter about. I'm going to miss Grandpa so much. He was amazing. Last of a breed."

"Maybe some of that stock is still in your blood?"

Jeff tilted his head and stepped back. "Well, you're

quite the philosopher, Becky Ashbourne. What are you doing around here?"

"Waiting to go off to uni in a bit."

"Which one?"

"Debating. Are you returning to Hereford tonight?"

"No, I've arranged to stick around for a week or so. Thought I'd offer Mum and Dad some moral support."

"Oh." Rebecca attempted to conceal her relief without much success.

Jeff half closed his eyes in a squint. "So, do you have a boyfriend?"

"In Coln Abbots? I didn't know there were any available."

Jeff snorted. "Welcome to the country. I meant back in London."

"No."

"Well, until the pub re-opens under new ownership, there's not a lot to do - day or night. Socially speaking, that is. I'm guessing you don't play Bridge?"

Rebecca giggled and shook her head.

Jeff went on. "If you wanted to go for a walk and a chat sometime, that might be nice."

"I'd like that."

"Great. When?"

"Drop by Pennycress Cottage whenever you're free. My calendar isn't exactly bursting with appointments at present."

"I hear ya. Don't knock it. Once you start at uni, a bit of quiet downtime might seem like a dream."

"I'll take your word for it."

"You do that. I'd better go and mingle with the other

guests, or they'll think I'm being rude. Nice meeting you, Becky."

"You too."

Rebecca watched Jeff walk across to the vicar and his wife. Moira approached her, eyes wide and face aglow. "Well, well, well, aren't you the little mover?"

Rebecca shrugged.

"Are you going to screw him?"

"Moira!"

"What? Oh, come on, don't tell me you're not interested in a piece of that? I know I wouldn't kick him out of bed for wearing wellies. Not that he wants to be a farmer, anyway."

"How well do you know him?"

Moira caught the note of uncertainty in her voice. At first she smirked, but then touched her friend on the arm. "Not *that* well, don't worry. I only met him while he was home for Christmas. That was a brief encounter, though not the romantic kind. But, if you don't get in there, some other lucky tart will."

"He's going to take me out for a walk sometime."

"You're very health conscious."

"Funny. What else are we going to do around here?"

"Kidding. That's great. And Josh is helping out on the farm for the time being?"

"Yeah. Hey, did you hear what happened with the fermenter?"

"I heard. Your Mum phoned later that day to unload. So, I got the full story over dinner. It's pretty freaky round here, isn't it? You'd better sleep with Jeff before something else happens to you, or you'll miss out."

Rebecca frowned and screwed up her nose. "Gee, thanks Moira. I can always trust you for a word of encouragement, can't I?"

"Come on. You haven't eaten yet, have you?"

"No."

"Well you've got to try the Victoria Sponge. It's to die for. We hope not *literally*, in your case.

Rebecca shot her a sarcastic grin. "Ha ha."

12

Robed and Disrobed

A long, relaxing soak after a hard day on her feet in the shop, had always been a treat for Jane Cowley. Plus, immersing herself in fragrant water might also cool the swelling from a wasp sting on her face. An affliction acquired the day before at Bob Faringdon's funeral. She opened both the taps on the bath. Her eyes were drawn to the scales sat underneath the basin. While the tub filled with water, she pulled out the weighing device and wobbled onto it. Her folds of surplus fat rippled. The woman leaned forward a touch to squint at the reading over the top of her belly.

"Oof." The gauge read higher than expected. *I need to cut out eating those surplus cream cakes in the shop. Time for 'waste' not 'waist.'* She chuckled at her clever mental play on words. *Ah well. The diet starts tomorrow. Famous last words.* She stepped back onto the bathroom floor and slid the scales back into place. The water level in the tub crept higher. Jane examined her figure in the mirror and winced. She always looked fatter in a reflection or picture than she imagined herself to be. *Best turn off the taps before I displace the contents all over the room.* The podgy lady brought the plumbing to heel.

She picked up a round bath bomb from a box and dropped it into the water. The aromatic product fizzed and spread into an array of petals floating on the surface. A tender fragrance wafted up from the steaming tub and invited her to enter. Jane dipped her toe into the water at first, to check all was well with the temperature. She didn't fancy ending up like a boiled lobster. The heat was about the level she liked it. A little higher than desirable to begin with, but it would cool while she lounged amidst the soapy bubbles. Her folds of flesh sank into the water. The level rose near the brim, but stopped short of overflowing.

"Aah. Perfect." Jane let out a long purr of pleasure. She rested her head back and allowed her arms to float on the surface. Already her tired and corded muscles were beginning to unwind and loosen. She daubed a few soap suds across the angry welt on her face. *Damn that Wendy Simpson. I'll bet this was down to her witchcraft.* She felt the muscles re-tighten and decided to let the offence go. No way was that creepy crone going to spoil her amateur spa treatment. Jane slid her arms in tender loving strokes across her body, massaging and caring for herself. The waves of relaxation were coming now and she closed her eyes. The woman brought both hands up from her tummy and over her chest. She pulled her neck forwards to relieve any tension that lingered there.

Down below, a delicate sensation like other fingers slid around the tops of her legs. Then a similar experience enraptured her stomach. Jane half-opened her eyes, a puzzled expression crossing her face. It almost felt like her husband was in there with her, although the bath was hardly big enough. The stroking tightened. Something gripped her legs and stomach beneath the water. She exhaled a sharp breath and attempted to clear the soap suds. In the paper the other day, she had read about a pet python escaping elsewhere in the country. It emerged through the plumbing into a family home and scared them half to death. Jane swished harder at the suds to peer beneath the surface of the water. The remains of the bath bomb cleared. Down below, two pairs of arms clamped tight around her torso. They appeared to be coming from somewhere beneath her. The logic of how this could be possible with her backside pressed against the tub, didn't even cross her mind.

She opened her mouth to let out a scream. The first note escaped, before another pair of arms burst forth with a splash either side of her head. Slimy, weed-covered hands clamped across her mouth and pulled the frantic bather under. Bubbles floated to the top while Jane Cowley was dragged into darkness. Her terrified eyes widened. A rectangle of light above marked where the bathroom light shone. But, she had descended into some fathomless, impossible chamber. It was as if the bottom of the tub had vanished, and now she struggled in a black and watery pond. Faces leered at her from the shadows. Further arms grabbed on to hold her fast. Dead eyes stared with vacuous indifference at the plump, panicked shopkeeper. Long-dead hair floated in watery slow motion, like hypnotic octopus arms. She tried to shake herself free; tried to scream again in abject fear. Putrid water filled her mouth and nose. Sinuous weeds floated up and tickled her lower limbs with sickening massage mockery.

Back in the bathroom, all remained calm and serene. A few minutes after those ghoulish hands dragged the bather below, her silent corpse floated back to the surface. Eyes and mouth lay fixed wide open, staring in soundless horror at the ceiling.

* * *

"What have you got on for today?" Elizabeth Ashbourne wiped her hands on a towel. Her husband kissed her on the cheek and deposited his coffee cup in a washing-up bowl.

"Taking the lees off that new batch of rudamel."

"How's the stickiness now?"

"In the room? Not too bad. I don't think we'll lose the tide mark around the edge until we re-paint the plastered sections. But, it adds character."

Elizabeth rested her head back against his shoulder.

Bob Faringdon's trusty old Land Rover ground to a halt outside. Jeff - his grandson - hopped out of the driver's seat and waved to the couple standing near the kitchen window.

"He's a nice lad. I spoke to him after the funeral," Doug said.

"Yes. Becky took quite a shine to him as well."

"Oh yes? I hadn't noticed."

Jess barked and bounded to the front door, tail wagging like a propeller. Bethany opened up and watched the dog leap and run around the student. He made a fuss of the animal and it licked his face.

The eleven-year-old giggled. "She likes you,"

"I've known her a long time. Is your sister about?"

"Yes, she's upstairs. Do you want to come in?"

"Yes please."

In the kitchen, laughter lines appeared around Elizabeth's eyes at the look of surprise on her husband's face. The couple had caught every word.

Jeff appeared in the kitchen doorway. "Oh, hello there Mr and Mrs Ashbourne."

"Good morning, Jeff," Doug said. "I see you're taking Bob's old Landy for a spin."

"Yes. That is, I wondered if Becky fancied taking a drive with me to Stow. If that's okay?"

Elizabeth pressed herself away from her husband and walked by the lad. "I'm sure she'd like that. Let me get her for you." She leaned on the banister to call upstairs. "Becky? Jeff Faringdon is here to see you."

A door whipped open above and the sound of hurrying footsteps thudded on the ceiling. The pace was soon brought under control. Rebecca regained her poise upon catching sight of Jeff in the hallway.

The lad took a step closer. "Hi Becky."

"Hi Jeff. Did you come by for that walk we spoke about?"

"Sort of. Dad let me use Grandpa's old Defender today. Anyway, I wondered if you'd like a drive in to Stow and a walk round the shops?"

"Would I?" Rebecca bobbed on the bottom stair. "Hang on, I'll get my purse." She turned and took the steps at a bound on her way back up.

Doug wiped fingers across his mouth to dispel a subtle grin. He looked at Jeff. "I'd call that a yes, then. How's Josh getting on at the farm?"

"He's a fast learner and a hard worker. We appreciate his help a lot, thanks."

"Don't thank me, it was his own idea."

Elizabeth joined in. "We're proud of him for doing this."

"I should say so," Jeff said.

"Okay, I'm ready." Rebecca launched herself off the last few steps like a gymnast dismounting the parallel bars.

"Have fun, you two." Elizabeth watched them leave, her arms folded in loose satisfaction. She eyed Doug as he made for the door. "That's the happiest I've seen her since we came here."

"It's more of an adjustment and less of an adventure at her age. Perhaps things will start going right now, Lizzie."

"Perhaps. Don't get so engrossed you forget to stop for lunch again, hey?"

"I won't, Darling. Love you."

"Love you too."

Rebecca got herself seated in the Land Rover. It was beaten, worn and smelled of oil. But, with Jeff at her side it might as well have been a Rolls Royce.

"I know it's not sporty or trendy, but she'll get us there." Jeff turned over the engine and crunched the gears.

The girl fidgeted. "It's nice to have a little independence again. I haven't been to Stow-on-the-Wold yet. Mum and Dad have been too busy to go many places."

"I'm sure you'll like it. Pretty town. High up. Filled with all kinds of boutique clothing and jewellery shops, eateries and coffee houses."

"Sounds cool."

"Yeah, it *is* pretty cool." He released the brake and the Landy lurched off down the drive.

At the base of the hill, an agitated crowd milled around near the shop.

"I wonder what's going on?" Rebecca's voice sounded quiet. Something was up.

"There's Mrs Leach. I'll see if she knows." Jeff pulled over and wound down the driver's window. Angela Leach caught sight of his puzzled face and strode over.

"Good morning, Mrs Leach."

"Good morning, Jeff. Oh, and to you, Rebecca."

"Good morning, Mrs Leach."

The vicar's wife fluttered her eyelashes. "Are you two off out on a jaunt?"

Jeff nodded. "We're popping in to Stow. What's happened here?"

"You mean you haven't heard? Gosh, well Jane Cowley drowned in her bath last night."

"What?" Both youngsters did a double-take.

"Yes. Terrible state of affairs. The police said she appeared to have been held underwater. They arrested her husband."

"He murdered her?" Rebecca gawped.

Angela sucked her teeth. "Honestly? I would be very surprised. Pete Cowley is the gentlest man I've ever met. He adored Jane. Oh, I know couples sometimes fight and things can get out of hand. But, if that was so, they kept their problems well hidden."

Jeff drummed his fingers on the steering wheel. "So what's the alternative, an intruder?"

"I suppose. Rural burglaries are on the up around here. Somebody might have broken in and happened upon her."

"GOD, how awful." Rebecca put her hand to her mouth and flushed. She looked at the vicar's wife. "Oh, I'm sorry."

Angela waved in a dismissive gesture. "No matter. Well, you two have a good time. Drive safe."

"We will. Thank you." Jeff rolled up the window and signalled to pull back out into the lane.

The Landy climbed the other side of the Coln Valley over Calcot Peak. Jeff turned right onto the A429 at the hill above Northleach. The occupants remained quiet until the car crested a rise near Cold Aston, on the descent to Bourton. Rebecca was first to speak.

"Drowned." She shivered. "Coln Abbots is starting to give me the creeps."

"You mean with what happened to Mr Compton, Grandpa and now Mrs Cowley?"

"And some near misses in our own household."

"What near misses?"

Rebecca swallowed hard. "You might think this makes me sound like a nut job, but I've got to get it out."

"Fine. Hey Becky, I'm pretty open minded about all sorts of stuff. I'll listen to what you've got to say."

"Are you 'handling' me?"

One corner of Jeff's mouth lifted. He wanted to say 'not as much as I'd like' in response, but good manners and a sudden lack of courage held him back. Becky was a babe. "Tell me what happened. We can discuss interpretations later."

"Alright then."

The vehicle crossed the old stone bridge near Bourton. It passed traffic lights before the turning for Lower Slaughter. Beyond the junction with the Burford road, they began the long ascent to Stow. All the while, Rebecca relayed stories of everything that had happened to her family.

Jeff shifted down a gear to make the hilltop. His face creased with concern. "That's amazing. Bloody hell. How close did each of you come to losing your life?"

"And by drowning. Hence my earlier musing."

"It's too weird to be coincidence. There must be something else behind it."

"So you believe me?"

"About the voice, faces and stuff? Hell yeah, why not? Okay, so one odd tale in three might be dismissible. But all three? I don't think so, somehow. Plus there's the way Grandpa died. I know what Mum and Dad have told the village, but I also know the truth. How could he drown in mead while sitting in his armchair? And there it is again as you say: drowning."

"Do you believe in ghosts, Jeff?"

"After growing up in the rural Cotswolds? Err, yeah. Okay, I've not had a specific, concrete encounter. But, I've seen, heard and felt some pretty weird shit over the years. Especially near that pond behind your house."

"That's where Bethany went in."

"So you said."

"What about demons and witchcraft?"

"I guess if you believe in ghosts, it's not too much of a jump to make. Is that what you think the voice was?"

"It didn't sound human. I know that's daft-"

"No," Jeff interrupted. "No, I can appreciate it. Okay, you were under stress. But sometimes that heightens perception rather than dulls it. You know, the *fight-or-flight* response, as they call it."

"It's nice to have someone other than my younger siblings believe me."

Jeff passed the entrance to Back Walls and pulled up at a red light by the top of Sheep Street.

Rebecca caught sight of the picturesque buildings stretching away downhill to their right. "Oh wow, this looks lovely."

"Wait until you see the marketplace. It's still got some old stocks. A favourite for tourist pictures."

The light went green. Jeff drove on and pulled up in a car park by a supermarket near the local recycling point. "It's free to stop here. Most visitors don't know it and pay to park on the hill. But, we're only a short walk to the market."

"Great."

They climbed out of the Defender. Jeff locked the doors and reached his hand towards Rebecca. The butterflies fluttered in her tummy again. He only held her for a second, while they set off in the right direction. But, it made her feel on top of the world. He led her into town, past the stocks and through the marketplace. If the girl was timid at first, she soon conquered any discomfort upon spying the retail delights of Stow. After an age examining clothing, earrings, leather goods and purchasing a few handmade chocolates, Jeff decided they could both use a breather. He knew that *he* needed one, anyway. This girl could browse and shop for England!

"Hey Becky, how about stopping for a coffee?"

"Great, where's good?"

"Loads of places. My favourite is in Church Street. Comfortable leather sofas, high stools, a sun terrace for the nicer weather. Great coffee and hot chocolate, too. Decent food if you're peckish."

Rebecca took his hand and swung their arms in a pronounced and playful gesture. "Lead on. Oh, Jeff?"

"Yeah?"

"I'm glad our 'walk' ended up being round here instead."

"Sure. Me too. Hey, let me show you this wicked church door."

"Wicked church door?"

He guided her down an alley into St. Edward's churchyard. They skirted the Cotswold stone cruciform structure and stopped by the northwest door. This double width, studded wooden portal was shaped into a Gothic arch with five small windows tracing its top. Two ancient yew trees stood sentinel on either side, and a large lantern hung overhead. The whole presented an almost mystical appearance.

"That's a bit special." Rebecca studied the curious architectural feature.

"Some believe it inspired Tolkien's *'Doors of Durin'* in *'The Lord of the Rings.'* No idea if that's true, but I still think it's cool."

"For real? Josh would love that. I'm taking a picture." She raised her mobile phone and snapped an image with the inbuilt camera.

They continued around the side and made their way along a narrow street to the coffee house. It was a smart place in a traditional building, full of rustic charm.

"So what do you think is behind all the sinister happenings at home? Any ideas at all?" Jeff sat side by side with Rebecca on a leather sofa. A waitress placed two coffees and a Pain au Chocolat on a low table in front of them.

Rebecca broke the pastry in half and handed some to her companion. "Moira Robbins thinks it's deliberate. Witchcraft. Hey, I didn't tell you about our midnight walk and the ghosts."

"You mean the witch hunters who head out from the pub?"

"Have you seen them?"

"No. Actually I haven't. The haunting is pretty famous in the village. I've never had occasion to go creeping around that late at night. Sounds like you got a good look, though."

"That was odd."

"Scary?"

"Yes and no. Scary to actually see something like that. But, it was a bit like watching an old projection. Nothing appeared to be after us, or even aware of us."

"How about Moira? She looks like the type to mess around with magic."

"Oh, she does. But it's only a curiosity with her. That reminds me, you'll never guess what we saw from outside Wendy Simpson's place."

"Creeping along lanes at midnight. Spying through windows. Should I be getting worried about you?"

Rebecca sipped her coffee. "I hope not."

"Let me guess. You've heard the stories about Wendy being a witch?"

"Not only *heard*. We saw her at a witch's altar with a dagger."

Jeff furrowed his brow. "It's called an athame, if I'm not mistaken. Okay, that's a bit harder to refute. I always thought it was mere gossip."

"That's what Mum thought. Doesn't change what I saw. Mum actually ran into a mysterious robed figure or figures up in the woods."

"So, what do you want to do: burn Wendy at the stake or drown her in Nevermere?"

Rebecca put down her cup. She watched people

walking up and down Church Street, through the large glass windows. "I know. It's crazy, isn't it? Even if she *has* got something to do with it, we're completely powerless. That's the scariest thing of all."

"Maybe that's why your folks are so dismissive. They don't want to consider the implications of what it means if you're all telling the truth. How do you fight magical or supernatural murders?"

"I don't know." Rebecca's eyes stared into space. "I just don't know."

* * *

Jeff honked the horn on the Land Rover. Rebecca watched the vehicle rumble away from Pennycress Cottage and waved.

Her mother was sat in the living room reading, when the teenager entered the hallway.

"How was Stow, Becky?"

"Fabulous. There are so many excellent shops there, Mum. We should go more often."

"I'll have to make sure we do. Been a while since I was last there. Have you eaten?"

"I had half a pastry. I'm not all that hungry. Jeff took me to a nice coffee house."

"So you two had a good time, then?" Elizabeth closed her book and watched her daughter glow with pleasure.

"Brilliant."

"He seems like a decent young man. Oh, Moira phoned to ask if you wanted to eat with them tonight. I told her you were out in Stow with Jeff."

"Thanks, I'd better give her a call. She'll be champing at the bit for all the juicy details."

"How juicy?" Elizabeth adopted an air of mock concern.

Rebecca grinned and walked across the hallway into the kitchen to call Moira.

"So?" The word popped out of the pink-haired Goth's mouth. The door at Box Cottage hadn't even finished opening.

"So what?" Rebecca knew she was going to enjoy winding Moira up a bit.

"Oh, come on, spill."

"Can I come in first?"

"Whoops. Yeah, of course." Moira stepped aside. "Hey, tell you what: Let's go for a stroll down the lane. Extra privacy and all that."

"Crumbs, it's not like we went to an orgy, Moira. Jeff took me shopping and for a coffee."

Moira winked. "That's how it usually begins." She leaned further into the hallway and shouted. "Becky and I are off for a quick walk, Mum. Be back in time for dinner."

Nancy appeared in the hall. "Do you have to? Becky's mother saw some weird people stalking around after dark."

"Jeez, we're only going along the lane. Anyway, it's not quite dusk. We won't be long. I *am* turning nineteen, you know. We're not children."

"And Elizabeth is forty-one. It didn't stop her being scared out of her wits." She looked from one girl to the other and realised they were in fact adults after all. "Okay. Well, be careful."

"We will."

"That's rather unlike your mother. She's usually so laid back," Rebecca said.

The girls checked the lane for traffic and set off on their walk.

"I know. Your mum has been laying it on thick about some robed figures she saw up in the woods."

"Did you hear about Jane Cowley?"

"The whole village is talking about it. When I heard she'd drowned, I felt like someone had walked over my grave. God, that's unnerving. Anyway, I looked up a protection ritual on one of my magic websites. It seems pretty straightforward. I was thinking we should try it tomorrow afternoon, while Mum and Dad are out. It could save our lives. Are you game?"

"I don't have to drink chicken blood or anything, do I?"

Moira grinned. "No. Wave a bit of incense and do some chanting, that's all. I understand the nudity is optional."

"Nudity? What? Get out."

"I'm teasing. It's pretty straightforward. Mum wouldn't like it, so we'll do it while we've got the house to ourselves."

"Guess it couldn't hurt. I told Jeff the whole story."

"And?"

"And it seems we're out of options for any kind of action. You're right. We need to fight fire with fire. Okay, I'm in."

"Great. So, tell me about Jeff and-" She paused, face whitening. "Oh fuck, Becky get down!"

"Wha-" Rebecca didn't even finish the word. Moira's hands dragged her into a patch of moist grass behind a dry stone wall.

Moira panted and whispered. "One of your mother's robed figures in the churchyard."

"Are you serious?" Rebecca could feel her pulse quickening.

The girls pressed themselves flat against the limestone barrier. Their heads lifted to peer between the upright 'cocks and hens' that topped it. A tall figure in a floor length, hooded black robe crept along the churchyard path. The cowl was large enough to frustrate any attempt to gauge the identity of the wearer.

Moira nudged Rebecca. "I'll bet it's Wendy Simpson up to no good. Let's follow her. I've got a fiver that says she'll be back off home now."

"You're on."

They waited until the hooded figure emerged from the churchyard gate. To their relief, it turned in the opposite direction and followed the lane downhill.

"What did I say? Next stop Gingerbread Cottage."

"We'll see. Come on."

The girls traced the wall until they reached its end. From there it was a case of trying to merge with hedges, or blend into assorted undergrowth that dotted the thoroughfare's edge. The lights of Gingerbread Cottage were lit for the evening. The mysterious pilgrim sauntered past without giving the place any visible recognition.

"Looks like you owe me a fiver," Rebecca said.

"It could still be her. Let's see where they're going."

Rebecca and Moira passed the cottage. A silhouette moved inside and Wendy Simpson appeared at the window.

"Shit," Rebecca squashed herself against the building.

Moira shrugged. "Okay, so not Wendy after all. Quick, before the creature loses us, whatever it is."

They approached the centre of the village. The robed figure stopped outside a house near the pub. It flicked the oversize cowl first one way and then the other. A slender hand emerged to rap a wrought iron knocker against the front door.

Rebecca and Moira attempted to slow their beating hearts that pounded at a gallop.

The front door opened. A well-built, sandy haired man in his early forties stood in the illuminated entryway.

Moira whispered. "That's Harry Aston. Do you think it's some kind of coven?"

Rebecca remained silent, her eyes fixed on the unfolding drama.

The robed figure entered the house and the door closed behind.

"I wonder if we can see anything through the window?" Moira stood up and raised a hand to cover her eyes. It was rather a redundant gesture given the lack of sunlight. Evening mist crept up from the Coln. It snaked between the aged and weathered stone structures.

Rebecca's gaze darted around. "What if we're seen? Moira, we could be pushing our luck."

"Haven't they already tried to kill you? Do you think it will make any difference if we're seen or not?"

"You're right, I suppose. Okay. Go easy."

A car rumbled past and the girls ducked for cover. Its taillights disappeared into the murky cloak of approaching night. The pair stole across the lane. Drapes hung open on a downstairs window. Rebecca and Moira eased alongside, cautious of announcing their presence through clumsiness. They spied the interior of a comfortable sitting room with inglenook fireplace and low ceiling beams. Bookshelves were fitted either side of the chimney, stacked full of volumes impossible to recognise from outside. A Suffolk latch raised on a white, wood-panelled door from the hall. Harry Aston entered the room. Behind him the cloaked figure followed. Two feminine hands lowered the hood.

"Holy shit, that's Angela Leach the vicar's wife." The words came with a squeak of shock from Rebecca, and louder than intended.

Harry Aston ducked to peer out the window, wearing a frown. Thanks to the light in the living room and the dark outside, the girls could see him but not the other way around. He tugged the drapes closed.

Rebecca and Moira moved away from the structure.

They stopped at the place where they had squatted to observe the ghost procession on their midnight stroll.

Moira shook her pink hair, disapproval writ large across that partially obscured countenance. "The vicar's wife? Bloody brilliant cover for a witch. Do you think her husband's in on it too?"

Rebecca shook her head. "I don't know. This is getting weirder by the minute. Could there be others in there?"

"Perhaps. They might be about to perform some kind of ritual. Maybe more will arrive later. Or…"

"Or they could meet their friends up at Nevermere after dark," Rebecca continued. "I wonder if they're the ones Mum saw?"

"Do you want to wait around and see if anyone else shows up?"

"Not really. Hadn't we better be getting back to yours for dinner?"

"Oh yeah, good call. Here." Moira pulled a five Pound note from her pocket and passed it across.

Rebecca handed it back. "Keep it. Anyway, we still don't know if Wendy is a part of all this. She looks to be involved, somehow."

The girls wandered back up to Box Cottage. Their steps moved in double time upon reaching the old spinster's place. Once it was behind them, both displayed a strong sense of relief.

13

Sinister Spinster

"Never fear, an extra pair of hands are here. Hey, have you heard the news yet?" Nancy Robbins appeared in the kitchen doorway at Pennycress Cottage.

Boxes and packaging covered the room, lending the space a ramshackle appearance. This was somewhat at odds with the state in which its owner usually kept it. Elizabeth sat at the table next to a considerable pile of soaps and candles. She grimaced and studied her neighbour. Mustering the energy or enthusiasm to hear more local gossip seemed like too mammoth a task.

"I'm glad you're here. As you know, Katie Benson is coming by later this afternoon to collect a load of stock for the shop trial in Broadway. We'll have to work hard to wrap and label everything in time. Whatever you can do to help would be great."

Nancy eyed the pile of homemade products. "That's why I said I'd pop up today. Did you want me to fetch Becky and Moira? They're only down at our place dossing around."

"No, that's okay."

"What about the rest of the family?"

"Josh is so busy working at Washburn Hill that I didn't have the heart to ask him. Bethany would help, but she always puts the labels on wonky or doesn't wrap things to a suitable standard. These need to look perfect."

"How about Doug, or does the meadery need his undivided attention today?"

"He's on the road taking taster samples around to farm shops and the like. Hoping to drum up some business in time for when the first major batch matures."

Nancy pulled out a chair and plonked herself down. "Well then, it's a good job I'm here."

Elizabeth nodded. "Thanks. So, what's the news you were going to tell me?"

Nancy's eyes lit up. "It seems Angela Leach - the vicar's wife, has been carrying on with Harry Aston. Leslie Aston went to a social in Bourton last night, only to find it cancelled. When she came home early, she discovered Angela and Harry naked and in the throes of passion. On the living room rug, of all places."

"Seriously?" Elizabeth bit her lip.

"Oh yeah. It all goes on in a small village, you know."

"What did she do?"

"Leslie? I understand she blew up at the pair of them and chased Angela out of there. After that, she had a barney with her husband and went to let off steam at a friend's house."

"Hence word getting round so fast?"

"It wouldn't have stayed under wraps for long. Leslie doesn't take any nonsense. No way would she have kept quiet for the sake of the vicar and his self-righteous community decorum."

"Sounds like he's the innocent party, though."

"Perhaps. I don't know what their marriage was like behind closed doors. David and Angela, I mean. It's funny, I've often thought I saw her looking men up and down with a bit more relish than was appropriate."

Elizabeth whistled. "And there I was thinking Doug and I would move to the country for some peace and quiet. This place is turning into a regular soap opera." She picked up one of the bars to stress the irony of the term, then passed some light blue tissue paper across the table. "Here. I'll stick the gilt-edged labels on the soaps and then you can wrap them. Let me show you the correct technique. That way we'll get a professional and uniform appearance on the products."

* * *

"Jess, come here." Bethany heard the sound of an approaching vehicle. She climbed onto a grass verge and grabbed hold of the dog's collar. A saloon car emerged around a bend and slipped by. Its engine was so quiet that the only sound announcing its presence appeared to be a rumble of tyres on tarmac. The driver noticed the eleven-year-old and waved in appreciation at her efforts to stand aside with her dog. The girl listened a moment longer. No further traffic in earshot. She decided to click the lead in place until they were at a spot where Jess could run free without danger. The pair carried on downhill along the lane. Trees on one side opened up to reveal the churchyard. Bethany stopped at the wall. She studied the eclectic mix of tombstones and other grave markers, old and new. Temporary wooden crosses were all that indicated graves of two recently deceased villagers: Adam Compton and Bob Faringdon. Crosses soon to be joined by a third for Jane Cowley. In time, more permanent headstones would replace those markers. Bethany watched the tall, slender figure of Wendy Simpson. She knelt by the cross at Bob Faringdon's grave. The old woman hunched forward. Her hands fiddled with something concealed from the observer's view. Jess finished snuffling around in the grass at the base of the dry stone wall. The dog pulled on her lead as if to usher her walker along. Bethany bent over to pat the Lab and stroke her. "Okay Girl, we're going now," She stood back up and found Wendy staring at her from the churchyard path. Bethany gulped. Piercing hazel eyes watched the young girl. They fixed on her from that triangular face beneath the grey and mauve volume curls.

Blood rose to the youngster's cheeks. She let Jess pull her along and turned to look at something else: anything else. Her gaze found a nondescript bush, to which she gave undue pretend interest. But the sensation of that fixed stare remained upon her. It locked her in place, like a prison searchlight that had located escaping inmates. The girl fidgeted. Jess decided that a patch of daisies on the roadside was of such olfactory interest, it required an abrupt and total halt. Bethany pulled the lead but the dog would not be dragged away from her sniffing.

"If she wants to smell them that much, you might let her." Wendy's voice sounded closer.

Bethany looked up with a start. The spinster stood at the churchyard gate. Her tone was soft and those eyes felt less severe at this range.

"I suppose so," the girl replied. She found it hard to maintain eye contact.

"You don't need to fear me or feel uncomfortable, child. I won't hurt you."

Bethany took a long, slow breath, then clenched her teeth. She managed to bring herself to look up at the curious lady.

Wendy slapped the top of the gate with one hand. "There, that's better. You're Mrs Ashbourne's youngest, aren't you? I remember seeing you in the shop with your mother."

"That's right. I'm Bethany Ashbourne." The girl tried hard not to stammer, with moderate success.

"I'm Wendy Simpson."

"Pleased to meet you, Miss Simpson."

"Oh goodness, plain old Wendy will do. No need for formalities around me. And who is that with you, Bethany?"

"Jess." The girl's taut muscles unclenched. Wendy's voice was actually quite soothing. Almost melodious. Not the evil cackling she imagined from story books about witches. If this rather odd and lonely lady even was one.

"My goodness, of course." Wendy drew a sharp breath. "Adam Compton's old dog from The Woolpack. I've never frequented the place, myself. But, I remember seeing her sat outside in the nicer weather or going with him for a walk."

"Yes, that's right." Bethany looked past the woman to the graves beyond. "Do you mind if I ask what you were doing at MrFaringdon's resting place?" It took some courage for the youngster to speak up in this manner. But, she felt very protective of Bob Faringdon. The day of his funeral had been especially hard on her. The sensitive young lady cried herself to sleep that night.

Wendy's eyes reddened and watered. She glanced down for a second before taking a moment to twist round and face the grave. "I was laying a bunch of flowers I grew in my garden and blessed for him."

"Oh. Blessed? But you're not a vicar, you're a wi..." Bethany's voice trailed off. The phrase had popped out without prior thought. She winced. It felt like she had dug a grave of her own and wasn't able to climb back out."

"A witch?" the woman completed the statement for her - face blank, voice calm.

The eleven-year-old blushed and pulled Jess close to her leg for comfort and protection.

Wendy sniffed and wiped the moisture from one eye. "Oh, I know what they say about me in the village. When you're born different and you don't quite fit in, people like to talk and make up stories. When I was your age, they labelled me 'quiet' or 'standoffish.' When I became a teenager, I was 'shy' or 'bookish.' By the time I remained single and lived unwed with my parents until they died, I was either 'mad' or a 'witch.' I have better hearing than most people round here seem to think. Either that or they don't care."

Bethany swallowed. "I'm sorry."

Wendy let out a soft and wistful rush of air. "It's not your fault, young lady. You only know what your elders have told you. People your parents raised you to respect."

Jess sat down and panted.

Wendy indicated the animal with one long, bony finger. "It seems like she could do with a drink. I have a spare water bowl at my cottage along the lane. Would you like to pop in for a visit?"

Bethany pondered the request with a myriad of reasonings. On the one hand her parents had always taught her not to go off with strangers. But then, this woman was sort of a neighbour. There were many local stories about the odd lady being mad, or a witch. But the girl also felt a pang of guilt about adding to the quiet woman's anguish, through her near accusation. At last she made a decision. "Err, okay then. Thank you."

"Marvellous." Wendy opened the churchyard gate and stepped out into the lane. "I don't get visitors very often. Not too surprising, given my reputation in Coln Abbots."

"Did you ever think about moving?" Bethany

walked alongside her, Jess loping at their heels.

Wendy sniffed. "The rumours would only start up again somewhere else. Besides, this is my home. I live in the cottage where I was born and grew up. The only home my parents had together before they died. I don't think I could ever bring myself to leave it behind."

"But what about the W.I. or something? Maybe if you joined them, people would treat you a little nicer and say less nasty things."

One of the slender old hands patted the eleven-year-old on her left shoulder. "You have a good heart, young one. I like to keep myself to myself. Unfortunately for some people, that's grounds for idle and malicious gossip. I tend to leave other folk alone, but they can't seem to reciprocate."

Bethany thought for a moment. "I was going to ask what you meant about blessing the flowers."

Wendy nodded. A mischievous light twinkled in her eyes. "Ah now, that's the other problem. Not all the stories about me are completely untrue." She rested her hand back on the girl's shoulder. "You see, I actually *am* a witch."

* * *

Although it was a warm day on the relentless march to midsummer, the interior of St. Mark's felt cool. To the silent woman sat in a pew by herself, the atmosphere seemed chilly in the extreme. Her face hung low over her lap; long, centre-parted chestnut hair unmoving like a shroud. The oblong head rose to reveal pale green eyes wet with tears. Angela Leach struggled to decide which had been worse from a list of possibilities. Was it her adultery with Harry Aston? The hurt caused his wife, Leslie, and the damage to their marriage? Then what about the anguish she had seen on the face of her own spouse? After Leslie Aston kicked her out of their home, Angela had run back to the vicarage in a flood of tears. David was ever the loving comforter, desperate to know what caused her such upset. She could have lied, of course. The flirtatious woman had been living a life of deceit for so long. Not only since her affair with Harry came about. Through all her years, Angela had struggled with what the Bible referred to as *'the desires of the flesh.'* She adored men and found both the fantasy and reality of sexual gratification like a drug. She wasn't a sex addict as such, but the nymph inside never seemed to stray far from the surface. How many times after a reading from scripture had she sat in this very spot, longing for repentance? But she wasn't sorry - not in truth. Only for the damage done to others, but not in relation to the acts themselves. It had been so thrilling to slip down to the village whenever Leslie was away. Angela always took precautions to avoid identification. Her own husband's reputation was central to his career and their way of life. She had never meant to harm either him or it. But the joy of tearing Harry's clothes off; the power and sensuality of his oral skills driving her wild, were too hard to resist. David was a good man, but confined all his licking to ice cream on a summer's day. Then there had been the thrill of possible discovery with Harry. A variable that heightened their frantic and forbidden intercourse. The reality of actual discovery proved somewhat less pleasurable.

No, Angela went home and told her gentle - if somewhat pompous - husband the whole truth. You couldn't keep a story like that secret in a village the size of Coln Abbots. She owed the poor man at least a little honesty. It was a tale that immediately brought David Leach down to earth with a bump, like Lucifer's prideful tumble from glory. The vicar remained unmovable in shock for a long time, fingers pressed together beneath his nose as if in prayer. Angela had no answers to his questions like 'but isn't my love enough?' and 'if you were unhappy, why didn't you talk to me?' She doubted that any one man's love would actually be enough. Even if she ran off with Harry Aston, her roving eye would soon fall on another. And then there was that delicious new man, Douglas Ashbourne, up at Pennycress Cottage. He had occupied several of her solo fantasies lately. Wherever might *that* lead, if she got close enough to try to seduce him?

Angela arrested her erotic mental wanderings in their course. *Why can't I change? Why is my libido so fierce?* She raised her head to regard the large crucifix hanging behind the altar. Tears came again. The forlorn, discovered adulteress staggered to her feet. They were feet that moved in aimless steps, one twisting in front of the other down the aisle. Her eyes regarded the large stone font. *I need to make a vow to myself that I will change, before I can ever approach the*

Almighty. She moved to one side beneath her husband's pulpit and slid back the heavy wooden cover. David was due to perform a baptism this afternoon and had already filled it in readiness. Angela leaned over to gaze down at her own reflection. She took a deep breath and spoke to herself.

"I will never look at another man with eyes of lust again, if David will only give me a second chance."

The words might have appeared sincere, but the woman knew her own nature too well to believe them. A tear dripped from her bulbous nose into the receptacle. It caused the surface of the water to ripple. When the ripple cleared, Angela discovered another face staring back at her, alongside her own. She instinctively looked to one side, unaware of any other person standing near the font. There was nobody in sight. The moment her head twisted back, a third head appeared in the reflection on the opposite side. The woman didn't even have time to raise her curious eyes again. Two sets of rotting, weed-encrusted arms pierced the calm surface. They grabbed her by the head and neck. Angela shrieked. Her cries reverberated through the empty structure, rising to the rafters. It was a quiet day in a small, Cotswold country church. No visitors were near and nobody would hear her screams. Screams soon deadened by the ingress of water into her terrified mouth. The high-pitched calls subsided into bubbling, like the noise of a geyser. Angela pushed her arms against the sides of the stone font, but the spectral hands held her head underwater. Inside, the vessel appeared bottomless. A deep and watery tomb from which uncaring faces rose up to watch life follow air out of her torso. It was as if they were pulling her down to join them. She was being baptised into a community of lost souls. Terror of hell and judgement for her previous actions, gave the woman one last burst of energy. Her legs shook and her hands pushed. But it wasn't enough to break free of those relentless, dead arms. The last bubbles floated up from her nose and mouth. Her body became still; eyes open, staring and lifeless, like those that witnessed her death.

If you entered St. Mark's at Coln Abbots on that peaceful day in early summer, a curious sight would have met your eyes. Slumped over the church font stood the lifeless body of a tall woman, hands wrapped around the sides. Her head anchored the rest of her frame in place, from where it rested beneath the lip of the large vessel. In a little while, the vicar and a family bringing new life for baptism would be in for an unpleasant surprise.

* * *

Bethany didn't know what to do. The thin, bony, but elegant fingers still rested on her shoulder. She stood before a quaint, pretty cottage on the way into the village. At her side, Jess panted and looked at her with large, puzzled eyes. The dog could sense the girl's discomfort but seemed unaware of any danger. The words Wendy had spoken still hung in the air about the stunned eleven-year-old's head. So, not only was she a witch, but the strange and lonely woman had admitted it. What happened now? Bethany's eyes fell on the name 'Gingerbread Cottage' adorning the gate. It was as if she had drifted into some kind of surreal parallel universe. One where she had become a character like Hansel and Gretel in a real-life fairy tale. Did the spinster actually kill and eat her victims, like the crone in that fable? Bethany had heard stories of serial killers on the news. They did little to assuage her concerns.

Wendy felt the faintest tremble ripple through her hand from the young shoulder. She smiled to herself and delivered a delicate rub of reassurance. "I imagine right now you are wrestling with all the tales you've ever heard about witches. Most of them aren't very pleasant, I shouldn't wonder."

Bethany swallowed hard. "Uh huh." She stammered. "And then there's the name of your house."

Wendy followed her gaze to the gate, then threw back her head and laughed with a musical trill. "Oh, I see. Well, if it makes you feel any better, I finished a nice plump child for breakfast and won't need to eat for a while yet."

Bethany frowned. She twisted to lock on to the hazel eyes smiling down at her. Wendy was teasing. That look and gentle sarcastic humour took the edge off the child's worry. She giggled in relief.

Wendy went on. "No, I'm no corpse cruncher, Bethany. Mother and Father named the place 'Gingerbread Cottage.' It was how they got together as teenagers. Mum baked him some gingerbread. They were inseparable ever after. The place received its title long before I was even born. Though, it was my mother who taught me the craft. She was a witch too, you know."

"Goodness. Are you part of an oven?"

"An oven? Oh, you mean a COVEN. No Dear, I'm a Hedge Witch. A solitary and solo practitioner of nature magic." She noticed Jess panting again. "But before we get into all that, how about some water for your thirsty dog?"

"Okay."

"Good." Wendy led her to a front door lined with foliage. It crept around and covered a good part of the building. This gave a more pronounced organic aspect to the natural-looking home. She inserted a key and opened the thick, studded wooden portal with a lingering creak from its hinges. "Come on in and make yourself at home."

Bethany stepped into a square, dark hallway that led into a comfortable kitchen/diner. A further open doorway indicated a possible living room with fireside staircase beyond. A tabby cat sprung into the hall and sat in front of the dog. Jess lowered her nose to watch a pair of luminous green eyes studying her.

Wendy noticed the exchange. "Don't worry about Tink. She won't aggravate your dog. Jess seems very well behaved around cats."

"Yes. That is, I've never been with her around cats, but she's such a gentle animal I'm not surprised."

"Would you like something to drink, Bethany? I make a pleasant elderflower cordial. They've been in season a few weeks now. It's my dear old mother's recipe. No spells or magic involved, so don't fret."

"Yes please. Shall I close the door?"

"Thank you. Then come and sit yourself down in the kitchen. Bring Jess and I'll sort out a bowl of water for her."

Bethany creaked the old door shut. She wandered into the kitchen and sat herself on a wooden settle near a rough and worn table. The interior of the cottage might not have been designed to reinforce 'witchy' fairy tales, but it still fired the girl's imagination. Most items had seen better days and definitely earned their keep. She wondered how poor Wendy must be. Or was it that each of these knick-knacks had such special meaning to her, she couldn't part with them? Had they belonged to her parents?

"There we go." The woman placed a bowl of water on the flagstone floor next to the black Lab. The animal lapped it up with repetitive and noisy slurps.

"Thank you, Wendy."

"You're welcome. Now for our own refreshments."

Tink shared some of the dog's bowl rather than using her own. The Labrador didn't seem bothered. After a few sips, the cat slunk over and rubbed herself against Bethany's legs. The Tabby's tail tickled her. Bethany stroked her fur and soon had the animal curled in her lap, purring with its eyes shut.

"You have a natural gift with animals." Wendy placed a pitcher of cordial on the table, along with two glass tumblers. She poured them both a drink and sat opposite the girl. "That speaks of an even nature.

Creatures are very sensitive, you know. Much more than humans."

"I'd heard that." Bethany sipped her drink. "Mmm, this is nice."

"I'm glad you like it."

"So what *is* a Hedge Witch?"

"Well now. In the same way there are many branches and practises among different religions, so there are in the magical community too."

"Does that mean you cast spells in a hedge?"

Wendy cracked the faintest hint of a grin. "Not so much, though of course many plants I use are found in them. Hedges were traditionally borders between parcels of land and villages. It's often thought the name came about from our ability to perceive and receive messages from the Other World. In other words we represent a border, of sorts. But Hedge Witches are often found in nature: learning about medicinal plants, using them for crafts, food and drink and so on. We focus on respecting the natural order, seeking balance in the world around us, and healing people."

"Oh. So you haven't been casting spells against my family then?"

"Your family?" Wendy's eyes widened.

"And Mr Compton, Mr Faringdon and Mrs Cowley."

Wendy sipped her cordial. She drew her limbs close to her body and her eyes puffed. "I've loved Bob Faringdon my whole life." Her voice sounded distant.

"Why didn't you marry him?"

"Well, I never summoned the courage to talk to him much at school. I've always been quiet and not one for socialising."

"You're socialising with me okay."

"Thank you, Bethany. One-to-one is my favourite. Bob was always so popular, though. A crowd went everywhere with him as a lad. Then he married a fine girl from the village and that was the end of that."

"And you never looked at anybody else or stopped loving him?" The girl sat open-mouthed.

"No. Oh, I'm sure it seems quite silly."

Bethany shook her head. "It sounds romantic. Very sad, but romantic."

"Anyway, after his wife passed away a few years ago, I suppose an old flicker of hope re-ignited inside. But by then I'd become so entrenched in my solitary life, that I knew nothing was going to change. When I heard he'd collapsed at home and died, my heart broke. That's why I was so angry in the shop the other day. I would have thrown myself in front of a bus to save Bob Faringdon. Silly, dried up old spinster that I am."

A tear slipped down one of her cheeks. Bethany reached forward and took her by the hand.

"Wendy?"

"Yes Dear?"

"There's more to how Mr Faringdon died than you've been told."

"How do you mean? And what's all this about spells being cast against your family?"

Bethany laid out the whole tale of everything that had happened: her own trauma with the bees and people in Nevermere, Rebecca, the shower and eerie voice, Joshua in the fermenter with those arms and faces, and the robed figure or figures her mother had encountered at night. She also filled in the missing and unexplained details about how Bob Faringdon lost his life after drinking her father's mead. An impossible drowning.

Wendy listened to it all without interruption. When the story ended, she sat bolt upright, lost in silent reflection for a long time. At last her concentration snapped back to the present and she eyed her guest. "I knew *something* was going on, even after they found Adam Compton. There was a weird and uneasy sense in the ether that my spirit picked up on. When Jane Cowley died in her bath, my suspicions were further aroused. But, I didn't know Bob's death in between had also been on account of drowning."

Bethany moved to explain but was halted by the woman's flat, raised palm. "Oh, it's okay. I understand why the Faringdons wanted to protect your father. There's enough idle chatter around here anyway, without wild tales getting exaggerated about how Bob died. Not that it needs much exaggeration, from what you've told me. The near misses you describe in your household and their sinister accompaniments are especially troubling. I'm not surprised to find someone practising dark magic up at Nevermere. It's been a broken place for almost four hundred years."

"Broken?"

"Yes. During the English Civil War, there were a series of witch trials in Coln Abbots. Something known as *'Ordeal by Water.'* A cruel practise that resulted in the execution of several villagers."

"Didn't they burn witches at the stake?"

"Sometimes. *'Ordeal by Water'* involved men attaching ropes to someone's ankles and throwing them into the pond. If they sank, the men hauled them up and they were free to go. If they floated, it was seen as evidence of the devil extending his protection. A sign of guilt. As you say, they were often then burnt at the stake, or - as in the case of Coln Abbots and Nevermere - weighted down in the pond to drown."

"That's awful. Were there many witches here?"

"I have no idea. But I do know the trials were a popular way for people to accuse those they didn't like. Greed, jealousy, revenge for adultery - those were all motives that could see you facing the ordeal. I'm sure many were innocent. I doubt those who may have been guilty were much different to my mother and I."

"Is that what broke the pond?"

"Something like it. I'm not sure exactly what, but there is a presence about Nevermere - something evil. The place is unbalanced. All the water in Coln Abbots is connected underground, one way or another. Like a network of sorts. Most things in the village somehow relate to the springs around your cottage. Springs that also rise into the woodland pond above it."

"Are there ghosts?"

"Not exactly. Oh, I'm sure it's haunted after a

fashion. A place of such tragedy might inevitably bear witness to restless souls unable to find peace. But there is something more. Legend has it that the darkness descended after the last witch trial. One final accused girl - the sister of a previous victim - was due to face the ordeal. But, she died during scuffles with a lynch mob."

"Is that the lynch mob of ghosts my sister saw at the pub?"

"Oh, she's witnessed 'The Procession,' has she? Yes. That's the same mob, repeating their final act of self-righteous justice. Or so the stories go, anyway."

"Have you ever known this kind of thing to happen in the village before, Wendy?"

"Not in my lifetime, nor my mother's. Something has awoken or caused the evil in the water to stir from its slumber. My guess is: practitioners of dark magic."

14

The Contract

"What time is your Dad leaving?" Rebecca reclined in a living room chair at Box Cottage. She and Moira had been catching some daytime TV when Nancy left.

"I'm not sure. But, the ritual won't take long to set up. We can perform it in front of the hearth here." The Goth swept back her brightly coloured mane with a carefree hand. "So, what do you think about Angela Leach then?"

"I guess our mothers will have a good old natter about it. I don't know what to think, if I'm honest."

"Bloody church hypocrites." Moira almost spat the words. "Not so fucking self-righteous now, I'll bet. I reckon the vicar's hung like a mouse and couldn't keep his wife satisfied."

Rebecca folded her arms. "Aren't you being a little harsh and stereotypical there?"

"Are you defending them?"

"No. I'm only saying people stray for all kinds of reasons. Their religious beliefs might not have anything to do with it. Nor their physical attributes."

"Well, I never warmed to either of those two. How wild do you reckon Angela got with Harry Aston? It must have been pretty steamy."

"And there we were thinking they formed part of a group casting spells against the village."

"Sounds like they worked a little magic on each other. Of course, we don't know what other sinister practises they might be a party to. Just because they've been bonking like bunnies, doesn't clear them of other possible charges. Don't forget the robe Angela wore."

Rebecca moved her mouth around like a cow chewing the cud. "More likely she was trying hard not to get spotted."

"Fat lot of good it did her."

"Yeah."

"So your mum's packaging up a load of soaps and candles for Katie Benson's shop?"

"That's right. Glad I'm not there. She was flipping out over it last night, worrying about how she will get everything ready in time."

"I'm sure my female parental unit will roll up her sleeves to help."

"Female parental unit? You *do* come out with some phrases, Moira."

The fulsome lips puckered. "The good news is, it will keep her away while we do the protection ritual. Once Dad goes out visiting clients, we're sorted."

"Okay girls, I'm off into Cheltenham for a bit." Howard appeared in the doorway.

The approach of wailing sirens disrupted the general peace. Blue flashing lights pulsed through the cottage windows. Two police cars and an ambulance roared by on the lane.

"What on earth?" Howard craned his neck to follow their route of transit. "Looks like they're pulling up at the church."

Rebecca and Moira raced to the window. The Goth grabbed her friend by the arm. "Come on. Let's go outside for a gander. I bet the vicar's either topped his wife or himself."

"Moira, that's not very nice." Howard wagged a disapproving finger at his daughter.

The girl scoffed. "Bet it's true, though. Come along, Becky."

The teenagers hurried out into the garden and stood near the boundary wall to watch the drama unfold. A group of well-dressed men and women milled about outside the place of worship. They fidgeted and pulled at their clothing, pausing now and again to make a fuss of a baby carried by one lady. The emergency vehicles disgorged their occupants. The crews hustled through the porch into St. Mark's.

Howard honked the horn of his BMW and waved to the girls. He drove past the church and disappeared from view round the sloping bend.

The female observers held their spot for some time, waiting to see what might develop. A white van arrived from the opposite direction and stopped at the church. Blue and yellow Battenberg stripes adorned its sides. Above that, alongside a police badge were emblazoned the words 'Forensic Investigation.' A male figure climbed out and hurried down the churchyard path, clutching a large bag.

After some time, Reverend David Leach appeared, his hands secured before him in rigid speed cuffs. Two police officers walked him to one of their cars and loaded the tearful vicar into the rear.

Moira punched the air with triumphant relish. "I bloody told you, didn't I?"

Rebecca touched her heart. The minister appeared to be in a state of total grief. "We don't know what happened, Moira. I'm sure this is only a routine procedure."

The pink-haired rebel was having none of it. "Crime of passion. I'll bet you any money he rogered her to death with a candlestick or something. Those uptight religious bastards can lose it when they finally let their hair down, you know."

Rebecca shook her head. "We have no idea what's even happened, or to whom."

"Let's see if we can find out." Moira waved at two children nearby - a boy and a girl about eight or nine years old. They had been ushered away from proceedings by their agitated parents, to play in the graveyard. "Hey Kids. Come here."

The young baptism guests approached, attired in their finest formal raiment. "Hello." The phrase sounded in chorus from a pair of timid mouths.

Moira winked. "Hi. Can you tell us what's going on?"

Boy and girl exchanged frightened glances. The lad broke their deadlock and spoke. "We came to watch our second cousin get baptised. But a lady has drowned inside the church."

Rebecca shuffled on the spot. "Drowned? You mean in the font?"

The boy shrugged. "I suppose. She had her head in a big stone thing full of water."

"What did I say?" Moira's tone rang with absolute confidence. "Okay, so not a candlestick, but-"

"That's terrible," Rebecca interrupted. She looked at the children with sad eyes. "Are you okay? That must have been an awful thing to see."

The girl didn't look too sure, but the boy nodded. "We only saw her from a distance before our parents brought us outside to play."

"Well, be certain and talk to them about it if you have bad dreams, okay? Don't bottle it up inside."

"We will." The boy grabbed the other child's arm. He dragged her back towards the path where their mother stood beckoning for them to return.

Moira snorted. "What are you, a secret child psychologist or something?"

"Crumbs Moira, can you imagine witnessing something like that as a child? That poor girl looked scared witless. I wouldn't like to see it myself, even now."

"Did you want to hang around and watch them bring the lady out in a body bag? It's gotta be Angela Leach. I'll lay you any money."

"Not particularly."

Moira's expression of sarcasm softened. "Okay. Well, Dad's gone now. How about I fix us a drink and we get down to business?"

"Sounds good. Moira?"

"Yeah?"

"Do you really think David Leach drowned his wife?"

"Probably, why?"

"It's the whole 'drowning' thing again."

"I know. Too weird. The sooner we get on with that ritual the better. That's what I say."

"You'll get no argument from me there."

They wandered into the house with somewhat less excitement than they had left it. Moira made for the kitchen and pointed to the living room. "You make yourself comfortable by the fireplace in there. I've got the sage out back, so I'll bring it through."

"Okay." Rebecca felt a shiver run down her arms. She rubbed them and noticed gooseflesh appear. The moment the teenager entered the living room again, she froze to the spot. A raven-haired girl in her early twenties lay before the fireplace. She stared right through Rebecca as though the blonde wasn't actually there. The young brunette's head rested on the hearth at a funny angle to her neck. Rebecca let out a shriek. The apparition blended with the fluctuating sunlight and vanished from view.

Moira ran to the door and found her friend shaking, hands clasped either side of her face. "What happened, Becky?"

"I... found a young woman sprawled in front of the hearth. She vanished."

A knowing light flickered in Moira's eyes. "Oh. You saw the ghost of Mary Blackwood."

"Who?"

"The story goes that she died here, long ago during the old witch trials. The cottage was a lot smaller, then. Not much bigger than this room, in fact. This is the oldest part of the building. I saw her once, myself. No more present than the spirits in that procession we watched."

Rebecca span on her heel. "How can you be so calm about all this stuff?"

"When you connect with the unseen world, you suspend modern disbelief. I suppose you get used to encountering the unusual or supernatural."

"I need the loo. Thought I was going to wet myself for a minute there."

Moira grinned. "No worries. Our downstairs toilet is out of action. It's been backing up, for some reason. Nothing to do with magic and curses though, I'm sure. More like too much paper and too little water pressure. You'd better use the bathroom. You know where it is."

"Thanks. I won't be long."

"We're good for a while yet. I'll fix us a glass of something cool."

Rebecca slipped off upstairs.

"Hey Becky?" Moira called from down below."

The blonde teenager's head appeared over the top railing, eyebrows raised.

Moira went on. "I left a lighter on my dressing table with a ribbon we'll need. Can you fetch them on your way back down?"

"Sure."

Rebecca relieved herself in the bathroom, then pushed open the door to Moira's boudoir. The Goth's dressing table stood crammed and draped with all manner of charms and arcane symbols. The Ashbourne girl lifted a couple and let them run through her fingers. *God she's into some freaky shit. But, it might save our arses today.* She pushed a hairbrush aside and found the lighter and a purple ribbon. Rebecca's gaze was drawn to a small and dirty metal box, about the length of a ruler. It sat atop a pine chest of drawers standing next to the vanity unit. It appeared rather old. The lid wasn't quite secured in place. The girl felt a wave of curiosity overwhelm her. She looked back over her shoulder. Moira was still fixing a drink and waiting downstairs. Rebecca lifted the lid and peered inside. The top fell from her fingers onto the wooden unit with a clatter. Her mouth dropped open, allowing a soft gasp to escape. Inside were all manner of personal items, wrapped in cord and stuck full of black pins. She lifted a piece of checked cloth, like the material of a shirt. Beneath that lay a folded handkerchief, embroidered with the initials 'A C.' Rebecca's hands shook. "Adam Compton? Could it be?" Her mouth went dry as she whispered the words to herself. Amidst other fragments of what appeared to be dress material, she located some tissues adorned with wizards. They were screwed up and stuck together by some long-dried goo or other. "Josh's tissues?" Rebecca glanced around the room to see if Moira had somehow purchased the same variety. Her tissues were plain white. She moved the mess to one side. "Oh my god!"

A tampon lay wrapped in cord and stuck with pins. Below that was a clump of familiar hair wrapped around a solid lump of old chewing gum. The discovery caused the teenager to let out an involuntary squeal. Her pulse raced and she ran a hand across her sweating brow. A folded, yellow piece of parchment was tucked down the side of the box. With quivering fingers, Rebecca opened it out. Some text had been written in what looked like quill script. Despite the document's obvious age, the paper appeared undamaged. The writing clear as the day it was written. She scanned the words, pupils dilating at what her mind read:

'The undersigned do hereby attest that they will - by all necessary means - deliver the mortal stroke upon seven souls from this village and its immediate environs. Said souls are offered in tribute to The Master, whereupon such sacrifice will witness him afford the undersigned power beyond all natural reckoning in this life. In the course of this undertaking, those souls already in thrall to The Master pursuant to their execution for witchcraft at Nevermere, will aid any signatory upon nocturnal request for the same. Once expiry occurs in relation to this mortal realm for the beneficiaries, they do hereby surrender their own souls forever to the ruler of this world. This promise shall be considered binding upon signature in blood.'

"Seven souls…" Rebecca's voice trailed away. She studied the bottom of the parchment, anxious to discover who had signed it.

"Find everything you were looking for?" Moira's voice cut through the stillness with sudden force. Her tone dripped with sinister mockery.

"You fucking bitch!" The response came out almost under her breath. Rebecca lifted an angry gaze to the pink-haired creature standing at the entrance to the room. She stepped back in surprise to find Moira's baby blue eyes had turned completely black. No whites or pupils could be distinguished in that unnatural and intimidating stare.

Shiny red lips curled over the occultist's teeth. She let out a long and inhuman laugh. "God Becky, you really are thick as shit, aren't you? Only now do you finally begin to understand."

Rebecca trembled with a mixture of fear and rage. "Understand what?"

Moira's voice deepened way below the ordinary range of her physicality. "The power that The Master has promised to His faithful."

The blonde swallowed hard. "You're completely mad."

"Am I?" the voice gloated. "Was it madness that drowned all those pathetic little villagers? Was it madness that almost added the souls of you and your big city siblings to the account? Why don't you lay down and die? Oh, that's right: you're about to."

Rebecca snatched up the lighter and flicked the top with her sweating thumb. On the third go a small flame ignited. "Oh yeah? What if your contract no longer exists?"

Moira folded her arms across her chest and leaned

against the door frame. "Try it."

The blonde called her bluff. She lowered the flame beneath the sheet of parchment. The flickering light darted around but had zero effect on it. It didn't even blacken or stain the hellish document.

"Extinctus!" A command erupted from the Goth in a resonant and animalistic tone. The flame went out and the lighter flew across the room from Rebecca's hand into her own. "We found the box concealed in the chimney, during some building work after we moved in. We'd been drawn to the house and village for a long while and then discovered why. Fire won't touch that paper, so you're wasting your time and energy."

"We?" Rebecca struggled to get the word out.

"The signatories."

At the base of the contract, three names had been added in blood; each inscribed by a different hand:

Howard Robbins. Nancy Robbins. Moira Robbins.

"B-but that means Mum's in danger."

Moira took a step closer. "Don't worry, you'll be joining her soon enough." She bared her teeth. "We still have three more souls to go."

Rebecca's face reddened. Her blood rose. "I'm going to rip your ugly black heart out, you dirty witch!" She flung herself at the Goth.

Moira held out an arm and clamped her hand onto the assailant's left shoulder. A burning sensation tore through Rebecca's body. She screamed and writhed in agony. The hand pushed her down to kneel on the carpet. The fake friend cackled with glee. "You'd better get used to that scorching fire, Rebecca Ashbourne.

Tonight you sleep in hell."

* * *

"That's good. Why am I not surprised you have a knack for packaging and presentation?" Elizabeth admired Nancy's handiwork on the wrapping. She peeled another gilt-edged label away and positioned it on the front of the next soap bar.

"Do I present the appearance of a neat packager, then?"

"No. Well, yes actually. That is, everything about your personal appearance, your home, catering and so on is always hallmarked by attention to detail."

"Gosh, that sounds like a compliment."

"I meant it as one."

"Thanks. I couldn't say whether it's the result of my inbuilt nature, upbringing, or years of trying to outdo friends and colleagues from the Chelts set."

"A blend of the three?"

"Could be." Nancy sat back in her seat at the kitchen table and allowed her gaze to wander around the room. "You've done a nice job with this place. I mean, I'd never been up here before your arrival. But, the changes you've made since we first met show good taste. But then the presentation of your products and the look of your website show a keen eye for aesthetics."

"One-all on the compliments score." Elizabeth handed the soap across and placed her palms flat on the wooden table.

A telephone rang on the wall. Elizabeth slid her chair out with a scraping noise of pine on ceramic and stood to lift the receiver. "Hello?" She listened to the voice on the other end for a moment, then twisted to signal Nancy. "It's Moira for you."

"Moira? Whatever has she got up to now?" Nancy took hold of the phone and Elizabeth sat back down to start on another soap. The Robbins woman listened, nodding from time to time and watching the wall. "Oh my goodness. Do you think it was Angela Leach? I see. They did? Well, that does seem to suggest she's the victim. I'll tell Elizabeth. What about the other thing? All taken care of. Good. Okay, Sweetheart. I'll see you later." She hung up.

"What was that all about?" Elizabeth didn't even look up, tongue poking out the side of her mouth in concentration.

"Angela Leach - or someone at least - has been found dead in the church. It looks like they drowned in the font."

At the second sentence, Elizabeth started and slipped. The label creased and attached itself at a jaunty angle. "Bugger." The woman eased the adhesive ticket away from the surface and checked for blemishes. The product remained in pristine condition. She lifted her head as Nancy re-seated herself. "What on earth is going on in Coln Abbots lately? Is Moira sure it's Angela Leach?"

"Well, the girls didn't see her body. But the police arrested David Leach and took him away. Some children who were due to attend a baptism, told them that a lady had drowned inside."

"I don't know David all that well. Do you think he could have done it?"

"After discovering Angela caught in adultery? Then the resulting stress on his marriage and injury to both career and reputation?"

"Well, when you put it that way, I suppose anyone could flip and go off the deep end in such a situation."

"All it takes is the correct provocation. Sounds like Angela pushed all the right - or wrong - buttons."

Elizabeth rested her nose on folded hands. "Drowning again." She shivered. "Doesn't anyone ever die of anything else round here?"

Nancy smirked. "Well, if you try hard enough, you might be able to give yourself a nasty paper cut with those labels. Could take a few to be fatal, though."

"We shouldn't be joking at a time like this, should we? It's in rather poor taste."

"Black humour. Same way the emergency services cope with the horrors they witness. They'd go mad, otherwise. Let's not forget you've had a few near misses with your kids. That's got to be taking its toll."

"I know. I've wanted to talk more about it with Doug. But, the whole thing sounds so crazy."

"Are you starting to believe the children now? The wilder aspects of their accounts, I mean."

Elizabeth shook herself. "I must be doolally. But I can't get away from the idea that something sinister is afoot. I suppose that incident with Jess and the robed figures by the pond was the clincher for me."

"What happened at the church sounds more like an

injured husband striking out at his wife with whatever means were to hand. I doubt David is some night-stalking devil worshipper." One corner of her mouth rose. "Although, I could be wrong."

"Like I said, I must be doolally. Here's the last soap. Once you've wrapped it, we'll get started on the candles."

Nancy's mobile phone lit up and vibrated where it sat on the table alongside her. She picked the device up, swiped to connect and raised it to her ear. "Katie, how the devil are you?"

Elizabeth fidgeted at the sound of the name. There was still a pile of work to do before the boutique owner arrived.

Nancy winked at her and waved a dismissive hand before continuing the phone conversation. "Well, we're finishing up on the soaps right now. Then there's a bit of packaging on the candles to do. You're going to love the presentation of these items. Elizabeth has done you proud. About an hour?" She tilted her head at the woman fiddling with candles.

Elizabeth rubbed her chin and performed some quick mental arithmetic. She rocked one hand back and forth in a gesture of uncertainty, palm towards the floor.

Nancy spoke into the phone again. "Can you make it ninety minutes? I'm sure we'll have everything ready by then. Okay. Okay. Yes, see you in a little while. That's correct, up the hill from our place. Pennycress Cottage. Right then. Ta-ta for now."

"Phew." Elizabeth let out a sigh. "Thanks for that."

Nancy put the phone back on the table and wrapped the final soap. "You need to take an assertive hand with Katie, sometimes. Otherwise she'll walk all over you. Not a bad sort. But she can be a bit bossy."

"A woman who knows what she wants?"

"That's a politer way of putting it, yes. There." Nancy placed the neatly packaged, fragrant item into a waiting box.

"Great. With the candles we only need a sticker placed underneath and bows tied around the mid sections."

"Why don't I take a turn at sticker placement for a change? The bows will be a little trickier and we're somewhat pushed for time."

"Sounds like a plan. Crumbs, I thought running a full-time cottage industry was going to be relaxing."

"Well, business is business. Most of the other folk I know who do this sort of thing, find that the pace moves in fits and starts. But I don't think any of them would go back to the employment treadmill."

"I hear you. Sunday afternoon dread, waiting for Monday morning. Commutes, office gossip, personality clashes, egos, red tape, HR and fighting to get permission when you need time off. Being paid by the hour to sit eight to ten hours in an office when you've done all your work in four-"

"Sorry for interrupting, but it sounds like you already realise the benefits."

Elizabeth laughed. "I must sound like a right old moaner."

"Honestly? You should become a self-employment

evangelist or something. Did you ever think about running seminars?" She paused. "What? Don't look at me like that, I'm serious. Passion is contagious and you have it in spades. I'll bet there's someone I know back in Cheltenham who'd be interested in having you over to speak. Could bring in some extra income."

"One thing at a time. Thanks, Nancy."

"Well look, why don't I put the kettle on while you're arranging those candles into our little kitchen production line?"

"Ta. I'll have a herbal tea. Second jar on the left in the cupboard there."

"Think I'll join you." She filled the kettle and plugged it in. "Is it strange living in your grandfather's cottage?"

Elizabeth positioned the candles on the table and pulled out a box of stickers and ribbons. "It was at first. Not uncomfortable as such, but I did feel odd redecorating his home. Still, I know he'd like it. Grandpa was a real pragmatist, even if he was also sentimental. He'd be delighted to find us using all the rooms again. So many of them sat empty after his children left home."

"And he'd no doubt be pleased you're caring for his bees." Nancy stirred a couple of herbal tea bags in two cups, squeezing them against the china with the back of a spoon.

"Yes. This life, my business, Doug's mead, the cottage - none of it would be possible without Grandpa. We have a lot to thank him for."

"How lovely." Nancy placed a steaming cup of

herbal tea next to Elizabeth. "Why don't you pause for five minutes and enjoy that, before the final push."

"The final push? Are we wrapping for victory?"

Nancy's eyes twinkled. She sat down and sipped her tea with a gaze that never strayed from her neighbour.

Elizabeth allowed her knotted shoulders to unravel. The familiar smell of the herbal tea brought relaxation to her muscles.

"Mmm. This tastes different. Sweeter. Did you put some of my honey in there or something?"

"Or s-o-m-e-t-h-i-n-g." The second word dragged out with a curious, lingering growl.

Elizabeth felt light-headed. She began to sweat and pulled at the neck of her blouse. The room moved around on its own, fading in and out of focus. She staggered to her feet. "W-what's happening? I feel so strange." The woman stumbled across the hallway into the living room and collapsed on the sofa. Groggy, half-closed eyes scanned around in an attempt to make sense of her predicament.

Nancy's piercing, bright blue stare flashed in front of the dazed face. Her wide, pink lips twisted into a hateful grimace. The words that came out, slurred through Elizabeth's foggy brain.

"Why do your family all seem to have nine lives? But your luck has run out at last. We have no more time to waste on silly games. So, our group have opted for a more direct approach."

"Doug," Elizabeth's whimpering and baleful cry seeped out of lips that fought to move. The cottage span as if she were drunk.

"Oh, Doug will be joining you, don't worry." Nancy ran a teasing finger across the drugged lady's brow in a stroking motion. At the last, she dug a fingernail in and scratched. "One way or another, Doug will be joining you."

* * *

"Thanks. I'll be back in touch when the first batch of regular mead is in saleable condition." Doug clasped a half-case sized cardboard wine box under one arm. With the other he closed a shop door on his way out. The characteristic bell jangled behind. The man smiled at a couple of beaming Japanese tourists. They bounced about and waved smartphones around on selfie sticks. He ambled along Victoria Street in Bourton on the Water, past a shop selling gemstones. His nostrils detected the pleasing sweetness of delightful fragrances wafting from the perfumery opposite. Beyond an independent clothing retailer, he hung a left back towards the river. It was a pleasant day, warm without being too hot. He'd acquired a keen local merchant as a customer and was feeling pretty pleased with himself. A footpath led southeast along the banks of the Windrush. He spied a tearoom serving local ice cream through a hatch, so decided to enjoy a treat.

Doug sat on a narrow wooden bench with his snack. He chuckled at a mongrel leaping around in the broad, shallow waters of the river. Silvery spray hissed in all directions and the happy animal let its tongue loll from side to side. This chocolate ice tasted rich and satisfying. The man patted the box resting on the ground between his legs. "No substitute for quality local produce," he said under his breath. *I wonder how Lizzie is getting on with that packaging? She was pretty stressed about it last night. Should I give her a call or leave her alone? Okay, a quick check-in to show I'm thinking about her.* He tugged a mobile phone from his jacket pocket and flicked up the land line number at the cottage. It rang and rang. *No reply. That's a bit odd. I guess she doesn't want to be disturbed. Things must be pretty fractious back there.* He tucked the device away. Crowds wandered back and forth across the many bridges that had earned Bourton the moniker: 'Venice of the Cotswolds.' The lovely quaint town proved a picture perfect dream of good, old-fashioned England. He crunched the last of his waffle cone and tossed the serviette in a nearby bin. There were no more potential mead vendors on his roster for now. Doug opted for a saunter around before making a slow journey home. Lizzie wanted some space. She'd even asked Bethany to stay outside with Jess and keep out of her hair today. Soon, normal service would be resumed. But not before Katie Benson collected the finished stock of 'Elizabeth Ashbourne' products.

The man continued southeast and crossed the river at Coronation Bridge. His eyes fell on the model village opposite. *Bethany would love that. We should have a family shopping trip in a day or two. I reckon we've all earned it.* Doug's steps brought him northwest along the High Street. He ducked down an alley between two limestone walls. Back by the Subaru, another coach of tourists unloaded at the Station Road pay and display.

The silver estate car slipped along in almost total silence. Its reliable engine ran like a sewing machine. Doug kept a weather eye on the Sat Nav, not following a prescribed route. He weaved through the Barringtons and Rissingtons, before joining the A40 at Windrush. Shortly before the junction, his eye was drawn to a memorial outside the village church. He pulled over to examine it further.

'To the memory of Sgt Pilot Bruce Hancock R.A.F.V.R. who sacrificed his life by ramming and destroying an enemy Heinkel bomber while flying an unarmed training aircraft from Windrush landing ground during the Battle of Britain 18th August 1940.'

Doug whistled. This quiet collection of villages were crammed with history. The Red Arrows started life down the road, too. He put the car back in gear and delivered a respectful nod at the memorial stone. "Brave chap."

Entering the Coln Valley again felt like coming home. Doug took this as a very positive sign that he was adjusting well to life in Gloucestershire. His old project management job in *'the smoke'* seemed a world away now.

About a mile from Coln Abbots, the Subaru started to misbehave. The engine revved itself and the steering became heavy, as if the power assistance had failed.

What on earth? This car is bulletproof reliable. Whoa! The vehicle lurched to one side. Doug narrowly missed an oncoming tractor. He took his foot off the accelerator, but the car continued to run. His arms felt like they would snap as the wheel spun right. The estate smashed through a wooden gate and careened across a mossy tump. Doug barely had time to catch a warning notice: *'Fishing Lake - Danger Deep Water'* before the vehicle plummeted into the depths. The cabin began filling with water and the car sank into darkness. He tried the handle, but found himself unable to push against the liquid weight holding the door shut. *Hammer!* Elizabeth had always been a safety-conscious woman. She insisted he install a window-smashing device in the front passenger foot-well, when they first purchased the car. His hand plunged into ice cold water and he located the small, bright yellow hammer. Doug took a deep breath and whacked the glass. The safety shards broke into a million pieces, flooding the remainder of the cabin and equalising the pressure. The man pulled himself free of the car and kicked towards the light above. Already he was running out of oxygen. His head broke clear of the surface, coughing, spluttering and gasping for air. With gargantuan effort he swam for the bank and hauled his cold, soaking torso onto the grass. An angler rushed over to see if he was okay.

Another voice shouted from the roadside. "Doug? Good heavens, it *is* you. I thought I recognised your car crashing through the fence." Howard Robbins stood next to his BMW. "I say, old man, are you alright?"

Doug caught his breath. "Steering locked up and the engine went berserk. I've never seen anything like it. Thank God Lizzie made me install that window hammer."

"Indeed." His neighbour's voice sounded neither pleased nor relieved. "Good job the rest of the family weren't on board too."

"Yeah." Doug straightened up from where he had stood doubled-over to recover.

"Well, why don't I run you home so you can dry off and sort out this mess?"

"Thanks Howard."

"No problem. Good job I happened by."

15

Rural Isolation

"Thanks for your help, Josh." Mike Faringdon clapped the lad on his back. 'The Girls' had completed their evening milking and once again the Ashbourne lad proved he could work like a Trojan.

"No problem. See you in the morning." Joshua strolled away from the farm buildings and climbed over a stile. The track brought him along the ridge of a hill that entered the woods above Pennycress Cottage. He always enjoyed the walk to and from Washburn Hill Farm. But - being all downhill - the return journey was the easiest and most relaxing.

From the overgrown track ahead, the boy could make out a familiar figure sat on a mossy tree trunk. It was a figure whose curves never seemed far from his mind. A preoccupation that amplified after the mind-blowing tug-job she had given him. His heart leapt at the sly and teasing grin flashed by the pink-haired Goth.

"Hey, Josh. Thought I'd find you here."
"How are you doing, Moira?"
"I'm good."
"Is Becky not with you?"

"We hung out earlier in the day. She's resting now."

"Resting? Lazy bint. So, you've worn my sister out?"

Moira flicked back the hair that covered her other eye and delivered a look of demure innocence. "Something like that."

"And now you're planning to wear me out too?" Joshua felt his pulse quicken. Ever since that erotic encounter in his bedroom - when the girl hinted at taking things further - he hadn't thought of anything else. Might this finally be the day?

Moira rose and moved closer to him. "I'd say it's your turn to wear *me* out, wouldn't you?"

Joshua gulped. "What did you have in mind?"

Moira got right up in his grille. She pressed her ample bosom close to his chest. Tender fingers stroked the boy's erection through his jeans. Her hot breath blew against his mouth. "Can you do anything else with your tongue, other than talk?"

Joshua tried not to pant.

Moira didn't wait for a response. "I know a quiet spot over the rise." She entwined her fingers with his and led him through the undergrowth. They emerged on the north-western edge of the hill. There stood the remains of a dry stone wall, in need of serious attention. Sections of the boundary still remained, interspersed with collapsed breaks in the whole. The Goth turned to face her aroused companion and slipped her arms around his neck. The kissing and wrestling of tongues came salty and hot. Joshua held Moira tight, her full chest squashing against his upper torso. The girl broke off the connection and backed towards the wall with slow, sultry hip wiggles. Her fingers traced the outline of those hips and slid beneath her short dress. Joshua gulped. The Goth pulled down her panties and slipped them over her feet. She pressed her back against the wall and sank down to rest her naked bottom in the soft grass. Athletic legs spread wide, Moira pulled up the skimpy black dress to reveal her full womanly glory. The boy's erection strained in his shorts. Feminine fingers slid across the girl's tummy, rubbing and pointing at her most intimate feature. She didn't take her eyes off the boy.

"How about returning the favour for me, Josh? Wouldn't you like a *taste* of the good life?"

The lad licked his lips with unconscious fervour. A rush of circulating blood roared in his ears. He wanted to hold Moira's sexy stare, but could hardly tear his gaze away from the pubic paradise on offer below. He took a couple of cautious steps forward, crouching at first then kneeling before her. Moira collected one of his nervous hands and slid the trembling digits up and down the full length of her nether regions. The moist and silky touch caused the boy to breathe more heavily. She flicked her tongue out in a licking motion then flashed her eyes down to indicate the intent of her desires. Joshua lowered his mouth to her abdomen. Moira grabbed the back of his head and pushed it further down. She rubbed his short hair in encouraging circles. Her voice sounded husky.

"That's what I want, Josh."

The lad stuck out his tongue to deliver a long, slow lick.

Moira moaned and panted. "Oh yeah. More. Come on, Josh. Give me more."

Spurred on by her sounds of pleasure and keen to enjoy the full range of this new experience, Joshua flicked and swirled. His urgency mounted with Moira's rising vocal responses and the increasing wetness of her womanhood against his tongue.

The girl looked to one side. A pile of chipped and broken limestones from the sagging wall had collected near one of the ragged sections. The stones appeared flat, sandy coloured and sharp. One hand still holding the enthusiastic boy's head in place, she reached out the other to grab a large stone. Joshua was distracted with his task. Despite his barely legal age and lack of experience, the oral he delivered was turning her on. Moira knew she couldn't lose control, or risk also losing the advantage. The sharp chunk of limestone rose above the boy's head. A second later she brought it down upon his skull with a sickening crunch. The tongue movement ceased even quicker than it had begun. The girl rolled the motionless teenager onto his back. Blood seeped from a gash on the rear of his head. The outline of his arousal still stood proud against the denim of his jeans. Moira placed her ear next to his mouth. There was breath there, faint but definite. She hadn't killed him, but he was out for the count. A trembling in her genitalia reminded the Goth how close the Ashbourne boy had brought her to the edge. She sat back down and finished herself off in the soft, warm grass, slaking it with her juices.

A curious mix of sexual release and erotic power

over the unconscious lad swam through her mind. She fished out a cell phone and keyed in a contact.

"Hello? Yeah, I've got the boy. He's unconscious, but I'll need help to get him to the site. Can you send someone up to the top? We're on the north-western edge near the break in the woods to Washburn Hill Farm. Okay, see you then."

She put the phone away and retrieved her knickers. "Sorry, Josh. You're only a means to an end for power beyond comprehension." The words rang in unconscious ears. The lad's chest rose and fell, his mind lost in oblivious blackness.

* * *

"What time did you need to be home? I can't have your parents worrying that you've gone missing. Especially if you were only supposed to be out taking the dog for a walk." Wendy Simpson glanced at a wooden-rimmed clock on the wall.

Bethany sat, still stroking Tink; the tabby asleep in her lap. "It's okay. Mum asked me to stay out with Jess as long as possible today. She's packaging soaps and candles for sale at a shop somewhere."

"Ah, I see. Your mother gets a little stressed when the pressure's on, does she?"

"She needs to be able to concentrate. Mum isn't much fun to be around if you get in her way when she's busy."

Wendy collected the glasses and placed them in the sink. "In that case, how would you like to learn to make some of that elderflower cordial?"

"Would I? Yes please."

"Good. I enjoy your company. There's a patch of elderflower growing nearby that we can use. For best results, you should always make the drink within a couple of hours of picking. A dry and sunny morning is ideal. The aroma tends to fade by afternoon."

"What else do we need?"

"Sugar, boiling water and a couple of large lemons. I have all that, so no need for extra shopping."

Bethany fidgeted with mild excitement. The emotive movement stirred the cat from its slumber. The animal stretched, sprung from her lap and disappeared into the living room.

Wendy picked up a wicker basket. "We should gather about fifteen elderflower heads. We'll remove the stalks and add the blooms to the sugar, lemon juice and zest - dissolved in boiling water."

Bethany followed the woman into the square hall, Jess close behind. "What happens then?"

Wendy opened the creaking front door. "Then it needs to be covered and left to stand for a couple of days, stirring morning and night. After that, I like to strain it through muslin. If you come by next week, I'll decant some into a bottle and you can take it home for your family to try."

"That would be lovely." Bethany stepped into the sunlight. From further up the lane, the sound of emergency vehicle sirens wailed and came to a halt.

Wendy frowned and locked the front door.

The two new acquaintances skirted the boundary of

Gingerbread Cottage. They came out near a hedge on one side of the River Coln. There was a commotion up above in the churchyard. Wendy stood frozen to the spot, as if sensing something beyond the range of normal human experience.

"What's wrong?" Bethany spoke in a subdued tone. She didn't want to break the woman's concentration.

"I don't know. Apart from the obvious arrival of emergency vehicles, there's something..." The woman's voice bore an element of pain. She winced and shook her head in long, confused sweeps.

"Are you okay?" Bethany tapped her leg. The Lab sat down patiently at their feet.

"Yes, child. Thank you. Now then, where were we? Ah yes, do you see the elders? They can be shrubs or small trees, with distinctive feather-shaped leaves. These typically come in groups of five or seven, with an even number of leaves on either side of the stem and one at the tip. They have serrated edges and hairs underneath." Wendy turned a stem round for the young girl to examine. "At this time of year, elders bear flat-topped clusters of creamy-white flowers. I'm sure you can smell the fragrance."

"Mmm, it's sweet. No wonder there are so many insects all around them."

"Well spotted. What an observant young lady you are. Now, you may be surprised to learn that the flowers and berries of the elder are mildly toxic. But they are edible if cooked, which takes away any danger and unpleasantness."

"What happens if you eat them raw?"

"Well, they have a bitter taste in that state. You might suffer a bad tummy for a while. Let's start gathering, shall we? If we fetch double the number I said, you and I can fix some elderflower fritters for a snack. Would you like that, Bethany?"

"Ooh yes."

Back at Gingerbread Cottage, the pair boiled up a batch of sugar and lemon syrup solution. Next they added some of their elderflower heads - sans insects - to the mix. Wendy taught the eleven-year-old how to make elderflower fritters and they sat down to a tasty repast. The afternoon wore on into early evening. The tall woman glanced through the latticed, leaded-light windows at an angry sky.

"It looks like there's a storm brewing." The spinster withdrew a leaf pendant from beneath her dress. She thumbed the item and studied the darkening clouds. "Perhaps you should run along, before you and Jess get soaking wet. Unfortunately I don't have a car, so I can't drive you up the hill."

"That's okay. I'm sure Mum must be finished by now. Thanks for a lovely day, Wendy. I'm so glad you invited me to join you."

Wendy leaned forward with her hands on a chair back. "I hope it won't be the last time. You are always welcome to pop in."

"It won't be. I'll be round for that elderflower cordial, remember?"

"Of course. Well, Tink and I look forward to your

next visit." She escorted her guest to the old cottage door. "Take care for traffic on the lane now, Bethany."

"We will. Come on, Jess." The girl attached the dog's lead and the pair bounded down the garden path and off up the hill.

Wendy stood in her doorway watching after them. It had been a long time since she'd had any company at Gingerbread Cottage. The faintest trace of nostalgia glistened in her hazel eyes. She squinted and raised her face to the heavens. *Thunderheads rolling in. Unusual this early in the year.* The hairs raised at the rear of her neck. *Something unnatural is happening. What was all that fuss at the church earlier?* She sniffed the air. The particles felt charged with ozone. The woman closed her door and looked down at the tabby. "It's going to be a gully-washer, Tink. Very strange."

* * *

Bethany entered the freehold surrounding Pennycress Cottage by the footpath that ran alongside their outbuildings. A sudden breeze blew with a surprising chill for the time of year. The girl rubbed her arms then reached down to hug the Lab as it snuffled around in the bushes. The sound of tyres on gravel switched her attention to the driveway. It was barely visible from their position. Bethany recognised the BMW at once. *Mr Robbins must have come for his wife. That's odd. Is he going to deliver the soaps and candles himself?* The car doors opened. The eleven-year-old climbed a few paces up the hill to see over the rooftops obstructing her view. *What are all those other cars doing here? Hey, that's Dad with Mr Robbins. But where is our car?*

"Looks like a regular village meeting. How many people has Katie Benson brought with her? Lizzie will be flustered by a lot of unexpected visitors." Doug indicated four other vehicles parked outside the cottage.

Howard shut the driver's door and pointed at a Volkswagen SUV. "That's Katie's car."

"So who are all these other people then? Hey Howard, hasn't one of your Cheltenham folk got an Audi with a paint job like that?"

"Yeah, now you mention it. Standard colour option though, I suppose."

"Ah well, best find out what's going on." Doug fished some house keys out of his pocket. "I'll let us in. If Lizzie's stressed up to the eyeballs, I don't want to get my head bitten off with a lecture about ringing the doorbell."

"I hear ya. I'd get the 'guilt by association' speech from Nancy, too."

Doug grinned and opened the front door. His water-logged clothing dripped onto the mat. "I hope I haven't made too much of a mess on your vehicle upholstery. Lizzie is going to go nuts when she finds out about the car. Of all the days this could happen. Ouch."

Howard clapped a hand on the home-owner's back from behind. "I'm sure she'll be relieved to know you're okay. That might ease the sting for you a little."

"Oh my God, Lizzie?" Doug caught sight of his wife laid out unconscious on the sofa. He rushed to kneel at her side. "Lizzie?" He patted one of her hands between his own.

Howard, Nancy and Katie Benson entered the living room from the kitchen. An assortment of others Doug recognised from the Box Cottage social joined them. They regarded the new arrival with vacant stares.

"Nancy, what happened? Did she hit her head? Have you called an ambulance?"

"An ambulance won't be necessary," Howard said.

"Huh? What do you mean? How do *you* know?"

Nancy's piercing eyes glimmered with a cruel light of elation. "Because she'll be joining your two eldest children as a sacrifice to The Master."

"What the fuck are you talking about?" Doug looked from the woman to her husband. "Howard, what's going on here?"

Nancy flicked her hand at two burly men standing near the fireplace. "We haven't time for this. An eighth soul will do no harm. Restrain him. He can go into the pond with the others. One less loose end running around."

Doug was halfway to his feet when the men reached for his arms. He threw his weight against the pair, sending the lot of them crashing into the inglenook. One reacted like a coiled viper, springing back to lock onto his arm. With his spare limbs, Doug staggered aloft and delivered a right cross to the face of the other. The force knocked the recovering man back down again. Howard stepped up and locked onto the dangerous, free-swinging hand.

Doug roared. "I'm going to take you apart, you bean-counting piece of shit!" He writhed and twisted in the grip of his assailants.

Katie Benson grabbed a lump of firewood from the fireside basket. She smashed it across the outraged man's brow. Doug blacked out and slumped like a rag doll.

At the open window to one side, a pair of eleven-year-old eyes widened in terror. Bethany hadn't liked the unusual situation at home. She sneaked up to the cottage from the rear. If there were a lot of adults and a stressy mother inside, she knew it was best to keep clear. But curiosity led her to crouch concealed outside the living room. From there she had spied Elizabeth on the sofa.

Nancy Robbins turned to her husband. "What happened with the car?"

"He broke the glass and escaped."

"You'd better tie him up. Dump him in the utility room out back. We'll have to make an extra trip to bring him uphill for the ritual."

A rumble of thunder rolled away in the distance.

Katie Benson put the log back in the basket. "What about their youngest?"

Nancy shook her head. "If she shows up, fine. But the girl is only eleven and doesn't know anyone round here. She'll either come home to find us, or an empty house. By the time she ever gets an adult to listen, her family will be history and their bodies disposed of.

One of Gloucestershire's great, unsolved mysteries."

Howard dragged Doug out towards the hallway with the other helper. He called back to the rest. "Speaking of which, you'd all better go and park your cars down at our place. I know people can't see much from the lane. But, we don't want some nosey dog walker helping police with their enquiries - after the fact. Your parked cars are a regular feature at ours. If anyone asks, we were having another cheese and wine social."

Bethany clamped her fingers across the Labrador's mouth. The dog sensed something was wrong. The first telltale hint of a whimper crept out.

Nancy's mobile phone rang. She answered the call, then paced up and down. Howard re-entered the living room. His wife signalled to him and the other man. "That was Moira. She's got Joshua, but will need help to transport him to Nevermere. Best take a few more cable ties and something to gag him with, in case he wakes up before time."

"Will do. Come on, Steve."

Bethany edged away from the building. She lay prone in the bushes at the base of the hill behind Pennycress Cottage. Howard Robbins and the other man who had held her father firm, stomped out the back door and ambled up the track. Ferns swayed as they passed by, not more than a couple of feet from the trembling girl. She held onto Jess with sweating palms.

"What are we going to do?" She whispered in the Dog's furry black ear.

Bethany couldn't say exactly where she found the courage to do what happened next. Was it sheer desperation, or a helpless sense of anger? The youngster couldn't run away without attempting to free her father. *They said they were going to stow him in the utility room.* The girl lifted the dog's nose to her own. "Stay, Jess. Stay."

Doug stirred. The cold tiles of the utility room floor pressed against his cheek. He lay curled up on his side in the foetal position, hands secured behind his back by what felt like plastic straps. Similar restraints clamped his ankles together. A twisted tea towel gagged his mouth. He became aware of a sudden draft. The back door opened a crack to allow a breeze. Approaching thunder announced its presence from a darkening, slate-grey sky. A lithe figure slipped through the opening to kneel at his side. The man saw the frightened face of his youngest daughter. Her ears strained for any sound that might indicate imminent discovery. Adult voices raised in a group chant, drifted from the living room. Nancy's voice - strangely altered with a deep, raspy growl - called out in English above the hubbub.

"Send legions to stand guard, that we might fulfil this ancient contract. Let none approach Coln Abbots to frustrate Thy diabolical purposes. And let none escape."

Bethany loosened the tea towel.

Doug whispered. "Good girl. I'm trussed up like a rabbit, Honey. Can you free the straps?"

Bethany tugged at the cable ties securing his hands and feet, but to no avail.

Doug sighed. "It's no good. You have to go and get the police."

Tears formed in the girl's eyes. "No, I'm not leaving you."

"We have no choice, Darling. If they catch you too, we're all done for. These people are insane. But above that, they're also dangerous. Don't trust any of the Robbins family or their friends, do you hear?"

Bethany stopped listening to him. She ignored her father and crept on all fours into the dining room. It was empty. The girl peered around the kitchen door. Empty too. She knew her mother kept a small pair of snips with some of her craft items in the kitchen dresser. Her mouth went dry and she fought to keep control of her bladder muscles. With laboured movements, Bethany edged towards the item of furniture in breathless fear. Across the hallway, she could see a group of men and women clad in robes. They stood in a circle, eyes closed. The eleven-year-old knelt to slide open a pine drawer. She winced at the noise her fingers made, rummaging around to feel for the metal tool. The familiar chunky handles were cold against her hands. The girl pushed the drawer to and retraced her route to the utility room. At any moment those chanting weirdos might finish whatever they were doing and discover them. Bethany went for her father's ankles first.

Doug whispered to her again. "Try the wrists first. I can sort my feet out afterwards."

The girl pressed the snips together with all her might, face reddening. A loud clipping noise seemed to echo like a gunshot through the structure. The chanting ceased.

Doug didn't pause. He grabbed the snips and clipped again to free his ankles. Every part of him wanted to storm back into the living room and rescue his beloved wife. Goodness only knew where Becky and Josh were. But the man was still drained from his desperate escape from the sinking car. Not to mention his battle with the cultists - or whatever the hell they were. He was exhausted, sodden, and couldn't risk re-capture. There were too many of them to tackle alone. Now he had to pull himself away and get help.

"What was that?" A robed woman stuck her head into the hallway. She twisted and spied the eleven-year-old girl helping her father to his feet. "Hey! The man's getting away."

Doug and Bethany tripped out the back door. It started to rain in stair rods. Doug was already too wet to care, but everything about the environment appeared to weigh a terrible cost on his actions. It felt like nature itself was fighting against him. He stumbled around the side of the cottage, avoiding the hill. *We must find help down in the village. Who knows how many other robed murderers are lurking up there in the woods?*

Bethany shrieked. The woman who had discovered their escape caught hold of her arm. That grip tightened and crushed.

A dark shape bounded out of the bushes with a loud bark. Jess clamped her ageing jaws around the cultist's ankle and dropped her like a sack of potatoes.

Doug turned back and grabbed his youngest daughter. He shouted at the animal. "Good Dog. Come on, Jess."

The Labrador raced after them. They crossed the garden at speed, slipping and sliding on the wet grass. The pair pushed a hole in the boundary hedge and stumbled downhill along the lane.

Nancy emerged through the front door and glared after the disappearing escapees.

Katie Benson joined her on the step. "Should we go after them, High Priestess?"

The Robbins woman shook her head. "No. It'll draw too much unwanted attention that we can't deny. They won't get far and no-one will come to their aid. We have the remaining three souls required for sacrifice. Once the ritual is complete, The Master will grant us power to deal with Douglas Ashbourne. Nobody will ever be able to stand against us."

Rain flowed downhill in a river of its own, running parallel with the Coln. Doug slipped and lost his footing. He fell onto his coccyx and jarred the entire column of vertebrae. The dog nuzzled his face.

Bethany blubbed in relief at their temporary escape. She helped her father up. "I heard them talking, Dad. They've got Josh, too."

"Along with your mother and sister. Come on, we've

got to keep going."

Doug winced from a mixture of pain and his continued exertions. The downpour was torrential, making it difficult to see far ahead. Bethany made out the moss covered, wonky sloping roof of Gingerbread Cottage.

"Wendy." She called the name above the roaring rain.

"Wendy?" her father repeated.

"My new friend. She'll help us." Bethany put an arm around her father's waist, more for emotional rather than physical support.

Doug followed his daughter's finger to a squat, characterful little Cotswold hovel. It was one he'd driven past a hundred times without noticing. "Do you mean that tall, mauve-haired woman people are always talking about?"

"Yes. She's a witch."

Doug frowned. "Bethany, we-"

"Listen," the girl interrupted. "She's a gentle, quiet lady. I know she'll help us, Dad. I promise."

"Guess we don't have much choice. I can make it that far, at least."

"Goodness me. Bethany, you're soaked." Wendy peered out from behind the creaking cottage door.

"Please Wendy. The Robbins family and their friends have captured my family. I managed to free Dad, but he's tired and injured."

"Come in, come in." Wendy pulled the door wide.

She helped a limping Douglas Ashbourne into the square hallway. Jess shook herself on the step and followed behind.

"Thank you," Doug looked into the kind hazel eyes fixed on him. "I'm more exhausted than injured. My car went into the fishing lake beyond the village. Then I got home and found our neighbours had drugged my wife or something. They attacked and tied me up."

The woman led him by the arm to sit on her wooden kitchen settle. She opened a cupboard and fetched a pair of large, fluffy towels. "You're both drenched. Dry off first and I'll make some herbal tea. It will help recover some of your energy."

A loud thunderclap echoed overhead. The resounding boom shook the cottage to its foundations.

Doug rubbed himself down. "Have you got a phone? We'd better call the police."

Wendy pointed to a land line unit resting on a small, round table in the corner. "Help yourself."

"Thank you." Doug lifted the receiver. His eyes squinted and he scrubbed one hand across his face. A second later he tapped the cradle buttons in rapid succession. "The line's dead." The man turned to his daughter. "Do you have your emergency mobile?"

Bethany pulled a bright coloured cell phone from her back pocket and handed it to her father.

Doug waved the device around. "Great. It says 'No Service.' What on earth is going on here?"

"Please sit down, Mr Ashbourne." Wendy applied gentle pressure to his shoulders. The man sank back onto the settle. "You've been through enough, without allowing emotion to drain you further."

Doug regarded her with a confused expression. "You're a curious lady. Bethany said you are a witch or something."

"Yes, that's right."

"Like the chanting scumbags about to sacrifice my family?"

"No, Mr Ashbourne. Nothing like that. They're devil worshippers."

"Is there a difference?"

Wendy poured hot water over a collection of herbs added to the bottom of a small jug. Steam rose from the infusion. A flash of lightning lit up the tiny home. It was followed a second later by another crack of thunder. Rain hammered down on the roof with a deafening roar. Wendy lifted three mugs from a rack on the wall, her back to the man. "You mean, other than the way we treat you?"

Doug flushed. "I'm sorry. I'm being rude and you're only trying to help."

"Wendy is a Hedge Witch," Bethany offered, as if this new information might clear matters up for her father.

Wendy poured herbal tea into the mugs and brought them across to the table. She seated herself opposite the guests. Tink wandered into the room and rubbed herself against the eleven-year-old's legs.

"There's no need to apologise, Mr Ashbourne. I've been aware of something going on in the village for several months now. So, the Robbins family are behind it, are they? I had a few suspicions about their 'visitors.' More often than not, they stay the night. Yet the group have been very discreet. It might surprise you to learn how organised and professional some followers of dark magic are. Not to mention the funding involved in it all."

Doug's brow creased. "That's very interesting, I'm sure. But, if we don't get help, those nutters are going to murder my wife and two of my children." He took a large gulp of tea. The refreshing effect was remarkable. He immediately felt like a new man.

Wendy thought for a moment. "The Faringdons."

Doug scratched his beard. "Yeah, Mike would help if we could make it back up the hill. But we'd have to pass Box Cottage. Goodness only knows how many of those robed nightmares are out and about looking for us."

Wendy sipped her tea and smiled at the pair. "There are other paths to Washburn Hill, if you know where to find them."

"Where on earth are we?" Doug recoiled. A soggy branch whipped back into his face.

Wendy pushed on ahead with Bethany and Jess beside her. The old woman pulled a heavy, hooded cloak tight about her shoulders and came to a halt. "You should recognise it now."

Doug took another step forward. Beyond the storm-tossed branches of the undergrowth, stood the familiar building silhouettes of Washburn Hill Farm. "Wow. Thank goodness." He pressed ahead across the open field, face angled down against the wind and driving rain.

Young Jeff Faringdon opened the farmhouse door, a flickering lantern clutched in one hand. All lights were off inside the structure. "Mr Ashbourne?"

"Hi Jeff."

"Come in."

"I've got Bethany and Jess with me. Oh, and this lady here."

Jeff hurried them out of the harsh weather. "Hello Miss Simpson. Please do come inside."

"Thank you. Good manners, like your late grandfather." Wendy lowered her hood.

"I'm sorry about the lights, the power's gone out. Dad recently got back on foot from the village."

Doug's puzzled face reflected in the flickering candlelight. "On foot?"

"Yes. A flash flood hit the bridge and washed it away. Dad was driving his pickup. He was lucky to get out in time and make it to the bank near The Woolpack. The truck's a goner."

"On its way down to Bibury by now, I shouldn't wonder." Mike Faringdon lumbered into the hallway, drying his bedraggled hair with a cloth. "Is everything alright, Doug?"

"No, it isn't. I know this sounds crazy, but the Robbins family and their friends have kidnapped Lizzie, Becky and Josh. They're part of some weird cult. Anyway, they intend to murder them at Nevermere."

"What the-" Mike began.

"I know, I know. But believe me, it's true. I only got away myself, thanks to Bethany here. There's too many to face down alone. The phones are dead, so I can't reach the police. I was going to ask if you could drive me-"

Jeff stopped him. "Grandpa's Landy. I'll get my keys. We can go to the police station in Ciren. Best bet if we can't find a working phone between here and there." He raced up a flight of stairs.

Doug put an arm around his youngest daughter's shoulders and looked at the farmer. "I'll go with Jeff. Is it okay for Bethany, Wendy and the dog to stay here?"

The man nodded. "Of course. They'll be safe with my wife and me."

Doug looked him square in the eye. "If you see anyone strange creeping around, bar the door and don't answer it. These are serious freaks, Mike. I hope we're not too late."

Jeff reappeared. "Let's go."

The battered Land Rover forded the flooded lane with aplomb. The road had become a tarmac backed, artificial semi-waterfall flowing down from north of the valley. But it presented no challenge to the faithful old machine's capabilities. Its occupants squinted through the dirty windshield. The glass wasn't even cleared by wipers on full speed. The sky darkened to such an extent that it gave the appearance of midnight.

"Whoa!" Jeff slammed his foot on the brake. The

Defender lurched to a halt, mere inches from an obstruction.

Doug opened the passenger door and hopped out. He splashed into cold water that ran around his ankles. A sturdy Beech tree had fallen in the storm and blocked the entire lane. He kicked the solid trunk. "Shit."

Jeff joined him. "That's not going anywhere and neither are we."

Doug studied him through the pouring rain with pleading eyes. "Is there any other way out of the village?" Deep down he already knew the answer.

"I'm sorry, Mr Ashbourne. The bridge at the southern end and the hill this end are the only roads in or out." Another tree swayed and creaked in the blustery gale. "We'd better head back before more of them come down."

Mike opened the front door at the farmhouse. Dark metal barrels of a side-by-side shotgun poked through the crack.

"It's us, Mike," Doug shouted above the din of rain and thunder.

"What happened?" the farmer allowed the dark figures access. He glanced down the track behind them, then closed and bolted the door.

Jeff flicked rain from his hair. "A Beech tree came down on the Winson road. We're completely screwed."

Doug tapped the barrel of Mike's gun. "I don't suppose you've got any more of those?"

The farmer shook his head. "It's Dad's old shotgun. Only got a couple of cartridges, too. I couldn't bear to dispose of it after he died, so I sorted out a license. He used to shoot rabbits with it for the pot, when I was a nipper. It hasn't been fired in years."

"Great." Doug paced back and forth, hands clamped beneath his chin. "I've got to try to rescue them. I've *got* to."

"Doug you can't go-"

"What do you think? I'm going to sit by and let my family get murdered?"

Mike sighed. "I was going to say: 'you can't go alone.' Wendy has told us a few home truths while you two were trying to get out of the valley. It seems Dad's death is as much to do with these people as anything else. I'm coming with you, at least."

"And me," Jeff said.

Mike held up a hand. "No, Boy. What if Doug and I don't make it back? Someone's got to look after your mother."

Jeff's eyes glistened. "They've got Becky, Dad. And now you say these people murdered Grandpa, too? I'm coming along. Just you try to stop me."

Mike's wife stepped into the candlelight and pulled on a coat. Daisy Faringdon was a slender woman with short, dark hair. Beside her, Wendy cast the cloak about her own shoulders and Bethany held tight to Jess. Daisy swept her gaze across the assembled men. "You're going to need every spare hand you can get, and there's no time for a village meeting. We're all going with you."

16

Something in the Water

Two women, two men, a lad at the end of his teens and an eleven-year-old girl squelched through Washburn Hill farmyard to the stile. A bedraggled black Labrador darted back and forth between the curious group. They followed the same route of travel Joshua had taken on his fateful journey home. Once under the leafy canopy of the hilltop wood, they finally experienced a little relief from the driving wind and rain.

Wendy held up a hand to stop the party. "We must be cautious from here on in. It's not unusual for these occult groups to place sentries around a site while performing a ritual."

"You seem to know a lot about this." Doug squinted at the odd woman, his jaw set firm.

Wendy met his stare for a brief moment and then continued without a word. She led them past a crumbling old stone wall. They stayed on the far side of the crest, a little below the skyline. The firmament loomed black and the storm's tumult masked their approach. But, it seemed foolish to risk placing their silhouettes against the sky. One eagle-eyed spotter could spoil what little advantage they might have.

Doug's mind raced. *What happens once we're discovered? Are there enough of us to put up a fight? And to think we left London partly to escape the violence. Jesus, even my youngest daughter is jumping into the fray. How desperate are we?* He watched Bethany keep the dog close by her leg. The recollection of her bravery in rescuing him from the utility room floor, came flooding back. The man felt his chest swell with pride. But the sensation was soon overwhelmed by heartbreak. Worries about what might happen if the cult defeated them, replaced his positive emotional reverie.

Lightning flashed and illuminated a hooded figure only a few yards ahead. The approaching group crashed to the woodland floor as one. A thunderclap hot on the heels of the electrical discharge, let them know the storm was now overhead. But it also concealed any noise of their hurried camouflage attempt. The silent watcher appeared to have its back to them. Doug exchanged a soundless grimace of determination with Mike. The farmer nodded and patted the old shotgun. Together the two men pulled themselves along the muddy ground. They split into a V-formation, flanking the figure on either side. Another strobe of white light pulsed against the tree trunks. Once the illumination dimmed, Doug rose to his feet. He placed one hand across the cultist's mouth - a man as it happened - and wrapped the other arm around his neck. Thunder shook the earth and the figures rocked from side to side. The robed sentry broke free of Doug's grip and shook him back against a tree. His triumph lasted only a moment. Mike appeared and walloped the butt of the old gun square into his face. The cultist collapsed in a heap of velvety material.

"Thanks." Doug took Mike's offered hand to regain his balance. His eyes fell on the unconscious man. Every part of him wanted to grab hold of that scum and beat him to within an inch of his life. But that wasn't going to save his family.

Wendy edged past and squatted by an old, moss-covered stump. They had reached the rise above Nevermere. The place Joshua tumbled down in his frantic charge to rescue his younger sister from the water. Bethany drew a sharp breath. Beneath them, a dozen robed figures lined the far edge of the pond. All but three carried bright lanterns. The remainder formed up abreast of where an extra trio of souls lay trussed together on the bank. Even from this distance in the occasional flashes of lightning, the eleven-year-old recognised her mother and two siblings.

Doug made an effort to stand, but Mike and his wife held him firm at Wendy's signal.

Down below, the cultists hovering over the remaining Ashbournes lowered their hoods. Nancy, Howard and Moira Robbins leered at their struggling prey. Nancy raised both her arms in an arcane gesture and let her voice ring out.

"Come, Dark Master. Receive these final three souls we offer in accordance with Thy contract."

A glimmer appeared beneath the surface of the pond. It was faint at first, almost like reflecting starlight. Or at least it would have been, were the stars visible through the thunderheads above. The glimmer intensified into a flickering white pulse that grew in size. From the depths of the water, several figures rose toward the surface. Their eyes gazed in wide and uncaring stares. Hands reached up as if waiting to receive a gift.

Nancy withdrew a dagger from beneath her robe and passed it to Moira. "Let the cries of fear from our sacrifice rise like sweet incense. An offering to the Lord of Darkness and salve to the Mistress of Retribution."

Moira crouched and cut free the gags from their victims. Cable ties still held each one rigid at the wrists and ankles. Lead weights lay fastened to their feet.

Rebecca shrieked. "You fucking demonic whore." Her voice collapsed into something resembling more of a squeal.

Howard motioned at two of the lantern bearers. "Put them in."

The robed cultists approached. With a puff they lifted Joshua first. Arms swung to gain momentum and they hurled him into the water. Ripples ran across the surface. The weights pulled the boy beneath. Those callous, spiritual water figures reached up to grab him in the ethereal light emanating from the depths.

Doug could take no more of it. He shook himself free

and vaulted the mossy stump. His body slid down the high bank, legs fighting for purchase on the slippery wet mulch that adorned it.

Elizabeth sank with a splash.

Doug reached the water's edge.

Rebecca screamed. Her cry disappeared with a gurgle as the sacrificial hauliers completed their task.

Jeff joined Doug a second later, his own desperate tumble initiated by watching Becky go in.

All about the pond, the robed figures chanted. "Ave Satanas. Ave Satanas."

Another thunderclap reverberated through the woodland clearing. Doug and Jeff dived into the murky mere, wild legs kicking them towards the terrifying underwater spectacle. Joshua, Elizabeth and Rebecca drifted below, surrounded by the morbid figures riding down alongside them like some spectral escort. When the would-be rescuers approached, those nightmarish ghouls turned their hollow eyes upon them. Wispy hands - indistinct in the rippling shadows and unearthly illumination - gripped onto the men and dragged them away. Doug fought hard, his face never leaving the struggling forms of his wife and two children. Their eyes bulged in panic, but the cable ties and weights offered no chance of escape. Pretty soon they would run out of air.

On the ridge above Nevermere, Wendy stood tall and proud. She extended her hands high across the body of shimmering water, palms facing downward. Mike, Daisy and Bethany did not comprehend the words that the woman spoke. But somehow Gaia stirred, came alive and echoed with the phrases pouring from the spinster's mouth.

In the depths of the pond, the apparitions loosened their grip. Weeds beneath their blurry feet swished and flicked about. The tendrils glowed and coiled around the ghost figures, like tentacles from an attacking giant squid. Doug didn't hesitate and swam straight for his drowning family. Jeff was at his side seconds later. His horrified eyes stared in helpless agony at Rebecca's panicked countenance. The older man tugged at the cable ties. Then he remembered the snips Bethany had used to free him. They were still in his trouser pocket. He fumbled around and tore the tool free. First to be clipped were the weights and ankle restraints. Jeff recognised his strategy and held onto Rebecca. Together they kicked for the surface, her hands still bound tight. Oxygen was the first priority. Wrists could wait to be unfastened. Joshua - ever the strong swimmer - rose to the surface the moment his legs were freed. Doug brought up the rear, clutching onto his wriggling wife with thankful arms. Their heads burst through the calming surface of the pond with a series of splutters. The sound disappeared amidst sheets of relentless rain.

"Seize them!" Nancy Robbins pointed and yelled.

"Stop." Mike Faringdon stood in clear view on the rise, brandishing his father's shotgun. He aimed it straight at one of the robed helpers who had taken a step towards the emerging swimmers.

Doug snipped Elizabeth's hands free. Her desperate

coughs and vomiting of foul water finally allowed the woman to catch her breath. Joshua slipped down beside them and offered his wrists to his father. His hands came loose in an instant.

"Jeff," Doug called to the boy cuddling his eldest daughter at the water's edge. Rebecca lay gasping and crying. Jeff looked up. Doug tossed him the snips and he released the girl's final restraints. She wrapped her arms around his neck and kissed him. Her lips feasted with an intense mix of passion and relief.

"We're not out of this yet," Jeff said when they both came up for air in a more figurative sense. His widening eyes scanned above the bank to where a series of angry-looking cultists edged closer.

"Do not fear. Who is your master?" Howard urged the assembled followers.

A male figure nearest Jeff and Rebecca took a defiant step in their direction. One of the shotgun barrels erupted from the ridge. The resonant boom of its report blended with more thunderclaps. The advancing man dropped to the grass with a yell. His hands ran across the bloodied material of his robes. He tugged against his chest. At this range, the young couple were able to hear the fellow rasping and wheezing for air. His body shook and spasmed for a moment. With a final foot twitch he lay still.

Nancy Robbins linked the index fingers and thumbs of her hands together to form a frame. She raised it to centre Mike Faringdon in the picture and spat out a curse with an inhuman slur. The shotgun backfired from the second cartridge and blew open the breach.

The farmer staggered in shock, his ears ringing. The barrels smoked, hammers a mess of twisted metal. Cultists ascended the wooded ridge on either side. Mrs Faringdon caught sight of Katie Benson leading the charge on their left. Her heart still ached at the loss of her beloved father-in-law. She threw herself into the fight with gusto. The pair rolled back down the bank. Their tumbling bodies knocked those following off their feet, like a human landslide. To the right, Mike caught sight of a chunky beefcake of a man. The thug grinned and lowered his hood. His knuckles cracked with eager anticipation. The farmer eyed his father's ruined weapon, hanging limp in his own hands. *Well it might not fire, but it's still a tool.* He swung the barrels around to connect with the solar plexus of his approaching enemy. The man doubled over, only to receive another wallop from cold metal on the back of his neck. He hit the wet, fern encrusted soil and didn't get up.

Two strong arms reached over the edge of the pond and hauled Rebecca from Jeff's grasp. She kicked and scratched the attacking man like an ensnared animal. The Faringdon boy jumped on top of him. The panting female fell aside as the two males fought.

Another hand clasped the girl's shoulder from behind. This time the grip burned with a familiar fire. Rebecca twisted her head to meet the angry and fearsome gaze of Moira Robbins. Her pupils had swollen to fill those eyes with a hideous blackness once again. She flicked the pink hair back across her shoulders. Fastened about her neck, a star-like pendant pulsed with a faint blue light. Rebecca had observed the same feature worn by both the Goth's parents, ever since they donned their ritual attire. Those pouting lips peeled back to reveal gritted teeth. They flashed like a row of freshly sharpened daggers. Her voice hissed with hatred.

"You can't win. Why don't you give up and die, Ashbourne?"

The cultist let out a yelp and her hair flew backwards. The burning hand released its hold on Rebecca. She watched Moira fall into the grass, her legs swept away from beneath. Two paces distant, Joshua staggered aloft clutching a broken tree branch. He frowned at the buxom seductress who shot him a fiery gaze of indignation.

Rebecca climbed to her feet and glowered at the girl. "You first, Robbins."

Moira moved along on her hands and knees towards the sixteen-year-old lad. Her eyes returned to their signature deep blue colour for a moment. "What's the matter, Josh? You don't want to hurt me, do you?" She stood erect and moved her hips in small, seductive steps. "Why don't we forget this mess and go somewhere quiet?"

Joshua spat at her. "You must think I'm completely stupid. Or believe you have more power over me than you do."

"Didn't take much to make you lick my pussy, did it?"

"Shut up."

"I'd make the most of it if I were you, dweeb. You're a pathetic nerd with a tiny dick. No girl is ever going to give a runt like you the time of day."

"Why don't you pick on someone your own age?" Rebecca clasped onto Moira's upper right arm.

"Oh, like you?" Moira whirled and gripped the offending limb with her burning hands again. Rebecca screamed, but the Goth intensified her magical delivery. The unholy pendant shone with increased luminosity. Joshua raised the branch above his head and went for her. Moira didn't flinch. She stretched her other arm level and connected with his chest. The searing heat that coursed through her fingers caused him to drop his makeshift club. Pain wracked his frame and he sunk to a kneeling position. Joshua watched his older sister writhe in agony. She squirmed beyond the halo of evil blue light that now seemed to highlight Moira's entire body. *They're connected. Her abilities and the charm.* Fighting against that relentless force to stand up, felt like holding your hands on a hotplate. The young man wanted to move in the opposite direction, but he couldn't let Rebecca suffer any longer. He reached out with arms so scalding they felt almost aflame. His fingers clasped the pendant from behind and he ripped it away from the Goth's neck. The symbol shattered in an explosion of light. The shock wave knocked Joshua off his feet. His head struck a rocky patch near the water's edge and he blacked out.

Moira twisted to watch her pendant fracture and vaporise. Her red lips seemed - to Rebecca at least - like they opened in slow motion. Then, the burning heat wasn't there anymore. The Ashbourne girl pushed Moira away with both hands.

"Oh, I don't think so," the pink-haired cultist reached out and gripped the girl's shoulder again. Nothing happened.

Rebecca watched her with unblinking eyes. "What's the matter, bitch? Not so tough without your magic necklace?"

Moira didn't get a chance to respond. Rebecca's clenched fist rocketed from below and delivered a resounding uppercut to her startled jaw. She flew backwards into the water. The buxom torso floated on the surface, alive but out for the count.

In the commotion of battle, Bethany had torn herself away from the friendly Hedge Witch. A part of her wanted to stay. Somehow being around Wendy seemed like the safest place in all this dangerous chaos. But the girl had to reach her family and do anything she could to help. She weaved in and out of assorted tree trunks, the black Lab close at her side. With each step, the youngster did her best not to draw attention to herself. So much was going on about them. She only hoped the distractions would continue until she reached the rest of the Ashbourne clan.

Doug hauled Elizabeth clear of the water. He was half way to his feet when Howard Robbins pushed him back to the ground. The cultist stood before him, legs spread. He unfastened his robe. The garment slipped down into the grass. One of the diabolical pendants glowed about his neck. He withdrew a dagger from a leather sheath at his waist and made long, swift cutting motions in the air. With each whoosh of the blade, the accountant uttered foul-sounding words in some foreign language. A laceration sliced across Doug's upper arm. A thin sliver of blood glistened in the flickering lantern light and intermittent lightning flashes. Doug clapped the hand of his other arm across the cut. He could feel the blood oozing out and coating his fingers. A saltiness formed on his tongue. Another stinging sensation incised his left calf muscle. Already it was starting to bleed. He forced himself to stand. A diagonal cut tore through his sodden shirt and sliced across the exhausted man's pectoral region. He dropped down again in pain, a cry of despair escaping his lips. Howard moved from side to side. With wild and freakish eyes he sized up his opponent, like a woodcarver considering which piece to take off next.

An eleven-year-old girl crouched with her dog in the undergrowth beyond. The Labrador's sad eyes watched the man she had come to love, ever since he first fed her table scraps while a guest at The Woolpack. A steady growl grew in both volume and aggression.

Howard brought the dagger around to his side in a balletic sweep, ready for the next strike. Lightning sparkled on the metal and flashed down the length of the blade.

Jess sprang from her hiding place. The dog's strong jaws clamped around Howard's wrist. He let the knife fall with a yell. The combatants flailed from side to side, the Lab frothing at the mouth in fury. Her saliva ran down the cultist's arm and mingled with the blood that the animal had drawn. Howard thrust his free hand against the sturdy brow of the enraged pet. His pendant pulsed and Jess let go with a yelp. But she didn't stay down for long. The dog squatted on her haunches and lunged back at his neck. Howard staggered against the weight and force of the assault. Gnashing teeth caught hold of the glowing emblem. The dog pulled back and snapped the item free. A fireball of blue light blew the pooch off into the bushes. Her torso struck a tree and fell to earth. She raised a limp paw, but had no energy left to get up again. Bethany rushed to hug her neck. The animal whined and looked round with large, forlorn eyes across the bizarre battlefield. She had given all she could.

Howard regained his footing and squeezed the bloody bite marks on his right wrist. A short distance beyond, a wounded and angry man staggered aloft. He rubbed the back of one hand on his short stubble beard, vengeful stare never breaking free of the wincing cultist. Doug clenched his fists and summoned every remaining ounce of strength. Witnessing the brave Labrador come to his aid had stoked the fire in his belly. Whatever it took, he was going to have a pop at Howard Robbins. He wanted to say something powerful and dramatic to launch his attack. In action films and TV dramas, the hero usually had a pithy, well-thought out line to deliver before landing the crushing blow. But Doug's mind went blank. He couldn't even form simple profanities in the dazed fogginess and heat of battle. Sounds came out of his mouth, but not as intelligible words. Yet the anguish, fury and desperation of that utterance would be universally understood by any observer. His intention was clear: Only one of them would be getting out of that clearing alive; Howard or himself. A line had been crossed. This was a fight to the death.

Doug's fist connected with the cultist's chin. Howard tumbled to the dirt with flailing limbs. He didn't even have time to sit up before his furious neighbour landed on top of him. Howard tore at his attacker with frantic arms to defend himself. Doug sat astride the man's waist like a horse rider. His knees pressed into the root-strewn mud. Fist after fist rained down upon the pinned man's face in a series of relentless blows. The father of three yelled like a thing possessed. He licked his lips. Some primordial and ancient urge delivered a curious sense of relish at the sickening and bludgeoning impacts. He pummelled Howard's face until it was an unrecognisable pulp; bruised, broken and stained crimson. The accountant lay motionless, though Doug could still feel the faint rise and fall of his chest beneath him. *Lizzie.* The thought caused him to look round. *Where is she?*

Elizabeth had found her second wind in time to see her eldest daughter drop Moira into the pond. It was at the point Jess latched onto Howard's wrist, that she clambered to her feet to confront Nancy Robbins. Off to one side, the High Priestess waved her hands at the figure atop the ridge. Elizabeth shielded her eyes from a burst of lightning in an attempt to identify the target. *Is that Wendy Simpson? What the hell is going on?* Nancy's occult pendant glowed blue. She chanted and swirled her hands about like two slithering snakes. Wendy clapped both palms together in the manner of a shield. Two balls of white light collided above the water with a bang to rival the rolling thunder. Elizabeth pondered the fact that Nancy's attention was at least drawn away from sacrificing her and her family. Then the anger rose again. She had recovered enough to feel the pain of betrayal. The rage of attempted murder and destruction of everything she held dear. *That monster tried to kill my kids, one by one.* She thought about the ghastly apparitions in the water who dragged them down. The stories of her children came rushing back. *All those weird 'accidents' were nothing of the sort. Then that bitch sought to finish me as well.* Elizabeth's hesitant steps formed into a bold stride, then a full-blown run. She threw herself at the High Priestess, disrupting another attempt to strike at the old spinster.

The noise emanating from Nancy's throat tore out like the growl of some vicious, predatory animal. It caught Elizabeth by surprise, but didn't stop her striking at the woman with frenzied fists. The pair rolled in the sodden undergrowth on the edge of the clearing. Nancy hooked one ankle around her opponent's legs and used a tumbling momentum to gain the upper position. She pressed her weight against the struggling blonde, locking her in place. Claw-like fingers came down either side of Elizabeth's face. Their touch burned like branding irons and caused her to scream.

A jagged lump of limestone whizzed through the air and struck a glancing blow on the cultist's temple. She became dazed enough for the woman beneath to slide out and crawl backwards several paces. Nancy regained her composure and whirled to find Rebecca standing on the banks of Nevermere.

"Leave my mother alone, witch!" the teenager screamed.

The High Priestess flicked her arms past one another, then made a gripping motion in mid-air. The amulet blazed with unholy fire. Rebecca's eyes widened and protruded from her face. She reached up to touch her throat, fighting for breath. The lack of oxygen dropped the girl to her knees.

"Becky!" Elizabeth wailed. Tears streamed down her cheeks. Fury rose again. The woman fixed her eyes on her daughter's attacker. Something inside snapped. She felt a strange vibration surge through her anatomy. It delivered a throbbing heat and sense of otherworldly power.

Down at Pennycress Cottage, the bee hives had remained quiet. Their occupants wouldn't venture outside during such a storm. Not under normal circumstances. But, at that precise moment the structures started to hum. Clouds of bees emerged from each hive, swirling about the garden. The insects gathered into one heaving mass and rocketed over the cottage roof towards the hill.

Nancy Robbins twisted her head to gloat at the heartsick mother laying in the grass. On the edge of the pond, Rebecca Ashbourne's face turned a dreadful shade of blue. Lightning lit up the scene. Thunder rumbled. Then a new sound rose above the fading clap. It approached like the hum of some industrial scale electrical transformer. The trees parted. A dark and living cloud descended into the clearing. The pulsing throng of bees swarmed and morphed into the silhouette of a man. His feet touched down on the bank. The head moved to examine Rebecca clutching at her restricted throat. One bee-comprised hand reached out and touched her on the shoulder. Rebecca caught her breath. Her shoulders rose and fell in a sudden attempt to take in as much air as possible. Normal colour returned to her cheeks. The bee man turned to stare at Nancy. The High Priestess raised her pendant like a protective charm. It glowed, but nothing happened. The humming shape took a step forward.

Nancy spun back to frown at Elizabeth, who watched from where she lay. "How is this possible? It's you. You're doing this."

Elizabeth remained silent and kept her gaze fixed on the panicked cultist. The bee man strode closer. Buzzing arms raised and reached out for Nancy. Her pendant shattered with a blaze of azure fire. Swarming hands gripped the slender woman's shoulders. She screamed and struggled. Her layered brown hair whipped from side to side. Then the stinging started. A high-pitched, blood curdling wail rent the sky. Nancy tried to run, but the shape held her rigid.

On the rise above the pond, Wendy Simpson studied the chaos with narrowed eyes. Elizabeth's attack on Nancy had ended the spinster's frantic use of defensive spells. The respite bought her precious time to bring something else to the fight. The woman touched her own charm and closed her eyes. Strong magical forces were at play here. She knew that nature must rise at her request to bring balance to these negative energies. Her eyelids scrunched tight, concentration writ large across her forehead.

Down below in the clearing, Nevermere blazed to life as if the old pond contained the sun itself. The ground shook and the waters rippled. A slow, clockwise set of circuits commenced on the surface. With the increasing current stirred by these rotations, a downward vortex formed in the centre. Moira Robbins stirred where she floated. The water carried her along with it, spinning faster and faster. She screamed at the top of her lungs and sunk into the mysterious hole. The cries ended as suddenly as they had begun.

Wendy's eyes snapped open, blazing with light reminiscent of two torch beams. She extended hands either side of her body, index fingers pointing like signposts.

A curious sound of cracking and snapping wood joined the tumult. In the clearing, tree roots and branches slithered out of the undergrowth. Doug had climbed off Howard with a dazed expression to watch the bee man free his eldest daughter. A series of branches coiled around his arms and legs. His face snapped aloft at the fiery eyes of the spinster casting her spells. Behind him in the bushes, Bethany cried out in shock. The man looked over his shoulder. Tree roots had almost smothered the eleven-year-old and their dog. Doug clenched his fists. *I knew we shouldn't have trusted that witch. Now she's taking advantage of what the cultists started.* More tree limbs fastened onto Rebecca, Joshua and Jeff. Doug had no idea where Mike and his wife were. Fighting somewhere up near Wendy, most likely.

Elizabeth drew in a sharp breath. Creeper-like roots wrapped around her upper body. It felt like the wood was coming alive and snaring some prey for a feast. A smell of damp vegetation filled her nostrils. The distraction caused her to break focus on Nancy. The bee shape lost cohesion. Moments later, the swarm rose into the sky and was gone. The High Priestess wiped a hand across her welt-smeared face. She stared at the pinioned blonde with a pained glint of vengeful malice. Those wide pink lips and slightly upturned smile spread with pure delight. A glint in the grass caused her to catch sight of Howard's dagger where it had fallen from his grip. She stomped across to retrieve the blade.

"Time to die, Elizabeth." The phrase dripped with venom. Nancy's piercing blue eyes locked back onto the immobile blonde.

The vortex in Nevermere accelerated to an incredible speed. A rushing wind - more than the result of the storm - rose with a howl.

Doug felt his torso pulled towards the pond, but the branches held him firm. He twisted to find Nancy pacing at his wife, knife raised above her head. The winds adopted an overbearing, suction-like force. The Robbins woman looked like someone trying to stride against a hurricane, while not making any progress. Television images of a police officer attempting something similar in the great storm of October 1987, popped into Doug's mind.

The glee on Nancy's face changed into a grimace of pure terror. The realisation that her quarry was not a prisoner but a protected person, came too late for the evil woman to escape. Unyielding suction pulled her head over heels through the air in the opposite direction. She tumbled into the rotating waters.

All about the clearing, robed cultists were dragged kicking and screaming into the gaping, spiritual maw of Nevermere. Howard and the body of the attacker that Mike shot earlier, went after Nancy. Even the unconscious sentry - knocked out by the butt of Bob Faringdon's old gun - joined his diabolical comrades on their final horrific journey. One last thunderclap boomed overhead. The waters slowed and their magical illumination faded. The rain stopped in perfect time with the stilling pond.

Jess licked Bethany's face. The girl giggled. Tree roots retracted around them with a gentle, almost paternal care. Doug collapsed as the living undergrowth released him. He crawled on hands and knees to cuddle his beloved wife. To their right, an aged piece of parchment burst into flames. Elizabeth sat up and watched it burn. "I wonder what that is?"

Rebecca squatted beside them. "An ancient demonic contract. I guess now the signatories are gone, it can finally be destroyed."

Jeff helped a stirring Joshua to his feet. The boy tapped his groggy head. "Thanks mate. Hey, what did I miss?"

Rebecca came over to give him a hug. "The biggest bloody plughole anyone has ever seen, I should think. It swallowed the cultists." She looked him square in the eye. "Thanks, Josh. You know - for what you did with Moira."

"No sweat, Sis. Can't say I'll miss her. Did she go down the plughole too?"

"Yeah. Good riddance to the lot of them. Don't believe a negative word she said about you either, you hear?"

"I'm my own man. Her opinion means nothing to me."

Rebecca slipped an arm around Jeff's waist. "It sounds like my baby brother is all grown up." They kissed.

"Thank God that's over," Mike Faringdon strode into the clearing with his wife. Both appeared battered and bruised, but generally in one piece. He motioned to the tall spinster behind them. "Or should I say, thank Wendy?"

Elizabeth stood and straightened herself to greet the new arrivals. "Yes. Wendy, I don't even have the words-"

The spinster raised an eyebrow. "For what?"

"Err. For defending us from Nancy with your... well, magic I guess. And then saving Becky and myself with that bee man. Not to mention sucking all our enemies down into oblivion, or wherever the hell they've gone."

"You give me too much credit."

Elizabeth frowned. "How is that even possible?"

"First of all, the bees were nothing to do with me."

"But they came when we needed them. Listen, I've been around bees almost my whole life. There's no way you can tell me that was normal."

"No it wasn't."

"Well what then?"

"The bees came because you called."

"Huh?"

"How far back do your family go in Coln Abbots, Mrs Ashbourne?"

"Grandpa's ancestors lived in the village dating back at least five hundred years or more."

Wendy nodded. "There's a little of the old Cotswold magic still in your blood, I would say. In any case, you summoned and controlled the bees, not I."

Elizabeth's mouth dropped open.

Doug nudged her. "There you are. I've always told everyone nobody handles bees like my Lizzie."

Wendy looked back at the water. "As to the vortex, that wasn't me either. Oh, the trees came at my request to keep you safe. But the final victory was only the natural order reasserting itself. Nature bringing everything back into balance."

Bethany bounded over to the spinster, accompanied by a happy and recovering dog. "I knew you were a great witch. You've so much power!"

Wendy's eyes became distant. "No, child. I was a tool in an unusual situation. My magic is the simple and non-spectacular healing spells and ointments you've already seen. Such power was never intended for humans to wield. Those who believe it is, are often led astray by their lust for it. People like your neighbours and their friends. But, will you help me do one last thing before we leave, Bethany?"

"Absolutely. What are we doing?"

"We must bless and purify the waters of Nevermere. The old curse is broken and the evil hold dispelled. Now we should assert our love for the life-giving waters that rise and flow throughout the Coln Valley." Wendy offered her hand and the youngster took it.

Elizabeth squeezed her husband as they watched the odd couple approach the bank. The spinster passed across a small vial of liquid. "Pour that into the water once I've performed the blessing."

"Okay." She uncorked the top and held the container over the water, ready to obey.

Wendy raised her hands and spoke with authority. "Negativity that invades this water, be banished now by nature's daughter. I break your power and seek to bless, this sacred pond with tenderness. May sweetness flow from springs below and ever cause new life to grow." She tapped Bethany. The girl tipped the liquid contents of the vial into the pond. The surface stirred for a single moment. Stars shone down from the clearing skies above and reflected in the mirror-like expanse.

Doug tried to hide a smirk and whispered to his wife. "Nice poem."

Wendy turned. "And still you doubt, after everything that has happened this evening?"

The man fidgeted. "No, you're right. I'm sorry, it was a stupid comment. Thank you, Wendy."

The mauve-tinted, curly grey hair bobbed in gentle acknowledgement. "Very well, Mr Ashbourne."

Elizabeth sighed. "Do please call us Doug and Elizabeth."

17

Milk and Honey

"This lavender oil you supplied me with makes an excellent beeswax polish. I'm looking forward to seeing if it sells at the village fete. I wonder if Pete Cowley would be interested in stocking some at the shop?" Elizabeth applied a label to a small, round tin of furniture polish.

Wendy Simpson sat back at the kitchen table in Pennycress Cottage to admire their work. "No harm in asking. He's quite an affable fellow."

Elizabeth paused from her activities. "Such a shame about his wife. Thank goodness the police cleared him of any wrongdoing. David Leach, too."

"Yes, our once self-righteous holy man has become a lot more humble since his own personal set of tragedies. He even stops to chat with me whenever I visit the churchyard."

"How about the rest of the village? Are they treating you any different?"

Wendy twisted her mouth. "Why would they? Some things will never change. No matter. I'm used to it."

"Well, you're always welcome at Pennycress Cottage, Wendy. Bethany tells me you two are off plant spotting later. She's become quite the budding botanist in the last couple of weeks."

"The girl has an affinity for nature. So rare in this generation. It's a pleasure to teach her."

A clunk sounded from the hall. Doug closed the front door. He appeared waving a folded newspaper.

"Well, it's all over the local front page: *'Mystery of the missing Cheltenham business people in Coln Abbots.'* The media are going to town over it."

Wendy tapped her fingers on the wooden table. "I'm not surprised. There have been reporters crawling around outside my front door all week. Hoping for a statement from a local, I imagine."

Elizabeth tilted her head. "Did you make one?"

"Only the same thing I told the police: *My neighbours often had people over at Box Cottage. Sometimes their cars remained all night. Other than that, I had little to do with them.*"

Doug grunted and sat down to flick through the paper. "We had officers show up canvassing the neighbourhood with their enquiries. It seems one of Howard's clients missed him after an appointment didn't happen. The police had already received missing person reports for most of the other cultists. Plod's relief was only temporary when they found the owners' cars together at one spot. Looks like their investigation won't get a lot further."

Wendy cracked a faint smile. "Not unless their jurisdiction takes them across into other dimensions. This is going to make *'The Campden Wonder'* look quite tame."

"Campden Wonder?" Doug and Elizabeth asked.

"Up in Chipping Campden. It's a famous local story. Almost twenty years after the witch trials here in Coln Abbots, a man named William Harrison went for a walk from Chipping Campden to Charingworth. It's only a couple of miles. Anyway, when he didn't return his wife sent their manservant to look for him. He also went missing. William's son went in search of both the next morning and found the servant. I won't go into the whole story, but the two of them continued looking and asking around. On the way back they recovered some of William's items, including a shirt and neckband covered in blood. During the ensuing investigation, the servant claimed he knew William had been murdered, but pleaded his own innocence. Instead he indicted his mother and brother, who denied the charge. Not too surprising. The servant insisted they had dumped William's body in the pond. It was dredged, but no body recovered. All three of them eventually suffered execution by hanging on Broadway Hill. The tower there stands on the site to this day. Their mother was actually executed first, since she was suspected of being a witch. The following year, William Harrison returned to England on a ship from Portugal. It transpired that he had been abducted and sold into slavery in Turkey. Curious for a seventy-year-old man, but who knows? After his 'master' died, he stowed away on a Portuguese ship and made his way home."

Doug dropped the paper. "That's incredible. What about the blood-stained items of clothing?"

"Harrison claimed some injuries occurred during the attempt to subdue him. Even our great Poet Laureate, John Masefield, wrote two plays about the matter. There is a popular story that Harrison's wife committed suicide after learning her husband was alive."

Elizabeth stroked her nose. "Could she have arranged the whole thing?"

Wendy clasped her hands together. "We'll never know."

Doug resumed reading the local rag. "Well, as long as the Robbins family and their ilk don't return out of the blue."

The spinster's eyes sparkled. "They won't."

* * *

"I couldn't believe it when Dad came up with the idea: Cheese. Of all the things he could think of. And why not, he's made it as a hobby for years? I guess your father's act of turning his own hobby into a business got him thinking." Jeff walked hand in hand with Rebecca through the woods above Pennycress Cottage. It was a warm and sunny morning. Shafts of light angled down through gaps in the leafy canopy. Even though only a couple of weeks had passed, it seemed an age ago that those trees came alive to protect them.

"You sound quite enthusiastic about it. I thought you weren't interested in dairy farming?" Rebecca's voice carried a note of uncertainty. She didn't want her curiosity to appear like a criticism.

"When the business was going down the drain with no future, there didn't seem much point. But Dad's idea to diversify into commercial cheese production with our milk, might actually work."

"So - if you add my parents' businesses to the mix - Coln Abbots has become the archetypal *land flowing with milk and honey*. What would your grandfather say, do you think?"

"I reckon he'd be delighted. This place was his whole life."

"He'd be proud of you wanting to get involved."

Jeff glanced up at the sky for a moment. "Yes, you're right. He would. As soon as I finish my business degree, I'm going to pull out all the stops to help Dad. We'll make a go of it, somehow. So, have you decided which uni you're going to choose?"

Rebecca's palms started to sweat. "Actually, I've had an offer from Hereford. Would that be too weird for you if I took it?"

"Are you kidding? I could see you every day. How cool would that be?"

The girl let out a long sigh of relief.

Jeff's mouth turned up at the corners. "What, did you think I'd have a problem with it?"

"I wasn't sure."

"Of course, I'll have to let all my *other* girlfriends know that an extra one is joining the party."

Rebecca giggled and thumped his shoulder. "Beast."

They reached the rise above Nevermere. Its still waters sparkled in the dappled sunlight. The fading fragrance of wild garlic hinted at a foraging season just ended.

Rebecca indicated a thick patch of grass near the mossy stump. "Do you want to sit down here for a bit?"

"Sure. This place has a nicer feel since - well, you know."

"Yeah." She fixed her moistening grey eyes on her boyfriend. "Jeff?"

"Huh?"

"There's something else I want to do before I start university."

"What's that?"

If Rebecca Ashbourne were a writer and they gave a prize for 'showing' rather than 'telling,' she would have been the absolute winner. She left Jeff Faringdon with little doubt of her intentions. They discarded their clothes in a breathless instant. Between the swaying ferns, their arching bodies rose and fell. Rebecca let out a sigh as her beau's girth entered her in its loving traverse. The girl's mild pain of first intercourse soon sweetened into a joyous warmth of wellbeing.

The naked couple lay staring up at the swaying treetops, in the afterglow that followed their passionate tumble. Losing her virginity to Jeff felt natural and right. She kissed the nape of his neck and melted into the strong arms that held her tight.

* * *

"I had better step aside. If people find me selling

your products, it could hurt business." Wendy Simpson studied the odd expressions of passing fete attendees. She stood behind a table laden with Elizabeth's wares.

Elizabeth placed a restraining hand on the spinster's forearm. "Nonsense. It's about time this village changed its tune." A passing woman from the W.I. caught her attention. "Maureen. How are you? Please come and have a jolly good look."

A fifty-something woman with a long nose and straight ginger hair squirmed on the spot. Maureen appeared torn between wanting to speak with Elizabeth and feeling apprehension at finding the odd woman beside her. She took a step closer and delivered a polite nod. "Is Wendy Simpson helping you, then?"

Elizabeth flung both her hands up in a gesture of delight. "Indeed she is. You should try some of this excellent lavender beeswax furniture polish." She twisted the lid off one of the tins, dipped in a cloth and wiped it across a short lump of demonstration wood. "The beeswax is from up at Pennycress, but Wendy made the oil from her own lavender at Gingerbread Cottage. No rotten chemicals, and as local a product as you could hope to buy. Far better than any mass-produced industrial equivalent, I'll wager."

Maureen studied the shiny piece of wood and ran her finger across the silken finish. "It smells so good, too."

Elizabeth beamed. "Thanks to Wendy, yes."

The ginger-haired woman fished around in her bag for a purse. "I'll take two, please. One for myself and one for my sister. She loves the aroma of lavender."

Elizabeth took the offered note and passed her two tins of polish in exchange. "There you go."

Maureen clutched the products close to her chest. "Thank you." She paused and made a point of looking straight at Wendy. "And thank *you*, too."

The spinster tried to conceal an unbelievable swell of emotion. It started in her tummy and spread towards her face. "You are most welcome."

Maureen went off to examine a cake stall. She almost tripped over a handful of young children who darted in and out of the colourful tables with squeals of excitement.

Elizabeth leaned across to her helper. "There you go. Small beginnings for us all."

Joshua sat on a low wall watching the River Coln bubble past.

"Excuse me?" a soft, enquiring feminine tone arose from behind.

The lad shifted his attention to a pretty brunette with short hair in a bob. Dark but happy eyes twinkled out above freckled, puffy cheeks. Her face may have been round but her figure was slender.

The voice came again. "I'm sorry to disturb you. I fancied chatting with someone my own age, if that's okay?"

Joshua nodded. "No problem. Are you visiting Coln Abbots for the fete?"

"Sort of. We moved in to Winson - up the road -

about a week ago now. I don't know anyone round here yet. Plus, I'm an only child."

"Sounds lonely." Joshua extended his hand and the girl shook it. "I'm Josh. Josh Ashbourne. My Mum is running the beeswax product stand over there."

"Oh? I believe mine just bought one of her soaps. I'm Mandy Green. Have you lived here long?"

"Only a few months. We moved up from London. I'm starting a new school in the autumn to study for my A-Levels."

"Me too. Not the London part - we're from Bristol - but I'm also going to be starting my A-Levels."

"Well great. So have you been to the Cotswolds before?"

"Only once, on a holiday when I was ten. It's so pretty, isn't it?"

"No arguments on that score."

"Do you find it quiet? If I'm honest, I like the quiet of the country. It's so peaceful. I don't imagine very much ever happens around here."

Joshua wiped a wry smile away from his lips with the fingers of one hand. They started to stroll and he glanced back up the hill. "Oh, you might be surprised..."

ABOUT THE AUTHOR

Devon De'Ath was born in the county of Kent, 'The Garden of England.' Raised a Roman Catholic in a small, ancient country market community famously documented as 'the most haunted TOWN in England,' he grew up in an atmosphere replete with spiritual, psychic, and supernatural energy. Hauntings were commonplace and you couldn't swing a cat without hitting three spectres, to the extent that he never needed question the validity of such manifestations. As to the explanations behind them?

At the age of twenty, his earnest search for spiritual truth led the young man to leave Catholicism and become heavily involved in Charismatic Evangelicalism. After serving as a part-time youth pastor while working in the corporate world, he eventually took voluntary redundancy to study at a Bible College in the USA. Missions in the Caribbean and sub-Saharan Africa followed, but a growing dissatisfaction with aspects of the theology and ministerial abuse by church leadership eventually caused him to break with organised religion and pursue a Post-Evangelical existence. One open to all manner of spiritual and human experiences his 'holy' life would never have allowed.

After church life, De'Ath served fifteen years with the police, lectured at colleges and universities, and acted as a consultant to public safety agencies both foreign and domestic.

A writer since he first learned the alphabet, Devon De'Ath has authored works in many genres under various names, from Children's literature to self-help books, through screenplays for video production and all manner of articles.

Printed in Great Britain
by Amazon